THE
DEVIL'S
DREAMCATCHER

ALSO BY DONNA HOSIE

THE DEVIL'S INTERN

THE
DEVIL'S
DREAMCATCHER

Donna Hosie

Holiday House / New York

Library of Congress Cataloging-in-Publication Data

Hosie, Donna.
The Devil's dreamcatcher / by Donna Hosie. — First edition.
pages cm
Summary: "Team DEVIL reunites and takes another journey to the land of the living—
this time, to stop a madman from unleashing the terror of The Devil's most prized
possession, his dreamcatcher"— Provided by publisher.
ISBN 978-0-8234-3390-2 (hardcover)
[1. Hell—Fiction. 2. Future life—Fiction. 3. Death—Fiction. 4. Time travel—Fiction.]
I. Title.
PZ7.H79325Db 2014
[Fic]—dc23
2014048387

For Team HOSIE:
Steve, Em, Dan
and Josh

Contents

Acknowledgements

The Devil's Intern was four years in the making; *The Devil's Dreamcatcher* was four months! Well, when I say four months, it took *me* that long to write it. Time increased exponentially once it went through my agent and editor, but I'm so glad it did. What you're about to read is a labor of love where every motive was questioned, and every line dissected. This book is humorous but also dark, and deals with subject matters that are hard. Yet at its heart this sequel is not a story about abuse, or even death. It is the continuation of a tale about friendship and love and loyalty.

So my friendship, love and loyalty go to the following:

EditorExtraordinaire, Kelly Loughman. The relationship between author and editor has its foundation in trust. I have never trusted anyone so implicitly with my writing before, and that is so empowering. You just *get* what I'm trying to say (half the time before I've even said it!). There are no words to describe how much I love working with you on these books.

AgentAwesome, Beth Phelan. You always have my back. You always ask the right questions. You love Ronald Weasley! Seriously, could you be more awesome?!

Jenny Bent and the Bent Agency in New York. I know when Jenny has tweeted about me and my books because my email starts going crazy! I'm so lucky to be signed to a literary agency where the entire team gets behind all its authors.

Aubrey Churchward, Sabrina Abballe, Mary Cash, John Briggs, Julia Gallagher, Sally Morgridge, Terry Borzumato-Greenberg and the wonderful staff at my second home, Holiday House. Thank you so much for all you do behind the scenes to get Team DEVIL out to the masses.

My husband, Steve, and my children, Emily, Daniel and Joshua. For keeping me in the clouds with excitement, and on the ground with laundry!

My mum and dad, Lorraine and Peter Molloy. It's hard having my family on the other side of the world when I want to share every moment of this with you. My sisters, Anna Lane and Katie Molloy, are awesome and I miss you both more than you can imagine. And to my gorgeous nieces and nephews, Poppy, Sam, Beatrice and Arthur. You're mentioned in a book now—you're famous!

Finally, a girl needs friends. Amazing friends. Friends who will support and encourage and promote like mad! No one does that better—or harder—than the following: Peggy Russell (I can't imagine ever writing a book and NOT thanking you), Erin Dolmage (total Goddess), Erna Brodocz (captain of the German Team DEVIL), Charlotte Evans (captain of the UK Team DEVIL), Melissa Lawson (the most amazing school librarian on the planet—I hope the book club gets a kick out of reading that!) and my New York Team DEVIL posse who made my visit there so magical: Elizabeth McIntyre, Tuuli Edwards and the adorable Sampo, Eileen Hegmann Connell, Denise Dowd, Moriah Moore and Kelly Bohrer Zemaitis.

1. Medusa

"How did you die?"

Why does every job application in Hell ask that question? If hiring devils bothered to read through the devil resources files that accompany the application forms, they'd know the answer.

Most of them don't bother, though. Or if they do, the information doesn't actually interest them. On the application for my current position as trainee patisserie chef, I wrote that I died after falling into a vat of meringue. The head chef, Michel Duberry III, didn't bat an eye. He gave me the job before I even sat down. He just thrust a red apron at me and told me to whip up three tons of custard.

Before that I worked in the law office. On that particular application form I wrote that I died after having an allergic reaction to dental floss. My supervisor there was a strange man, even for Hell. His name was Dominic Shayman. He was enormous: tall and fat, with a stomach that made him look like he was nine months pregnant, yet he had a tiny bald head. His favorite pastime was making female devils cry—and he was very good at it. The misogynistic pig made a pass at me once. After that, I told him exactly where he could shove his job, once he removed his tiny head from it first.

I haven't had a lot of luck with bosses in Hell. That's one of the reasons that I'm so desperate to get the other intern position in the accounting office, because accounting interns report to Septimus.

Septimus is The Devil's head accountant and right-hand man. He's a former Roman general, and he's also the coolest person in Hell. All of the women in the kitchens have the hots for him, but then, a lot of them died in menopause so they have the hots, period. I guess we all do, though. Hell is a furnace.

I like Septimus because he remembers my name when he visits the kitchens. My new name. The one I was given by the Grim Reapers at the HalfWay House after I died. For me, the name meant a fresh start—even in death. That might not seem like a big deal, but when you exist in the heat and monotony of Hell with millions and millions of other dead souls, fresh starts aren't exactly easy to come by.

So, for the first time in my death, I'm going to take advantage of that good feeling and be completely honest on a job application— and not...*weird*, as some of my *former* friends here have called me.

I start writing.

Name: Medusa (formerly Melissa) Olivia Pallister
Age: 16
DOD: December 2, 1967
How did you die? I <u>fell</u> from the Golden Gate Bridge.

I underline *fell* twice in thick red ink because I'm telling the truth here, and I want the truth to be clear. This really matters to me. Truthful words are important, even the ones that remain unsaid. Today I manage to put my truth on paper. But I'm still not willing to talk about it.

I've never been this high up in the central business district before. It's a good thing I don't suffer from vertigo. Hell's kitchens are on level 267. Now, for the first time in over forty years of death, I've made it to level 1. I'm trying not to get nervous, but I really, really want this job. Not only would it be awesome to work for Septimus, but getting out of the heat of the kitchens might help calm my hair down.

Maybe I should have tied it back. When people talk to me, they don't look at my chest, like they do with my *former* friend in Hell,

Patty Lloyd, but they don't look at my face, either. They're mesmerized by my hair.

Now I'm starting to feel self-conscious. I look down at my clothes: long black shorts and a bright-red shirt. My Converse sneakers are bright white. Too casual? I can't wear a skirt and heels. I'd look like a baby giraffe trying to walk for the first time in that kind of outfit.

Patty Lloyd has just swept past me decked out in exactly that kind of outfit, except it should be illegal to call what she's wearing a skirt because it barely covers her ass. I've got longer underwear than what she has on. She ignored me, which is no loss. She had an interview as well, but everyone knows she only applied for the job because she wants to nail the other accounting intern, Mitchell Johnson.

I have my own, very different, reason for wanting to meet Mitchell, and—after wanting to work for Septimus and calming down my hair—that's the final reason I'm here.

I can hear voices coming from behind the smoldering stone door of the accounting office. The deep drawl is definitely Septimus's, and I'm guessing the exhausted, I've-lost-the-will-to-exist voice is coming from Mitchell.

But there's another voice: slightly hysterical and high-pitched.

Is that The Devil? Goose bumps break out on my skin. Shivers . . . now, that's a sensation I haven't felt in forty years. I press my ear against the door. I've never heard The Devil speak before. Except for pictures, I've never even seen him.

"I want to see it now, Septimus!" screeches The Devil. "He has pushed me to the edge of reason. I want to see the virus tested now. He has sent me an invoice for the damage the cherubs have done to the Pearly Gates. He says I have corrupted them. I'll show Him corruption. He won't be whining about graffiti when I have unleashed Operation H on His foul, vile, disgusting angels. We'll be hearing their screams from here. In fact, I intend to record their agony and will release it as a free download— Oh, hello, Mitchell, I didn't realize Septimus had company."

I'm jerked back from the wall against my will; I think a shadow just yanked my hair. There seem to be more shadows up here than on my floor. They're a lot bigger, too.

I don't like shadows. I don't like anything that creeps around silently. It reminds me too much of the last few years of my life before I died.

Shaking with nerves, I sit back down and straighten my shorts. My skin is hot. Maybe I should have worn long pants. By now I have sweat stains on my clothes.

Unfortunately, there's no time to even think about going back to the dorm to change, because the door to the accounting chamber opens with an eerie creak, and a head belonging to a guy with spiky blond hair sticks out. He looks left and right, and I immediately notice his pink eyes.

Mitchell Johnson clearly hasn't been dead for very long.

"Is Mr. Septimus ready now?" I ask, hoping beyond hope that The Devil won't be present during the interview. If I have to stand in a room with the master of Hell, panic is likely to dissolve me into something that hasn't been categorized by social services yet. Devils black out all the time in Hell, from fear, or despair, or pain. They say it's like dying again, because you panic with primal fear, just before your existence goes black. If The Devil's coming to my interview, I'm going back to the kitchens and crazy hair. I don't need reminding of my death—it's not something I can ever forget.

"Miss Pallister?"

Naturally, Mitchell's talking to my hair.

"Yes."

A phone starts to ring. Mitchell ignores it, but his voice mail picks up for all to hear.

"This is Mitchell Johnson, The Devil's intern. Please leave a message after the screams. . . ."

The Banshee-like wails are cut off as the devil on the end of the line disconnects the call.

"Sorry about the wait. Septimus has had to leave," says Mitchell.

"Oh." My stomach plummets to my white sneakers. I wanted The Devil to leave, not Septimus.

"It's okay," replies Mitchell quickly. "Septimus asked me to do the interview. Do you want to come in for a minute while I pack up?"

I follow Mitchell into the accounting chamber, which looks like a bomb hit it. Cabinets are overflowing with folders that are too fat to be filed properly, and stacks of paper cover every surface. Plus, there's a strange smell, like Mexican food gone bad. This office definitely needs a woman's touch.

And a hosing down.

With bleach.

"Septimus gave me some money to take you out," says Mitchell. His face is inches from a computer monitor, and his right hand is maneuvering a mouse across a pad that has an image of The Devil on it.

My eyes narrow. Is this a joke? Mitchell Johnson had better not have placed that ad as a ruse to get girls up here. He may score with Patty Lloyd—most devils do—but I'm more likely to smack him with the baseball bat if he tries anything with me.

Mitchell has obviously sensed my discomfort. He raises his hands and blushes furiously. His cheeks now match the color of his eyes.

Pink eyes are very cute on a boy.

"No, no, no!" he exclaims, stepping back. He trips over a wastepaper basket. "It's not like that, honestly. Septimus gave me some money." He shows me a thin wad of bills. "I don't have this much money—in fact, I don't have any money! Plus, I thought we could meet up with my friends. If they like you, that's good enough for me. And you aced the written test with the best score by a mile. I'm not pulling a fast one on you or anything like that. Septimus was here just a second ago, but The Devil came in and..."

The words are tumbling from his mouth, and here I was, thinking verbal diarrhea was something only I suffered from. Mitchell looks so worried, I can't help smiling. Sensing he isn't about to get pummeled, he slowly inches around the desk.

"So are we cool?" he asks.

Mitchell looks down at me; I look up at him. I'm not all that short—I stand around five foot seven in my socks—but Mitchell is definitely over six feet tall.

I remembered him being tall.

"You don't remember me, do you?"

Mitchell looks wary. Is he thinking of lying? I hope not, because I hate liars. It's one of the reasons Patty Lloyd and I fell out a few years ago. Mitchell's eyes have narrowed, and he's biting his bottom lip.

"No, sorry," he mumbles eventually. "We've met before?"

"San Francisco—1967," I prompt. "Does it mean anything to you?"

Mitchell shakes his head. "You're getting me mixed up with someone else. I wasn't born until 1992, and I died in 2009. And I've never been to San Fran—" Suddenly he breaks off and his pink eyes widen. His mouth is a perfect circle.

I make a whistling sound, which is easy because I have a small gap between my front teeth. "And there it is," I say. "You do remember me."

I've played this moment over and over in my head, ever since I found out I'd gotten an interview for the second accounting internship and knew I'd have a chance to speak to him. I first saw Mitchell in Hell a few weeks ago, when I was working in the kitchens. He was with Septimus, carrying a pile of dry cleaning and a tray of coffee. That was when I knew he worked with Septimus. They only came in for a strawberry cheesecake—which was added to Mitchell's pile—and then they were gone. I didn't get a close look, but I was sure it was him: the embodiment of an apparition I was certain I saw while I was still alive, many years before, on the night *he* died.

The feeling of being remembered by Mitchell is just as great as I hoped it would be. It may be just a brief glimpse of me that he recalls, and he may have needed prompting to get there, but I *am* in someone's memory.

I wasn't forgotten after all.

Mitchell is still in a daze. "There was a house. We—I mean Alfarin, Elinor, and I—couldn't remember why we were there, but that was you," he gasps. "You're the one I saw at that house. They were taking a man away in an ambulance. I saw you—and you saw me."

"Yes, yes!" I say excitedly. "So that pretty girl with long red hair was Elinor? And the huge guy—that was Alfarin? Are they here in Hell, too? What are they like?"

"They're the best."

"I knew what you were as soon as I saw you. I mean, I knew you were dead."

"How?"

"You were surrounded by light. I thought you were angels."

Mitchell snorts and digs his hands into his pockets. For some reason, he's shaking. "Yeah, right idea, wrong direction."

"So you've only been dead for four years?"

"And counting," replies Mitchell. "I . . . I got hit by a bus."

I'm overwhelmed by a strange urge to hug him, but I don't. I'm not like Patty Lloyd and her dorm sorority of the Underworld. I would sooner throw myself into an actual vat of meringue than throw myself at a guy, regardless of how he died.

I have so many questions for Mitchell, now that we're finally talking. What was he doing that night outside my house, for a start? And how was he there in 1967, *dead*, when he hadn't even been *born* yet?

Unfortunately, Mitchell beats me to the punch. "How did *you* die?" he asks. "Septimus said you've been dead for over forty years. You must have passed over not long after I saw you."

It's that question again. Arching my back, I glare up at Mitchell. And to think we'd been getting along so well. The strange urge to hug him vanishes. Instead, I turn around and jab my elbow into his stomach.

"*Ow!*"

"I don't like talking about it, and you'd know the answer if you'd bothered reading my devil resources file."

"According to the first page in your devil resources file, you talk about everything. Nonstop," he retorts.

So Mitchell Johnson has read at least some of my file, then. He must be the first devil who's done that. I wonder why he didn't bother to read the rest. Then again, I've never bothered to read my file, either—but why would I want to, when I already know all too well how I died?

"Knowledge is power," I tell him. He grins and ruffles my hair. No one is allowed to touch the hair, so I flick his forehead with my finger. He retaliates with "Leave it, short-ass," which is rich coming from someone who looks like he's been stretched out on a rack.

"Your face looks like you're covered in fluff," I retort. "Not enough testosterone in that puny body to grow a beard?"

We aren't even at the door yet.

"Why are you called Medusa?"

I point to my head. "Have you not noticed the hair?"

"Can't miss it." But his reflexes are quicker this time, and he jumps out of my reach with a bark-like laugh. I smile in spite of myself.

"The Grim Reapers at the HalfWay House gave me that name. They misheard me in the processing center," I explain. "I decided I liked it, but not just because of my hair. It separated me from the Melissa I was on earth. It sort of allowed me to start again, you know?"

"That's actually kinda cool."

"Thanks."

"You have dimples," says Mitchell. "You look like the Raggedy Ann doll my mom used to keep on her bed."

I think that was a compliment, kind of. We stand there staring at each other, but it starts to make me feel strange. Not as awkward as in some of the encounters I've had with guys in Hell—trying to talk to the ones who are still stoned from their accidental OD back in the land of the living, for example, is a pretty ridiculous endeavor— but this is enough to make me feel self-conscious.

"Do you believe in fate, Medusa?" asks Mitchell.

"Yeah, I do," I reply. I don't add that I don't consider this a good thing.

But perhaps meeting Mitchell is finally the beginning of something okay in this hope-forsaken place. I just need to give it a chance. I just need to trust. And call it a sixth sense, but I feel like I know Mitchell already.

Maybe that's because, like Septimus, Mitchell remembers me.

"I never used to believe in fate or any of that crap, but I think we'll make a good team," he says. "I have a pretty good feeling about this."

"Does this mean I have the job?"

"Yeah, why not?"

What? Easiest interview ever! (Apart from the one for the kitchens, of course, which was over before it even started.)

"Oh, let me be the one to tell Patty Lloyd," I beg under my breath. *"Just this once, let* me *be the devil to hold something over* her."

I pause for a moment when a little voice in my head reminds me that I didn't always feel this way about Patty. The truth is, when she first arrived, I looked after her. She was terrified and would sob into her pillow every night. But after a while she got comfortable and chose another crowd, which wasn't difficult because there are hundreds of us squished in the dorm. Now I can always hear her, cackling away, saying mean things about how I look and dress and talk. That witch and her cronies are always trying to lord their superiority over me.

But finally, brains and wild hair have beaten out boobs and tattoos. Mitchell turns off his computer and extinguishes a couple of candles with his thumb and forefinger. Today is going to be a good day—a rare day; I can feel it in my bones. And wiping the smug smile off Patty Lloyd's face will be the icing on the cake.

2. **Team Devil**

"So does Septimus usually give you money to take devils out?"

"Are you kidding?" replies Mitchell. "That was a first. When he said he wanted to do another interview, I could have cried. I couldn't believe he was seriously going to make me keep working. These interviews have made today the day from Hell. After the fifth one, I figured this was how Septimus had decided to punish me."

"Punish you for what?" I ask.

"Uh, nothing."

We push through the crowds in silence. I still desperately want to ask Mitchell what he was doing outside my house forty years ago. Seeing him and his friends that day was the first time I thought there might be something beyond the wretched life I was being forced to live. An honest-to-goodness afterlife. Not that I wanted to die, but knowing there might be something else … well, it gave me hope.

But I'm worried about badgering him, and I don't want to annoy the guy who's just hired me. I've waited this long to finally find and speak to Mitchell alone, and a little while longer won't kill me— metaphorically, of course.

I decide to play it cool.

"So how long have Alfarin and Elinor been in Hell?"

"Alfarin's a Viking. He died in battle over a thousand years ago," replies Mitchell. "Elinor died in the Great Fire of London in 1666."

"And how did you all meet? You aren't the kind of guy I would expect to see hanging out with Vikings—no offense, Mitchell."

"Why wouldn't I hang out with Vikings?" he asks indignantly. "I can handle myself."

"Says the boy who got hit by a bus. Wasn't it big enough for you to see?"

"I was…distracted."

"By a girl in a short skirt, no doubt."

I'm only teasing, but Mitchell isn't smiling. At first I think I've offended him—I'm not very good at making jokes—but then I realize he isn't paying any attention to me at all. He's looking at *her*. She's clearly been waiting for him in the shadows, ready to pounce like a leopard. A mangy one. With fleas.

"Uh, hi, Patty," mumbles Mitchell at the figure swaying toward us. Honestly, if she moved her hips any farther from side to side she'd dislocate them.

"Hello, Mitchell." Patty flutters her eyelashes at him and then glares at me, but her pink eyes don't have the same ferocious intensity as red, and she's years away from that. I smile sweetly because I know it will annoy her.

"I have some free time right now," she says, turning her attention back to Mitchell. "I'm doing the late shift at the library tonight. I thought we could practice some of the things we'll be doing together in the office."

The Easy-Lay-from-the-Library licks her lips and winks. I don't know whether to laugh at how obvious she is, or push her annoying dead ass over the balcony. I once pushed Patty into a vat of crème caramel when she came by the kitchens to heckle me, and she dragged me in with her on her way down. It took me a month to get all that sugar out of my hair, but it was so worth it.

Mitchell's voice brings me back to the present. "Sorry, Patty, but Septimus meant it when he told you you're too valuable to the library to leave it," he says. "And also, Medusa got the job." The tone of his voice fills me with confidence. He seems pleased.

Patty looks horrified. This is even better than if I'd told her myself! "Well, we'd love to stay and chat, Patty," I say. "But Septimus gave us some money for a date, and it's burning a hole in Mitchell's pocket. Enjoy your night shift—alone."

Mitchell is still laughing as we reach Thomason's Bar. I'm on such a high that if we weren't trapped underground, I'd be touching the clouds Up There. This was the best revenge I could have wished for after Patty and her friends' latest prank on me. Last week they thought it would be funny to make hundreds of posters with ESCAPED ANIMAL written in bold letters across the top and my picture below. They plastered the posters on every free surface in the library. I took them all down myself, one by one. I wasn't going to ask for help. I didn't need anyone's help. But I spent every moment wishing someone would at least offer. After what just happened, I have a feeling that if Mitchell had been there, he'd have given me a hand.

Inside Thomason's, I recognize Alfarin and Elinor at once. Alfarin is built like a house. He has long blond hair and a beard with tiny braids in it. His enormous frame is balanced precariously on a stool as he stands on tiptoe, poking at something on the ceiling with a double-bladed axe.

Elinor has the longest hair I've ever seen. It cascades down her back like a red waterfall. It's so pretty—and straight. I would love to have hair like that instead of always looking like I've been electrocuted. For some reason, she's grabbing the back of her neck like she's nervous about something, which, judging by the wobbling Alfarin, is probably his balancing skills.

"Will ye get down from there, Alfarin?" begs Elinor. "Ye cannot kill a fly with yer axe. Ye will fall and hurt yerself, ye big oaf."

"I will make this pestilent creature rue the day it decided to buzz around my princess," says Alfarin grimly.

Seconds later there's an almighty crash as Alfarin topples off the stool and breaks the table where Elinor is sitting. Glass shatters. The unharmed fly buzzes past my ear and is then caught and swallowed by another Viking about to take a large swig of beer.

"*Alfarin!*" roars a bald man from the other side of the room. He has a golden moustache and a long, matted beard that reaches his stomach. He's clutching a black mace, which is swinging like the pendulum on a grandfather clock.

"My apologies, father brother," calls Alfarin. He is trying to extricate Elinor from shattered glass, which is glinting like a pool of fire in the torchlight. "I will gladly repair any damage."

"Who's the Viking with the mace?" I whisper to Mitchell. "And what's a father brother?"

"That's Magnus, Alfarin's uncle. That's what Vikings call a father brother. And the Viking behind the bar is Alfarin's cousin, Thomason. He owns this place. And see the guy with the long dark hair and short beard, throwing darts at that guy tied to the spinning board? That isn't a guy at all. It's actually Alfarin's great-aunt Dagmar."

I stick out like a sore thumb in this sea of enormous people and weaponry, and it isn't long before everyone's eyes—deep bloodred, of course—start drifting from the puffing Alfarin to the girl who looks like she has snakes for hair.

"Mitchell!" squeals Elinor. "Alfarin, look. Mitchell has brought someone to meet us. And it's a girl!"

"Mitchell, my friend," booms Alfarin. His heavy boots crunch through the glass as he scoops Elinor up and over his shoulder. He's still carrying her as he makes his way over to us.

"Put me down, ye fool!" she cries.

"Alfarin, Elinor, this is Medusa," says Mitchell, ignoring the mess. "She's going to be working with me in the accounting office as the other intern."

"Lovely to meet ye." Elinor beams and then kisses me on both cheeks. It's the first time a devil has ever done that to me. Actually, it's the first time *anyone* has done that to me, alive or dead.

I want to like it, but trusting people in Hell is as difficult as trusting people in life.

"Alfarin, son of Hlif, son of Dobin," says Alfarin very formally. He isn't smiling, and I'm a little alarmed as he swings his axe upward, catches it in his right hand and then drops to his knee.

"Your devoted warrior from this day forth," he continues. "You need only say the name of any foul devil who has slighted your person, and my faithful axe will slice open his entrails, which shall be tied around his neck until he is throttled—"

"Get up, Alfarin," scolds Elinor. "We don't want to frighten Medusa off before she even knows us."

"Yeah, let her get to know us first, and *then* she can make a run for it," says Mitchell.

"It's nice to meet you all." I try smiling at them, but my top lip sticks to my teeth and then my bottom lip starts to betray me.

Stop it, Medusa, I say to myself. My hands are in my pockets, so I pinch my leg—hard. I am not a crybaby. I've never been a crybaby. Life made me tough; death made me tougher. I will not lose it because I've finally found the three angels who were outside my house that day.

Devils, I correct myself. They were devils. They only looked like angels.

"Ye frightened her, Alfarin," says Elinor, and she rubs the back of her neck again. "I'm so sorry. He is lovely once ye get to know him. Please don't be worried, Medusa. It will be so nice to have another girl on the team."

"It isn't that," I say quickly. "It's just…" But I can't quite bring myself to say it aloud.

Mitchell steps in and explains for me in a hurried whisper. "Guys, I know this is crazy, but Medusa has seen Team DEVIL before. When she was *alive*."

Elinor and Alfarin exchange worried glances.

"How is that possible?" asks Elinor softly.

"Remember San Francisco?" Mitchell says quietly.

"What? San Francisco!" Alfarin exclaims.

"Shhhhh," hisses Elinor, frantically flapping her hands. She looks about wildly to see if anyone has heard us.

"Elinor is right. I am sorry, Mitchell," says Alfarin. Then he pats my hand awkwardly. "And I apologize for the throaty manliness of my voice, Medusa. I do not possess Mitchell's ability to whisper like a girl."

"Thanks for that, Alfarin," says Mitchell. "Look, Septimus gave me some money, so let's go get something to eat. Somewhere quiet, so we can talk without being overheard."

Alfarin, Elinor and I all turn and make a quizzical face at Mitchell. Somewhere quiet? In Hell? You can't go to the bathroom without an audience. Privacy is left with your pulse back in the land of the living.

"You know what I mean," says Mitchell, rolling his pink eyes.

The four of us leave Thomason's. Vikings are still watching us. Watching me.

The boys follow their stomachs, and Elinor and I follow the boys.

As we walk, I can't help thinking how strange this all is. I'm just not used to devils being so nice to me. I can't help worrying that I'm not going to be very good at being a friend—if that's what they eventually want me to be. I *hope* it's what they eventually want me to be. It's lonely sometimes, being on the outside of a crowd.

Yet there's something about Team DEVIL that seems so . . . nice. They give me this feeling of familiarity that's warm and snuggly, like clean sheets.

"So, how long have ye been in Hell, Medusa?" asks Elinor. She's wearing a long white dress and satin slippers, and she appears to float above the floor as we push through the bustling crowds of devils.

"Over forty years," I reply. "I died in 1967."

Elinor opens her mouth to say something, but she catches my eye and quickly closes it again. I know what she's going to ask—it's what every devil asks—but I appreciate the fact that she doesn't.

"How long have you known Alfarin and Mitchell?" I ask.

"I searched for Alfarin for nearly one hundred years after I arrived in 1666," she says. "Mitchell was easier to find, once I knew which logbooks to read."

"Why were you looking for them?" I ask, intrigued. "You lived too late for Alfarin and too early for Mitchell to have known them in life, right?"

Elinor gasps, and her pale hands with their long, delicate fingers fly to her mouth. Mitchell and Alfarin stop walking when they hear her, and she and I bump right into them.

Okay. Clearly, Elinor feels she's revealed something to me that she shouldn't have, and Mitchell and Alfarin know it. I have no idea what their issue is, but I do know there's definitely more to Team DEVIL than meets the eye.

Rumors have been flying lately that Hell is running out of food, but not for people like me who know where to look. I guess there are some benefits to having worked in the kitchens for so long.

A little while later, after I've managed to swipe four pizzas and a strawberry cheesecake from the kitchen prep area, we all head back to level 1 and the accounting office. Elinor is biting her nails, and Alfarin is actually attempting to tiptoe as we make our way through the corridor where shadows are fighting on the walls.

I want to make a good impression for many reasons, so I keep quiet, even though the shadows freak me out.

"I don't like this," whispers Elinor. "What if security finds us? What if The Devil is still in his office? I don't like being up this high."

"I would agree with you, my princess," replies Alfarin. "But, alas, my need for a meat feast pizza is greater than my worry of meeting the Overlord of Hell. If he should find us, know that I will sacrifice myself, so you may flee."

"Once you've eaten the chicken and spinach pizza first, you mean," says Mitchell, catching my eye. He's very funny for someone who's only been dead for four years. Most new devils spend their first ten years in a state of total hysteria, but Mitchell is pretty stoic.

We reach the thick stone door of the accounting office and I notice that something creepy and dark is dripping down its center. Mitchell puts his finger to his lips and we all stop dead in our tracks. We're holding our breath, which is ridiculous because we're dead and we don't need to breathe.

A feeling of recklessness comes over me. I want to get into the accounting chamber. I need to know why these devils were outside my house, and why *then*. The evening I saw them was the evening that Rory—the evening that *he*—was taken away. Forever.

That was the evening that should have changed my life for the better, but it didn't.

I gently push past Mitchell and open the door. The chamber is bathed in a strange, pale haze as sparks from blue currents zap and splinter along the walls.

"Get in quick," says Mitchell urgently, and he pulls Alfarin and Elinor inside behind me.

"What are those, Mitchell?" I ask, pointing to the electrical bolts that crack like whips.

"It's a sign that The Devil is in a foul mood. It happens all the time these days. Let me just listen in on the Oval Office. If he's still in there, we need to run. Don't worry, Medusa. You'll get used to the crazy stuff up here—eventually."

But it isn't the fact that The Devil might be in the Oval Office that's worrying me at the moment. It's the fact that I'm going to be working in an office that has electricity moving along damp walls. If I come into contact with one, my hair is going to explode into its own mushroom cloud.

Mitchell puts his ear up to another door and closes his eyes in concentration. Alfarin has his axe clenched tightly between his plate-sized hands, and Elinor is shaking so hard she looks as if she's about to drop the box with the strawberry cheesecake.

I take it from her trembling hands. "Save the cake first" is my motto. Gingerly, I step over discarded coffee cups that have clearly been thrown *at* the recycling bin instead of *in* it, and I place the cheesecake box on the messiest desk I've ever seen. And I thought lawyers were disorganized.

"Thank ye, Medusa," whispers Elinor. "Can ye hear anything, Mitchell?"

"All quiet on the Devil front," he replies. "Now, who has the pizza?"

Alfarin has placed the boxes on a chair, so we all sit on the warm stone floor, and it isn't long before we're munching away in silence.

Their quietness is companionable. Mine, I'm not so sure. I don't make friends easily. I've always been suspicious of strangers, even in Hell. If I couldn't trust people in life, who can I trust in death? The way the girls in my dorm turned on me with a pack mentality that wolves would be proud of was proof to me that the answer is *no one*. Yet I have to admit that the four of us make a very comfortable square as we all stretch out our legs and rest our backs against a wall, a safe, a desk and a dark oak wardrobe that's covered in symbols and runes.

"So, Medusa," says Mitchell, wiping his mouth on his sleeve. "Since we need to get to know each other, and since you're the newbie, it's only fair that you should get to ask us the first question."

I swallow my last mouthful of strawberry cheesecake and wipe my fingers on my black shorts. My questions tend to be blunt and awkward, and I'm always being told by other devils in the kitchens that I ask too many. I'll ease into this slowly, I decide.

"Why do you call yourselves Team DEVIL?"

"It's the initials, *D-E-V-I-L*," replies Elinor quickly. "It stands for Dead but not Evil Vanguard in Life. Mitchell thought of it."

"And it's just the three of you?"

"Yeah," says Mitchell, but there's a strange, abstract look on his face, as if he isn't quite sure. He looks to the others for support, but they all have the same confused expression.

"What's wrong?" I ask.

"It's just...well...we..." stutters Elinor.

"What my princess is attempting to say, Medusa," says Alfarin, "is that there were three of us who returned to Hell after our journey back to the land of the living. Yet there are shadows in our recollections of our time away. Empty spaces that do not make sense."

Aha. Here's the opening I've been waiting for.

"How did you get back to the land of the living in the first place?" I ask. "No one can leave Hell."

"We took—borrowed—something from the safe, in this office, that helped us," replies Elinor.

"Well, technically I did," adds Mitchell sheepishly.

"But what?" I ask.

"Have you ever heard of a Viciseometer, Medusa?" asks Alfarin.

A Viciseometer? I thought that was just another urban legend in Hell. You hear all sorts of crazy myths and stories down here, but the Viciseometer is one that's stayed with me. It's a time-traveling device, supposedly used to introduce new inventions to the earth. So *that's* how Team DEVIL got back to the land of the living. I try to wrap my head around the idea that Viciseometers are real and these three devils managed to get a hold of one.

"So why did you come back to Hell?" I ask. "I don't get it."

"Neither do we, Medusa," says Mitchell. "I mean, we know we came back because we found out we couldn't control our fates the way we thought we could, but there's more to it than that. Something happened to us back on earth, and we don't know what it is. It's like we're being haunted, but we can't see or hear what it is. In fact, the more I think about it, the more I believe you might be able to help us."

"I still don't get it."

"We think we did something, something we shouldn't have done, and we've been trying to figure out what it was ever since we got back, M," says Elinor. She looks up at me and blushes. "Oh, I'm sorry—do ye mind if I shorten yer name to M?" she asks. "Medusa in the Greek legend was nasty, and ye seem so nice."

"Sure, if you want."

I pinch myself again. My answer to her question came out sounding harsh, but thankfully Elinor just beams. She has the prettiest smile; it lights up her face. She would have made the loveliest angel.

"The point is," continues Mitchell, "—and by the way, none of you are shortening my name to anything, so don't even think about it—the point is, the three of us don't know why we were in San Francisco that day. It was like we opened our eyes and we were there, on that street, in that time. So don't you think it's more than just a coincidence, Medusa? You were there, you saw us, and then from all the billions of devils in Hell, it's *you* who Septimus told me he thinks is the most promising of all the applicants for this job? It's just strange, that's all."

"If there is one thing I have learned, it is that nothing in this death is an accident," says Alfarin solemnly.

"Fate," adds Elinor, nodding.

Fate. Mitchell spoke about that earlier. My grandmother used to talk about it all the time. She used to say our destinies were already mapped out for us. It was just up to us to take the right road, and even if you took a wrong turn, there would always be another way.

I don't think Team DEVIL will laugh at me if I tell them that. Well, Mitchell and Alfarin might because they're guys, but Elinor wouldn't. There's an innocence about her that's childlike, but she doesn't seem to take any crap from Mitchell and Alfarin, either. She's the absolute truth. The kind of person I always wanted as a friend in life, but never gave myself the chance of finding because I was scared they would get hurt, too.

But I don't get the chance to say anything, because just as I'm about to lay myself bare, a red light in the accounting chamber starts to flash. A terrible wail, like a person screaming in fear and pain, fills the office. Mitchell jumps to his feet.

"That's The Devil's panic alarm!" he cries. "Something's happened, right here on level one! Something really bad. This will be the first place they come!"

"*Run!*" Alfarin roars.

3. Lockdown

Alfarin is already at the door, but Mitchell pulls him back.

"We can't run," he says. "We have to stay here."

"We cannot remain!" cries Elinor. "We're in Hell, Mitchell! Act first, think much, much later is the rule here, ye know that!"

"Mitchell's right," I say. "We haven't done anything wrong, but if we're seen running away from level 1, it'll definitely look suspicious."

"Then I will trust in your judgment, my friends," replies Alfarin, backing down. His next words are drowned out by a sudden increase in the volume from the screaming siren. I can feel it piercing my eardrums, like needles. The pain of the person screaming is actually inside my skull. And then I recognize the voice. It's mine. It's the sound I made when I fell to my death.

Elinor has her fingers in her ears, and she's the first to collapse to the floor.

"Make it stop, make it stop!" she screams. "I can feel the flames again."

Alfarin is moaning about fangs and knives. His axe slips to the floor as he's forced to block out the sound with his hands. The flashing red light is getting darker. Liquid is dripping from its base onto the stone floor below.

The liquid is blood.

I don't like blood, especially the blood of the dead, because it looks like lumpy gravy. I start to sway.

"It's programmed so . . . so that every devil hears his own . . . death again," groans Mitchell. His pink eyes are rolling in their sockets.

I drop to my knees as the room starts to spin. My relentless scream is now accompanied by Septimus's deep, drawling voice, which seems to be coming out of every fissure in the stone walls.

"HELL IS NOW IN LOCKDOWN. YOU ARE STRONGLY ADVISED TO STAY EXACTLY WHERE YOU ARE. FAILURE TO COMPLY IS UNWISE. HELL IS NOW IN LOCKDOWN. . . ."

It's the last thing I hear before I pass out.

I wake to the sensation of something cold and wet being splashed on my face. Aside from the goose bumps I got when I heard The Devil screeching only a few hours ago, I haven't been cold for four decades, and the feeling is strange and unnerving. There's a bitter taste on my tongue. I can't quite open my eyes yet, but I sense someone crouching over me, watching me. Expecting the worst, I immediately lash out with my arms and legs, but it's only Mitchell's voice that responds.

"Watch it! Jeez, you're seriously bony, Medusa. You could take an eye out with those elbows."

I stop flailing and manage to open an eye. Mitchell, Alfarin and Elinor are already awake, although Elinor's pale skin has turned a jaundiced shade of yellow. Alfarin is the only one standing; Mitchell now has his long legs drawn up well away from me, and he's placed his head between his knees.

"HELL IS NOW IN LOCKDOWN. YOU ARE STRONGLY ADVISED TO STAY EXACTLY WHERE YOU ARE. FAILURE TO COMPLY IS UNWISE. HELL IS NOW IN LOCKDOWN. . . ."

The screaming siren has stopped, but Septimus's prerecorded warning still booms out of the rock at intermittent moments. I look up, both eyes open now, at the connecting door to the Oval Office, and see that the flashing light has also been extinguished. The only proof that it was ever in use is a thick puddle of blood, the circumference of a car tire, which is bubbling away below it.

"I see that not even the dead can rouse you easily, Miss Pallister." Only then do I see Septimus, standing behind a desk with a crooked smile on his face. "Let me assure you that this is not a further aptitude test to see whether you can cope with working on level 1."

He places a cup of water on the desk. I'm guessing he's the one who splashed me awake.

"That alarm is the sickest thing I have ever heard," groans Mitchell. "I could hear my bones crunching."

"As you know, it was designed that way to make devils listen, Mitchell," says Septimus. "It was programmed for each of us to hear our deaths once more. I am sorry for the distress it caused you all, but as an alarm, it is extremely effective. Even I stop everything at the sound of a sword slicing through an intestinal wall and the resulting harmony of dying moans caused by infection."

"How long do we have to stay in lockdown, Lord Septimus?" asks Alfarin. He's mopping at his face with the edge of his tunic.

"A while longer, I'm afraid, Prince Alfarin," replies Septimus. "There has been a grievous breach in security in the master's private chambers. The HBI and Sir's own private security team are currently scouring the central business district for that which has been taken."

"Someone stole something from The Devil?" I ask incredulously. "Only someone insane would try that."

"This is Hell, Miss Pallister. So yes, I would say chances are likely that the person or persons involved are almost certainly insane."

"HELL IS NOW IN LOCKDOWN. YOU ARE STRONGLY ADVISED TO STAY EXACTLY WHERE YOU ARE. FAILURE TO COMPLY IS UNWISE. HELL IS NOW IN LOCKDOWN...."

"Is there any way we can turn that thing off, boss?" asks Mitchell. He looks as if he's going to hurl—and then he does.

"Actually, I find it quite comforting," says Elinor. She is sipping from another glass of water. "Yer voice is very soothing, Mr. Septimus, sir."

"Why, thank you, Miss Powell," replies Septimus. "Now, can I trust Team DEVIL to not go...wandering? It is vitally important that the four of you remain here. There may be creatures roaming the corridors over the next few hours that no decent devil should meet."

"My axe and I will guard the door, Lord Septimus," announces Alfarin. He has more color in his face than the rest of us put together. "No one will go out, no one will get in."

"Then I place my faith in you, Prince Alfarin, and my first intern, once he stops vomiting pizza," says Septimus, grimacing at Mitchell. He then turns to Elinor and me. "Ladies, as it is in death as well as in life, you are both in charge, of course."

"Will you come back?" I ask.

"You have my word, Miss Pallister."

"HELL IS NOW IN LOCKDOWN. YOU ARE STRONGLY ADVISED TO STAY EXACTLY WHERE YOU ARE. FAILURE TO COMPLY IS UNWISE. HELL IS NOW IN LOCKDOWN...."

"Have ye ever known Hell to be in lockdown before, Alfarin?" asks Elinor. Septimus has gone and she's on her knees, cleaning up the large pool of blood under the light by the door. I take a deep breath and go to help her.

"Only once in my time here," replies Alfarin. "It was in 1348. The bubonic plague was eating away at the living in medieval England. Millions of devils arrived in Hell after Up There closed the gates. There were so many that the Black Death came with them."

"But devils can't die again," I say. "So what was the problem if the Black Death came to Hell?"

"Remember, the dead in Hell can still feel pain and suffering, Medusa," Alfarin says. "That was one of the edicts of the Highers. When the Black Death came here, devils erupted in pustulating boils. Hell went into lockdown while the affected devils were being treated. But many devils disappeared around that time, taken away, it is said, to be experimented on."

"That's awful!" exclaims Elinor.

"Operation H," mutters Mitchell. "Oh, no..."

"What?" I ask.

Mitchell shakes his head. "Nothing, ignore me."

But I know when someone is hiding something. I remember hearing The Devil talking about an Operation H when I was waiting for my interview.

"Do ye think the same thing is happening now?"

"No," I reply. "Septimus said something has been taken from The Devil's private chambers. I wonder what it is."

"HELL IS NOW IN LOCKDOWN. YOU ARE STRONGLY ADVISED TO STAY EXACTLY WHERE YOU ARE. FAILURE TO COMPLY IS UNWISE. HELL IS NOW IN LOCKDOWN...."

This time, the sound of something vibrating on a hard surface follows Septimus's message. A red glow lights up the office, and for a moment I think the warning light is going to start raining blood again. But Mitchell staggers to his feet and starts digging around among the empty pizza boxes. He emerges with a cell phone in his hand.

"Why does your cell phone do that?" I ask.

"It only glows red when the person on the other end is the devil who happens to be my boss," replies Mitchell. "Yours will probably do the same thing from now on."

I don't tell Mitchell that I don't have a cell phone in Hell. I did once, but the messages I received weren't the kind I wanted to read.

Mitchell puts the phone to his ear and falls into a big leather chair that has been wheeled into a corner.

"Hey, boss....All fine....Yeah, I've stopped puking my guts up....No, Medusa hasn't fainted again....No problem....Okay.... What?...Are you kidding me?...But you know we had nothing to do with it!...But Medusa was here...." At this, Mitchell looks over at me in alarm. "...Then we're coming, too....I'm not panicking....Easy for you to say....I said I'm not panicking....But she was here the whole time....My voice is *not* high enough to shatter glass....Okay....We'll wait for you....Bye."

Elinor puts her arm around me. At first I think she's trembling, but when I look down at the glass of water in my hands, I see that it's me.

"Septimus is coming to get you, Medusa," says Mitchell. "Apparently the security team wants to interview you."

"But she was here!" cries Elinor. "M didn't steal anything. She's been eating pizza with us."

"Actually, I ate most of the strawberry cheesecake." My voice is breaking as I attempt to diffuse everyone's obvious panic with humor. "Maybe the head chef knows I took it from his private storeroom."

Mitchell's voice sounded shrill on the call with Septimus, but mine could summon dogs. I haven't even started working on level 1 yet, and already there's a lockdown for the first time in nearly seven hundred years, and somehow they think I'm involved. That must be a record for screw-ups.

"You've been with me since the interview, and that was hours and hours ago," says Mitchell. "You've got nothing to worry about."

Elinor is holding my hand when Septimus and four suited men arrive to take me in for questioning. I don't want to, but I pull out of her grasp and wrap my arms around myself. I want the ground to open up and swallow me whole. I feel so humiliated that I've already dragged three devils into a situation that had nothing to do with them.

In single file, we are led along the level 1 corridor past the elevators and straight toward a blanket of darkness where the light from the flaming torches doesn't reach. A caustic smell starts to wrap its disgusting tendrils around me. It's like fish left to rot in a warm pantry.

"Oh, no!" cries Elinor as the smell reaches her. "Not here, not for this."

I don't know what the big deal is. "Try holding your nose, Elinor," I suggest.

"It's not the smell my princess is worried about, Medusa,"

says Alfarin, far behind me. "Mitchell, are you thinking the same thing as I?"

"You got your axe, Alfarin?" Mitchell responds.

"Naturally."

"Then we stand on either side of them when we get there, okay?"

"I am with you as always, my friend."

Mitchell and Alfarin have their own language, an understanding. Like true friends. But at their words, the HBI agent who is leading the way suddenly stops and turns around. His stubby fingers flick back his jacket to reveal a handgun nestled in a black leather holster.

"I wouldn't try anything silly if I were you, kiddos." He sounds as thuggish as he looks, and I shrink away from him. He couldn't kill us, of course, but a gunshot wound would still be agony.

"Oh, please, ye fool," replies Elinor sharply. "Alfarin could kick yer ass with his eyes shut."

"HELL IS NOW IN LOCKDOWN. YOU ARE STRONGLY ADVISED TO STAY EXACTLY WHERE YOU ARE. FAILURE TO COMPLY IS UNWISE. HELL IS NOW IN LOCKDOWN. . . ."

Septimus's voice continues to sound the lockdown alarm, and it's so loud that it almost covers the sound of the real Septimus laughing behind me.

"Don't mess with Team DEVIL, Roger," he calls. "Their ingenuity and cunning have been known to impress even me, and as Caesar can testify, I am notoriously hard to please."

This makes me feel better—until I notice that Septimus has maneuvered himself next to me as we walk into the darkness. I can't help thinking it's for my protection.

Tiny red lights begin illuminating the stone path as we make our way forward. The increase in gradient makes my thighs ache. We are traveling upward.

"Where are we going, Septimus?" calls Mitchell.

"To the security offices."

"I thought level 1 was the highest floor in Hell."

"This is an area that is out of bounds, Mitchell. We do not advertise its existence."

"Am I in trouble?" I whisper.

"No, Miss Pallister," replies Septimus firmly. "But a review of the security cameras in the master's private chambers has revealed something we would like your input on. You have nothing to fear."

"Septimus...that smell," says Mitchell, and I'm reminded of Elinor's reaction to it just a moment ago.

"I repeat, Mitchell, you have nothing to fear, not while I am with you."

The stench is getting worse, though. I've never been able to break the habit of breathing—there are very few devils who can— and no matter how hard I try to stop, the rotten smell gets into my nose anyway. My eyes stream with the effort of trying to see in the darkness. For the first time in ages, I wish I were back in the steam and sweat of Hell's kitchens. At least there, the aroma of fresh bread and roasting chicken didn't make me gag.

What in Hell is causing that stench?

The illuminated lights on the floor turn sharply to the right and begin traveling up the wall beside me. I realize they're marking out a large entrance. Sure enough, two of the HBI agents each push open a door in that very spot, and a flood of white light blinds us.

"Inside. Quickly," commands the one named Roger.

I blink rapidly as my eyes become accustomed to the change. All of us have tears streaming down our cheeks—except Septimus, who isn't blinking at all.

"A few words of caution before we enter the security briefing room, Team DEVIL," he says. "It would be unwise to mention the smell, even though it is quite unbearable. It would be deemed rude, and trust me, you do not want to offend Perfidious."

"Who is—"

But Septimus raises a hand to silence Alfarin.

"I will answer all questions once this exercise is over, Prince Alfarin, but I beg your indulgence. An item was stolen earlier from Sir's private chambers—his bedroom, to be exact. It is critical, for a number of reasons that I will not divulge now, that this item is found and returned. Hell will remain in lockdown until The Devil's property is back in his possession. Miss Pallister is wanted for questioning, not as a suspect, but because she may be able to assist in tracking the person we believe is the culprit."

I nod, although my instincts are telling me to run as fast as I can, as far as I can.

"Your new friends may of course accompany you during the questioning, Miss Pallister, if that is your wish," says Septimus kindly.

"I don't want them to get into any trouble." I sound like a four-year-old, but I'm terrified.

"We're staying," says Mitchell.

"Very well," says Septimus. "Do not panic, and do not resist what is about to happen." He directs his words to Mitchell and Alfarin. "As long as you obey, you are in no danger, you have my word."

The bright light is suddenly extinguished. I feel hot hands on my arms, and I wrestle with them as I'm hustled forward.

"Get off me!" I scream. My fists are on autopilot and are fighting for all they're worth.

"Don't touch her!" yells Mitchell, and I hear someone grunt, as if they've been punched.

"Remember, do not resist," calls Septimus. "Miss Pallister, please trust me."

His voice is like a soothing balm. Although every instinct I possess is pushing at me to fight back—hard—I drag my fists back to my side.

We're forced into a room with a long mahogany table in the center and a large mounted screen at the end. Telephones with rows of flashing red lights line the torchlit stone walls.

I gasp and stumble backward when I see what is standing in the corner of the room. It's a gray-and-white wolf. Only it isn't a wolf; it's a man dressed in a wolf's pelt. The skinned animal's cranium is sitting on top of the man's head, and its teeth are long, black and bared. A growling noise shudders through the air.

But it isn't the wolf head that's growling. It's the man beneath it. I notice for the first time that unlike everyone else in the room, he has black irises.

"Team DEVIL," drawls Septimus. "Allow me to introduce Perfidious, the leader of the Skin-Walkers."

4. **Perfidious**

Stunned silence meets Septimus's introduction. My throat constricts. I glance at Mitchell, Alfarin and Elinor, who are standing in a straight line a few yards away from me. Their movements are very subtle, but both boys edge forward a couple of inches, just enough to put themselves in front of Elinor, who is pulling at the back of her neck again. Mitchell looks over at me and jerks his head. He wants me to move closer to the group—the team—but Septimus stops me before I have a chance to react.

"Stay where you are, Miss Pallister," he says very quietly.

I don't want to look at Perfidious, but his presence is like a magnetic force. I'm drawn to it, but not in a way that makes me feel safe—far from it. Even without the bared black teeth and rumbling growl, I know he's dangerous. There's a distorted aura around him that I can actually see. It's a shadow that swirls around his entire body, moving and twisting like smoke.

The team of HBI investigators is standing back, too, because they're as scared as we are.

What have I gotten Mitchell, Alfarin and Elinor into?

Next to the large mounted screen is another door. It opens, and in walks a small, portly man with a big white beard and long white hair. He's wearing a red suit, which is bulging at the seams, and I am instantly reminded of Santa Claus, albeit one with ruby-colored eyes.

"Thank you for all coming," he says. He speaks with an accent that sounds Scottish, like that actor who played James Bond when I was alive. "My name is Sir Richard Baumwither, and I am the director of the HBI."

He pauses and looks around the room as if expecting a round of applause. He doesn't get one. Perfidious gives him a look of contempt that would unnerve the bravest of devils. The leader of the Skin-Walkers—whatever they are—looks like he wants nothing more than to bite Sir Richard Baumwither's head off. Then Perfidious licks his lips with a black tongue, and I swear I see that same movement mirrored in the lupine skull resting on his head.

"Everyone take a seat," commands Baumwither with an officious wave of his pudgy right hand. He either hasn't registered the wolf-man's reaction or he doesn't care. He simply picks up a remote control device and presses a square red button at the top. The mounted television flickers to life, and I can't help gasping as a familiar image fills the screen.

I suddenly know why I'm here.

At the same moment I open my mouth, Perfidious throws back his head, and the animal pelt comes alive as a shocking scream rips through the room. A set of crystal glasses in the center of the table shatters into tiny fragments. Alfarin springs to his feet with his axe in his hands, but the blade is torn from his grip by some invisible force and goes spinning through the air. It thuds into the table, inches from Baumwither's liver-spotted hands.

"I did not do that," booms Alfarin as two HBI agents foolishly try to grab him. He flings one, and then the other, against the wall.

Mitchell and Elinor are now standing again with fists clenched, ready to hit anyone who comes near their friend. I suddenly notice that I'm doing the same thing, and for a split second the shock of this realization makes me forget the image on the screen. I've always had to defend myself, but this might be the first time in my existence that I've had the instinct to physically protect someone else.

Then Perfidious's continuous howling brings me back to reality. He ignores the chaos in the room, and the shadowy aura surrounding him stretches outward, like groping fingers. It claws at the screen, and I realize it's the aura that's howling in anger, and not Perfidious or the gaping wolf head he's wearing.

I want to howl right along with it, because there is no question in my mind that the face leering down at me from the TV is the same face I see in my nightmares.

It's my mom's husband, my stepfather. His name is Rory Hunter. And he's the reason I'm dead.

The aura's howl reaches a fever pitch, and Baumwither smacks his hand on the table.

"That is enough, Perfidious!" shouts Baumwither. "Kindly recall that you're here because I have personally invited you into the master's inner sanctum. So please show some decorum."

The shadow stops clawing at my stepfather's image and slinks back toward Perfidious. It covers him in darkness, the antithesis of the light that I saw around Mitchell, Alfarin and Elinor that night outside my house.

The night I thought I was rid of Rory Hunter for good.

"Sir Richard," says Septimus calmly, "perhaps you could explain to Miss Pallister why she has been brought here? Despite her forty years in Hell, I would like to remind all of you"—Septimus pauses to glance around the room at everyone, including Perfidious—"that she is sixteen years of age in mortal terms, and this must be quite overwhelming for her."

"Thank you," I whisper, and I slowly sit down again. The palms of my hands are soaked with sweat. All I can think about is the inevitable bad dream that will invade my sleep tonight. I have a certain amount of control over what I do when I'm awake, but I'm a slave to my nightmares. Seeing Rory again after all this time is a brutal shock. It's been so long, and yet not long enough. I already know that tonight I'll fall asleep, and then I'll dream, and then I'll scream, and then I'll wake up everyone in the dorm, which will result in a new vat of crap and taunts from them. My nightmares are the reason Patty and the other girls started calling me an animal in the first place.

Mitchell walks across the room and sits next to me.

"We're here, Medusa," he whispers. "We won't let them hurt you."

I want to believe him.

"I take it by your reaction that you recognize this man, Miss Pallister," says Baumwither. His chubby, pale fingers are interlocked and resting atop his enormous chest.

I nod, and I feel light hands on my shoulders. Elinor has also crossed the floor and is now standing directly behind me. She is so kind that I feel like I'm contaminating her just by being near her.

"This meeting is being recorded," says Baumwither, and he points to four cameras, high up in each corner of the room. "So if you could verbalize your answers, it will save having to repeat the question now, or at a later date."

His ruby eyes are shining, but there's no warmth there. Not like what I see in Septimus's eyes, or Team DEVIL's. Baumwither doesn't remind me of Santa Claus anymore. Now he reminds me of a judge in a courtroom. I keep expecting him to condemn me to death, but he can't because I'm already there.

And it's *his* fault, I think, flicking my eyes to the screen.

"The man is Rory Hunter. He was my stepfather," I reply.

"*Was* your stepfather?" asks Baumwither. "According to our records, he still is. At the time of his death, on the eighteenth of June, 1967, he was still married to your mother, Olivia Alice Pallister, was he not?"

I nod. Baumwither raises a bushy white eyebrow. "Yes," I say aloud.

"Then he remains your stepfather."

"Why does it matter?" demands Mitchell. "You still haven't told Medusa why she's here."

"Miss Pallister is here," replies Baumwither, "because Mr. Hunter is now the chief suspect in a theft that took place earlier today."

"But I haven't seen him since…since my mom…since he and she…"

I can't seem to get the words out, but I recall every detail of that evening with terrible vividness. I can remember the sound of the gunshot, and racing down the stairs. I can remember the blood all over my mom's hands. There was so much blood that at first, I thought it was my mom who was shot. Then two medics were there. They just appeared out of nowhere. I ran out to the porch, and Jancye, a neighbor, came and helped me. I was covered in blood, too. It must have come from my mom's shirt when I hugged her, because I didn't go near Rory's body.

I hate blood.

I hate *him*.

Septimus turns to one of the HBI agents. "Would you get Miss Pallister some water, please?"

"Do I look like an assistant?" replies the investigator.

"It wasn't actually a request." Septimus's eyes narrow as he rises to his full height.

The investigator mutters something under his breath but leaves the interrogation room.

"Have you seen your stepfather at all in the forty years you've resided in Hell?" asks Baumwither.

"No."

For the first time, Perfidious moves. He leans forward at an unnatural angle, moving his arms in time with his long legs. It's almost as if he is deliberately stopping himself from loping on all fours. And then we hear his voice. It's unlike anything I've ever heard before. Half human, half animal. The words are elongated with a sonorous rumble that vibrates in my bones.

"The Unspeakable has been accounted for—every second, of every hour, of every day," growls Perfidious.

"Until today," says Baumwither tartly.

I hear Mitchell swear under his breath; Septimus does, too.

"Sir Richard," says Septimus. "I believe it would be prudent to show Perfidious a little more respect. He is, after all, the leader of the Skin-Walkers, and The Devil himself would accord Perfidious the deference his position demands."

"Septimus," replies Baumwither, "you may be The Devil's number one civil servant, but I am the director of the HBI and have been for nearly a century. Today Hell is in lockdown due to one of the most serious security breaches it has ever seen, which came about as a direct result of one of the Unspeakables escaping from the Skin-Walkers' realm, breaking into The Devil's private chambers and stealing his most valuable possession. So I will show Perfidious respect when Rory Hunter is back where he belongs—in spiked chains with the other vile cretins who once preyed on the living—and when that which has been stolen from the master of Hell is returned."

"I haven't seen Rory since the day he died," I repeat, hoping to redirect the conversation. "This has nothing to do with me, and it certainly has nothing to do with the others who came here with me. Please let them go."

Baumwither picks up the remote control and presses the red button again. I glance at Septimus, but he's watching Perfidious. The wolf-man has closed his black eyes and is standing quietly once more, as still as a statue. Yet there's a wry smile, almost like a smirk, on his cracked brown lips. I don't like that smile. I've seen it before, back in the land of the living. It's the look of someone who's plotting something.

The screen flickers again, and my stepfather's face disappears and is replaced by a black-and-white image of a small dais surrounded by drapes. There are clumsily written words splashed across the flat surface, as if someone had scrawled them in paint.

"Do not panic, Miss Pallister," whispers Septimus, but he's still watching the immobile, smirking Perfidious.

The words on the dais read: *You can have it back when I get my life back.*

Baumwither presses the remote control again, and the black-and-white image takes on color.

"Is that writing in blood?" asks Mitchell faintly.

My head is swimming. I don't understand any of this. Why am I here? I don't know anything. Rory is dead. He died over five months before I did. I've done everything I could to forget he even existed, so why am I being punished? It isn't my fault.

"*This isn't my fault,*" I say aloud.

"Indeed. This has been quite enough, Sir Richard," says Septimus sharply. "It is perfectly clear that Miss Pallister and her new friends have had no contact whatsoever with the Unspeakable. I am taking them back with me, and they will be provided with bedding and food in the accounting office until the lockdown is over."

"Now look here, Septimus—"

"I am taking them back with me, and that is the end of it. Far be it from me to tell you how to do your job, but I will remind you that I have been dead for two thousand years and my knowledge, experience and authority—excuse my language, ladies—pisses over yours, Sir Richard. Now, instead of interrogating an innocent sixteen-year-old girl, you should be putting your considerable resources into tracking down the Unspeakable, and more importantly, retrieving the Dreamcatcher. You are aware, I am sure, of its enormous power and the danger it could pose in the wrong hands."

The aura around Perfidious is moving again. The dark shadow is dancing around his body. It swirls and stretches to form the black outline of eight other wolf heads with wide-open jaws and bared teeth. They are shuddering.

No, they aren't shuddering, they're laughing.

"I reserve the right to question Miss Pallister again," blusters Baumwither, but Septimus is already herding Mitchell, Elinor and me to the door. Alfarin edges around Baumwither to retrieve his axe from the table. On our way out, we pass the HBI investigator returning with my glass of water. I ignore him and keep walking as fast as I can.

"HELL IS NOW IN LOCKDOWN. YOU ARE STRONGLY ADVISED TO STAY EXACTLY WHERE YOU ARE. FAILURE TO COMPLY IS UNWISE. HELL IS NOW IN LOCKDOWN...."

Septimus takes us back to the accounting office.

"Prince Alfarin," he says, "we will need to push these desks back against the wall. You may be here some time, and I would like you all to have as much space as possible."

"It will be an honor, Lord Septimus."

"I can help," offers Mitchell.

"Ye can move the pizza boxes and the chairs, Mitchell," says Elinor. She is already starting to tidy up as Septimus and Alfarin drag a desk into the corner. "The chairs have wheels to make it easier for ye."

I want to laugh at the indignant look on Mitchell's face, but I don't. And I don't want space. I want to be uncomfortable. I'll be less likely to sleep then.

Septimus moves toward the door. "All of you, listen carefully. Do not leave this room," he says. "I will send blankets and food for the evening in a while, but for now I must attend to Sir, who is very distressed at the loss of his Dreamcatcher."

"They won't come for Medusa, will they? If you leave us?" asks Mitchell, voicing exactly what I was thinking.

"They will not," replies Septimus, "but you must prepare yourselves for the possibility that Miss Pallister's usefulness in this disturbing incident is not yet over."

"We will stand by her until it is," announces Alfarin.

"She's part of Team DEVIL now," says Elinor with a weak smile. "And Hell knows I need another girl to help keep these two boys under control."

Before my brain has caught up with my legs, I'm at Septimus's side.

I hug him.

"Thank you, Septimus," I whisper. "Thank you for believing me." I quickly let go.

Septimus seems stunned, as if he hasn't been hugged in a long time. I immediately regret doing it, but he smiles, displaying brilliant-white, very crooked teeth.

"Good night, Medusa," he says. And then he's gone.

5. A Severing of Ways

A small man dressed in a white toga appears at the accounting chamber door not long after Septimus leaves. His eyes are so round and so red that they look like brake lights. He doesn't blink once as he unstraps four pillows and four camping mattresses from a belted contraption—like a backpack without a cover—from his hairy back. He's also carrying a square box filled with bread, fruit and what looks like a small plastic bucket of chicken drumsticks.

"Thanks, Aegidius," replies Mitchell.

The Roman doesn't reply. He pads away on bare feet that make a sticky, squelching sound. I'm totally grossed out because even his stubby toes are covered in thick black hair. Alfarin shuts the accounting chamber door behind Aegidius with a solid thump and moves Mitchell's desk in front of it as a makeshift barricade.

Elinor deals out the bedding. I take my pillow and mattress and lay them down in the corner farthest from the door to the Oval Office. If that alarm starts going off again, I want to be as far away from the blood as I possibly can.

The tension in the room is palpable. I know that everyone wants to talk about what we've just seen, but no one wants to be the first. So the elephant—or should I say Unspeakable—in the room isn't mentioned.

I don't actually know what an Unspeakable is, but if my stepfather is one of them, I have a good guess. But what are Skin-Walkers?

I think Perfidious is human, even under the guise of a wolf, but his irises are black. Black! Everyone knows the only devil in Hell who has black irises is The Devil himself.

It sounds strange, but I had never been really terrified in Hell before today. Nervous? Yes. Scared? Occasionally. Pissed off? Always. But now I have a twisting, churning feeling in the pit of my stomach that's making me sweat and shiver at the same time. I can taste a metallic bitterness. I know this sensation. It is the feeling of deep fear.

And it reminds me of living.

"I cannot stand this silence," Elinor finally says. "We are all thinking it, so we should talk about it."

"I don't want to talk about it," replies Mitchell. He has a drumstick in his hand, but he hasn't taken a bite.

"We need to be careful, Elinor," says Alfarin. "We do not know who could be listening in."

"Is this room bugged?" I ask.

"I don't think so," replies Mitchell. "We get it swept every week, and there isn't a devil in Hell who would dare bug Septimus, anyway."

He looks over at me. "I think we need to pick up the conversation where we left off when Hell went into lockdown. This is all because of San Francisco. We need to remember what was going on that day. If we remember, we can help Medusa."

"But we've tried, Mitchell," says Elinor. "Not one of us can remember why we were there that day."

"But we saw him, didn't we?" says Alfarin solemnly. "That man—Rory. We saw the Skin-Walkers, and what they did to him."

"What *are* Skin-Walkers?" I ask. "What do they do?"

"The Skin-Walkers were the first murderers, the first evil," replies Elinor. "They are the gatekeepers of the final dwelling of the Unspeakables: those who are so heinous in life, they cannot be left to mingle with others in the afterlife. The Unspeakables are the true tortured souls in Hell." Her voice has grown so monotonous, it's almost as if she's reading out of a guidebook. I wonder if that's because she's scared, or if her brain is just a scary repository of knowledge. Maybe it's both.

"The Skin-Walkers rip out the tongues of rapists, child abusers and murderers who kill for kicks," adds Mitchell. "No one knows where in Hell the Skin-Walkers are kept, and apparently they can track their victims—future Unspeakables—while they're still alive."

"We saw two Skin-Walkers take away your stepfather, Medusa," says Alfarin. "That evening, in San Francisco."

"There was a struggle with a gun," I whisper. "Between Rory and my mom. I didn't see what happened. They—the doctors—said he had lost too much blood. He died that night in the hospital."

"Did he hurt you?" asks Mitchell. "Your stepfather?" His pink eyes are glistening in the torchlight.

There's no point in hiding anything from them, so I nod. They don't ask for details, and I don't offer any. But I see deep sadness in their eyes. They understand without needing an explanation.

"And now he has escaped," says Elinor, leaning back against the wall. She yelps as a shadow pulls at her long red hair.

"How, though?" asks Mitchell. "And that message he left—what was that all about?"

"'You can have it back when I get my life back,'" says Alfarin, quoting the message scrawled in blood. "*It* must mean this Dreamcatcher."

"It sounds just like him," I said. "As if he's the victim of an injustice." Rory *would* see himself as the victim. He always did.

"What's a Dreamcatcher?" asks Elinor. She's slowly turning a bright-red apple between her pale hands. Like Mitchell with his drumstick, she hasn't taken a bite.

"They're Native American objects," I reply, trying to describe one with my hands. "You get a hoop, I think made of willow, and then you weave a web in the middle of it. Then the Dreamcatcher is decorated with feathers and beads. I've seen some before with little bells attached, although I'm not sure if that's considered very respectful to the culture and legend."

"But what do they do?" asks Alfarin. "Elinor and I are learned, but in all the years I've spent reading in Hell's library, I have never heard of such a thing, either. From your description, this Dream-catcher is very small. Why is Hell in lockdown over such an object? If it were a mighty weapon I could understand, but for feathers and beads, it does not make sense to me."

"If I'm remembering this right, I think some cultures believe that when you're sleeping, Dreamcatchers will filter out nightmares and trap good dreams," replies Mitchell.

"So, this Rory has stolen something with The Devil's good dreams in it?" asks Elinor.

"It looks like it," I reply, "but I have to agree with Alfarin. Why put Hell in lockdown? Why can't they just make The Devil a new one? It doesn't make sense."

We all look at Mitchell, who now has his head in his hands. The chicken drumstick is lying on the floor next to his sneakers.

"What's wrong, Mitchell?" asks Elinor. "Ye are closer to The Devil and Septimus than any of us. Do ye know something?"

"Think about it, Elinor," replies Mitchell. His face is deathly white. "A good dream for one of us probably involves eating food, or hanging out together or even living our old lives...." He trails off. All three of them are suddenly interested in the floor.

"But The Devil's good dreams are probably our worst night-mares," I finish quietly.

Mitchell nods.

"The dude is nuts, completely cuckoo crazy," he whispers. "All he wants to do is get revenge on Him and the angels. The Devil's good dreams would be filled with blood and screaming and torture and probably war against Up There. His idea of Heaven would be way worse than anything in Hell. This Dreamcatcher is going to be filled with the worst things imaginable."

"So The Devil's Dreamcatcher is actually the opposite because of who he is," I say. "It still captures good dreams, but his good dreams are so twisted...."

"Exactly," replies Mitchell.

"Could the Dreamcatcher serve as a weapon?" asks Alfarin. "If it holds The Devil's good dreams, as vile as they are, could these dreams become reality?"

"Yeah," I answer slowly. "I'm guessing the Dreamcatcher *would* be a physical manifestation of evil."

"Conquest, war, famine and death," whispers Elinor. "The apocalypse in a nice, neat package for anyone crazy enough to take it."

"It's the only explanation for the panic," says Mitchell. "I don't think Perfidious and the Skin-Walkers care—they just want Medusa's stepfather back with the other Unspeakables. But the HBI and that Baumwither dude are scared about the Dreamcatcher. Septimus is, too, and that's the really terrifying thing, because the boss isn't afraid of anything."

"What if the Unspeakable has escaped Hell?" gasps Elinor. "Medusa's stepfather has to be stopped if he's gone back to the land of the living with a weapon from The Devil."

"No one can escape Hell, Elinor," I reply, but my eyes widen as I suddenly remember that I'm sitting with three devils who have done exactly that.

"You all got out of Hell with a Viciseometer," I say. "What if Rory got out the same way?"

"If he did, the HBI might think we were all involved!" cries Elinor.

But Mitchell and Alfarin are vehemently shaking their heads. "Septimus knows we had nothing to do with this, Elinor," says Mitchell. "Plus, as far as I know, the Viciseometer we used is still locked in the safe, and I still don't know the new combination."

I shake my head. This morning, when I woke up in my crowded dorm, the only things worrying me were the fact that someone new was sleeping at the bottom of my bed because we'd run out of space, and the fact that I couldn't find my favorite sneakers to wear to the interview. I eventually located them hanging from a torch out on the balcony—and I'm pretty sure my feet don't smell so bad they walked out on their own.

But now everything has changed, in no more than the space of a day. Because now I've found out that my hated stepfather has been tortured in Hell by man-wolves called Skin-Walkers for more than forty years, and the bastard has retaliated by stealing a weapon from The Devil himself.

"Are you okay, Medusa?" asks Mitchell. He crawls over to my mattress. "You don't look so good."

"Probably because I'm dead."

I don't know why I use sarcasm and one-liners when I'm stressed. But unlike other devils, Mitchell doesn't seem to mind, which is another reason I'm really starting to like him.

"They'll find Rory, Medusa. The Skin-Walkers will track your stepfather down and take him back to where he'll rot."

"What if they don't, though?"

Just the thought of Rory being on the loose in the Under-world . . . I'm not so worried about the missing Dreamcatcher right now. I'm worried about *him*. Finding *me*.

"They will, M," says Elinor firmly. "The Skin-Walkers will find him, somehow." She turns and tries to fluff up her thin pillow. "Now, I think we all need to try and get some rest. We have no idea what will happen tomorrow, and Mitchell gets very cranky if he doesn't get his beauty sleep."

"What?" exclaims Mitchell.

"You may have my pillow, my princess," says Alfarin. He throws it to Elinor, but he's so strong, it hits her full in the face and sends her toppling backward over Mitchell's chair.

Full of remorse and apologies, Alfarin rushes over to help her, tripping over the discarded pizza boxes.

"Still up for joining Team DEVIL?" whispers Mitchell into my ear. A tickling sensation swoops down my back as I feel the brush of his hot skin against mine. "We're a classy and coordinated bunch, as you can see."

"Do you still want me? This mess is all my fault, you know."

"I don't think any of this is your fault, Medusa. If there's one thing I've learned, it's that life isn't fair, and death is even worse. So, once more, are you up for joining Team DEVIL? I need a girl around the office to fetch coffee and stuff, and plus, if we turn you upside down, you'll make a handy broom."

I elbow him. Hard.

"Ow."

"*Fetch coffee?* Get off my mattress, you gross boy. You're sweating on my bed."

"You think I smell?" asks Mitchell darkly. "We're in an enclosed space with Alfarin, and he's eaten two meat feast pizzas. If you weren't dead already, you would be by morning. Suffocated by farts."

"Ye should not use language like that around ladies, Mitchell," calls Elinor. "And Alfarin does not fart, he exudes manliness."

I don't remember falling asleep. I never can. I can always remember the fight that goes on with my eyelids beforehand, though, and never more so than tonight. Mitchell and Alfarin and Elinor may have happy dreams about their past lives, but not me. A Dreamcatcher would be wasted on me. I only ever have nightmares. They're all I'm capable of having. What's worse is that I don't just see them, I feel them. And I can't fight off the terror they bring. Ever. The only thing that helps is waking up.

"Medusa…Medusa!" someone calls.

It's Mitchell's voice, but my fear from tonight's dream is still too close for me to answer. This one was a nightmare I haven't had before. There was a small child, a boy, with a thick mop of blond hair that looked like straw. He was crying, but not wailing like most children his age would when they're throwing a tantrum. His tears were streaming silently down his pink cheeks. Then I saw his ruby-red eyes, and I noticed that his tears were no longer clear. He was crying blood. It was slowly dripping from his nose, too. He held his arms out, as if he wanted to be picked up. Then Alfarin was there, holding someone back. I realized it was Mitchell. I couldn't see Elinor, but there were another two people in the nightmare. They had a halo of light around them. One was a guy, maybe a couple of years older than I am, and he was dressed in an old brown army uniform.

The other was a stunningly beautiful girl with light-brown skin and long, wavy hair as dark as coal.

"Jeanne, you can't help him," called the army boy.

That's when I started to scream.

"Medusa!" Mitchell calls again. I feel strong hands holding my wrists. I stop fighting, not because I think I'm safe, but because I don't have the energy to battle the nightmare anymore.

"Were ye having a bad dream?" Elinor wraps her arms around me and strokes the curls away from my sweaty face. No girl in my dorm has ever done that before. I feel safe.

"I saw a little boy," I pant. "He was crying blood."

I drink some water from a cup. It's Septimus who passes it to me. When did he come back?

"I do not have words of comfort for you, Miss Pallister," he says. His deep voice sounds like a double bass being plucked. "Considering the events that transpired yesterday, and unfortunately, those events that may yet come to pass, I fear the nightmares that plague your sleep may only intensify."

"Have you found him? Have you found Rory and the Dreamcatcher?" I ask.

Septimus shakes his head. "Alas, they have not been recovered. I understand that Perfidious and the Skin-Walkers have now severed all communication with the HBI and The Devil's office and will act of their own accord. There will be meetings all day today about the recovery of the Dreamcatcher, and in the absence of Sir Richard Baumwither, I have been asked by The Devil to chair. It is apparent, however, that Mr. Hunter has departed Hell."

"It had nothing to do with us, Septimus," says Mitchell quickly. "I don't have the combination to the safe anymore, not since—"

"Mitchell, if I were to unlock the safe now, I have no doubt that Hell's Viciseometer would still be sitting on the shelf," interrupts Septimus. "No, I do not believe the Unspeakable left Hell with either our travel timepiece, or indeed the one from Up There. He wouldn't need it. The Dreamcatcher absorbs immense powers from The Devil, and it won't surprise you to learn that that includes his ability to travel to any place, to any time, at will. I believe the Unspeakable left Hell via the power of the Dreamcatcher." He pauses, and a frustrated look crosses his face. "How the Unspeakable knew the way to wield it, though, is something I have yet to ascertain."

"Is the Dreamcatcher a weapon, Lord Septimus?" asks Alfarin.

"You are very astute, Prince Alfarin. In the wrong hands, it could certainly be used for nefarious activities."

"Septimus, sir?" asks Elinor timidly. She's rubbing the back of her neck again. I make a mental note to check her for eczema or some other skin condition when the boys aren't looking. I doubt they've even noticed she does that.

"Yes, Miss Powell?"

"Ye said ye will be chairing the meetings today. Why? Doesn't Sir Richard want to be involved? That's his job, surely?"

Septimus sighs. It is a long, sad exhale. Too long, especially for someone who doesn't need to breathe.

"I warned Sir Richard Baumwither that it would be prudent to show Perfidious more respect. To challenge a Skin-Walker in such an arrogant, foolhardy way as he did yesterday..."

"Something's happened to him, hasn't it?" I ask, even though I have a feeling I don't want to know the answer. Perfidious's very presence in that room was a terrible reminder that just because we devils can't die again doesn't mean bad things can't still happen to us here.

"We found Sir Richard this morning on level 43...and also on level 99, and then on level 427. I believe his head was found floating in a toilet on level 666," replies Septimus. "He had been butchered, torn into pieces by what the rather nervous new head of the HBI says was an animal."

At that, the loudspeakers crackle and whistle. We all jump, even Septimus. And every devil in Hell hears the howling laughter of wolves.

6. **Thieves**

Hell is no longer in lockdown, but it doesn't matter. After the Skin-Walkers' little public service announcement over the loudspeakers, most devils are too terrified to leave their dormitories.

Septimus has given the four of us permission to stay in the accounting chamber, but Alfarin wants to check up on his family, and Mitchell decides to go with him. I don't have any family here—at least, as far as I know. My dad ran out on my mom and me when I was little, so even if he were here he could go screw himself. Mom is definitely still alive, because if she were a devil, she would have found me.

Because that's what moms do, isn't it?

"Do you have any family you want to check up on, Elinor?" I ask.

"No. Our John and our William were the only ones I really worried about," she replies, "and they went Up There with our Alice. My brothers, Michael and Phillip, are in Hell, but they are older than me and can handle themselves."

"Won't they be worried about you?"

Elinor's bloodred eyes lower to the ground. "I doubt it. They've never really bothered with me. Death didn't change anything there."

"I didn't have any brothers or sisters, at least not any that I know about," I say. "Maybe one day, when we know each other better, we can be sisters to each other."

I could kick myself. What in Hell made me say something as stupid and sentimental as that? But instead of laughing at me, Elinor smiles.

"I would like that very much, M," she says. "I don't know why, but I feel like I know ye so well already."

And I know what she means, because I feel it, too. It's as if there's a dark veil in my mind, and I'm overwhelmed with the feeling that if I grab hold of it somehow and pull it back, I'll be able to remember something really important. I've never believed in reincarnation or anything like that—with my luck I would return to life as a bug or a hairy spider and I'd get squished within seconds—but fate I can believe in, for better and worse.

I rub my temples. Maybe I can't remember anything because I'm too busy trying to get the image of Sir Richard Baumwither's head floating in a toilet out of my brain. I wish I had never met him. Or Perfidious.

And I wish they didn't know about me.

I had nothing to do with Rory disappearing, but are the Skin-Walkers going to believe me? Would they care?

"What are ye thinking about, M?" asks Elinor. She's sitting on Mitchell's chair and plaiting her hair into a thick red braid.

"I was just thinking about the Skin-Walkers."

"Ye mustn't. They're evil."

"I know. That's what scares me."

Every sound, both inside the accounting chamber and outside on the level 1 landing, is magnified tenfold. My overactive imagination is fooling me into thinking I can hear the Skin-Walkers. In the corner of my eye, I think I can even *see* the Skin-Walkers. They're laughing at me, hunting me, because of my association with Rory.

"Elinor, that night outside my old house in San Francisco, was that the only time you've seen the Skin-Walkers?"

Elinor lets her hands fall to her lap, and the long braid immediately falls apart.

"No," she says. "We had seen them before, the same night we left Hell."

"Were they chasing you because you were running away?"

"No. They were heading in the opposite direction. They had an Unspeakable with them. It was horrible, M. They were torturing him."

I'm not an evil person at all, even if I am in Hell, but I don't share Elinor's obvious horror. I'm glad these Unspeakables are punished in the Afterlife. They deserve it.

"How many Skin-Walkers are there?"

"We saw eight that first time, and then two of those again in San Francisco. Yesterday was the first time we saw Perfidious, though."

"And how many Unspeakables are there in Hell, do you think?"

"I don't want to think about it," replies Elinor, once more starting to braid her hair. "It is too much evil to understand. The Skin-Walkers haunted us while we time-traveled. They came at us in the darkness. When I sleep, I still see them coming."

"Tell me more about the Viciseometer," I say. "I always thought that being able to change time was a Hell myth. You know, a story to torment devils, to make us hope for a different future. But if you managed it, why don't more devils try? Why doesn't everyone get out of here?"

Elinor stands up and walks over to the safe. It's huge and built into the black stone wall.

"I think others have tried to get out of here," she replies. "But death is something ye can't cheat, not in the end. Ye can just try to make it easier, if ye are lucky."

"So how did you use the Viciseometer?" I ask, watching Elinor trace a circle with her fingers on the safe door. "What did you want it for? And how did you get out of here in the first place?"

Stop it, Medusa. I pinch myself. I have so many questions, but I shouldn't overwhelm Elinor. I need to slow down. When I was a kid, I was always being told off for asking too many questions. Then I stopped talking altogether, but nobody noticed. Then I got mouthy again when I got to Hell. I can never seem to get the balance right.

"If I tell ye, ye must promise never to say a word to anyone," says Elinor, turning around to face me. Her red eyes are glistening, and for one horrific moment, I think she's going to cry blood, like the little boy in my nightmare.

"I won't say a word to anyone," I whisper.

"Well, ye already know that the Viciseometer is a time-traveling device," begins Elinor. "There are only two, apparently, one in each immortal domain. Mitchell used Hell's Viciseometer to take us all back in time, to the moments of our death."

"You wanted to watch yourselves die?" I exclaim. "That's horrible, Elinor. Didn't you want to stop it from happening? *Why* didn't you stop it from happening?"

"It's a long story, M," says Elinor, and she bites her bottom lip. "It wasn't as simple as stopping our deaths. In the end, only Mitchell really wanted to do that, and then he realized that he couldn't, because he would have changed everything and M.J. would never have been born."

"Who's M.J.?"

"Mitchell's little brother."

"And he's still alive?"

Elinor nods. "Mitchell's parents were divorced and his mom remarried after he died. We time-traveled to Mitchell's grave and saw his mom and her new husband. They had a little boy with them called M.J. It was Mitchell's little brother, who was born after Mitchell died. He was ever so upset."

"The kid?"

"No—Mitchell. He thought he had been replaced, ye see. So then we time-traveled to Washington to the point where Mitchell died, and Mitchell was going to prevent his death, but he realized if he did, then M.J. would never be born. So he chose not to change his death. And then..." Elinor suddenly stops talking. She's looking at me strangely.

"What's the matter?" I ask. "Are you okay, Elinor? You don't look well."

"And then..." She pauses again. "Then we ended up in San Francisco because we were looking for something," she says, gazing at the wall. "But we don't know what. Not one of us can remember."

"Couldn't have been important, then," I reply, trying to lighten the black cloud that suddenly seems to be filling the office. I see movement in the corner and realize the shadows are with us. I think they're listening.

Elinor is grabbing at the back of her neck again.

"Why do you do that, Elinor?" I ask. "Does it hurt? Would you like me to look at it?"

"It's a habit," she replies. "I've been doing it for hundreds of years now. I just like to check...you know..."

Elinor is suddenly very preoccupied with tidying the papers on Mitchell's desk. It looks like question time is over for now. My priorities shift. I really want to change out of my clothes. I'm still wearing my black shorts and the red shirt I wore to the interview that never was, and I hate wearing the same gear for more than one day. Not because I'm vain like Patty Lloyd, who changes five times a day, but because I sweat a lot. This is Hell, you know. Fire and brimstone and more fire. My grandmother used to have a saying: *Horses sweat, men perspire, women glow.*

I say that's bullshit. No one glows in Hell. We *all* sweat. I bet when they were deciding the rules of Up There and Hell, the Highers allowed angels to fart rainbows, but devils have to feel pain and sweat and bleed blood that looks like custard.

"Elinor, I need to go change. We could go together if you want."

"I only have this dress," replies Elinor, pointing to her long white gown, "but I will go with ye if ye would like the company." As she speaks, Elinor's eyes widen and she leans forward just a fraction. I'm good at reading body language. I had to be when I was alive, and I was usually looking out for the warning signs that something bad was about to happen. But what I read here is only that Elinor is expectant, hopeful. It kinda chokes me up. I wonder if Elinor will want to hang with me, share clothes with me and, you know, just be like a normal dead girl with me, once this storm of crap is over.

Unfortunately, getting into my dorm is hopeless. There are just too many devils. They fill every corridor, every gap. For the first time,

I truly appreciate just how many of us are in here. Elinor and I trudge back toward the accounting office and find level 1 practically deserted. No one wants to be near the Oval Office. We hang out by the elevators, watching as men in black suits prowl the torch-lined corridors. The slightest noise makes them jump.

It's been over twenty-four hours since the alarm was sounded.

It's been over twenty-four hours since my stepfather took The Devil's Dreamcatcher.

And over twenty-four hours since he disappeared from Hell.

I find I'm glad when Mitchell and Alfarin step out of the level 1 elevator. They're carrying backpacks and bulging paper bags, and Mitchell has changed into a white V-neck shirt and olive-green cargo pants, which he's complaining about. Loudly.

"The pants are fine, but the pockets kill me. This is why I normally wear jeans. I shove too much stuff in the pockets, and then I forget what I've stashed where. See?" He pulls what appears to be an ancient granola bar out of a pocket by his right knee. "I didn't even feel this! Who knows how long it's been there?"

"That is why I prefer not to wear pants with any pockets at all, my friend," Alfarin replies. He's wearing a pale-blue tunic over baggy black shorts that skim his knees. "At least these shorts allow my manly calves to breathe."

At this point, Elinor and I are doubled over with laughter. "Have ye two been shopping?" asks Elinor, gasping.

"Men do not shop," replies Alfarin, offended. "We fight, drink beer and make merry with women."

"And how many on that list have ye done, Alfarin?" asks Elinor as the Viking passes her a large brown paper bag.

"I am very good at fighting," mumbles Alfarin. His round face is bright red and sweaty. I can't help grinning. Mitchell smiles shyly as he hands me a bag. His pink eyes look tired.

I open it up and pull out a white T-shirt, a pair of red Converse sneakers and some jeans that I know right away will be too long, but I don't care because it means no more stinky clothes.

"Where did you get this from?" I ask.

"We knew you girls would never get back to your dorms in this crush, so we got some stuff for you," replies Mitchell. "I'm not very good at guessing sizes, but it was the best we could do."

"And who is Primrose Weaver?" asks Elinor, holding up a pair of cream-colored ballet flats with black marker pen etched on the pristine soles.

"Er," says Alfarin.

"Um," says Mitchell.

"Did you steal these?" I ask warily.

"Ye thieves."

"We're devils. We improvised," says Mitchell indignantly. "But look, they're practically brand-new, Elinor. You won't catch anything gross."

Just then, another suited man walks past us. I recognize him as the devil who Septimus asked to fetch a glass of water when I was being interrogated.

"It was really nice of you to think of me, Mitchell," I say quietly, "but I'm not sure wearing stolen stuff is going to help me right now, seeing as everyone in Hell is looking for a thief."

"I wasn't thinking," says Mitchell, stricken. "I'm so sorry, Medusa."

"It's cool, honestly," I reply. "I can't believe you even thought of getting us fresh clothes."

"That's me, Mr. Considerate."

He ruffles my hair—again. I flick his forehead with my finger—again. I get called "short-ass"—again.

"Ever get the feeling of déjà vu?" I ask.

"Constantly," replies Mitchell.

Mr. HBI walks past again, just to ruin the moment.

"Can we help ye?" asks Elinor, and she smiles sweetly.

"Lord Septimus may have vouched for you lot, but I'm watching," replies the man. His finger is pointed at me. It's small and stubby, with a blackened nail that is far too long.

Mitchell and Alfarin immediately square up to him.

"And if you continue to harass Medusa, I'm going straight to The Devil himself," says Mitchell. "Let's see how brave you are when your ass is hauled into the Oval Office."

The HBI dude says nothing, although judging from his flaring nostrils it's clear he would like nothing better than to continue the argument. Alfarin swings his axe onto his enormous shoulder, and the man slinks away into the shadows.

"Let's go inside," mutters Mitchell, opening the door to the accounting office. "Septimus might be back with an update."

But as we walk into the office, it's clear that someone has been in there, and that person wasn't Septimus.

Before, it looked like a bomb had hit it. Now it looks like a nuclear device was detonated. Papers are burning in piles on the floor, a table has been tipped over and the chairs have been ripped apart in long, serrated strips.

"What in Thor's name has happened here?" exclaims Alfarin.

Mitchell says nothing. He climbs over the broken furniture to the safe and sinks to his knees. The door is open, and every shelf is completely bare.

"Well, if we weren't in deep shit before, we are now," he groans.

"What happened?" I ask.

"It's the Viciseometer. It's gone."

7. Angels Are Coming

"How long were you away from the office?" Alfarin asks Elinor and me. He reaches over Mitchell and sweeps the empty shelves with his thick fingers. I have no idea what he's expecting to find up there, except dust. Everything has been thrown onto the floor, where Mitchell is now sitting.

"Not long," replies Elinor. "We went to M's dorm but turned back because we couldn't even get inside."

"They're going to blame me," I whisper. "The HBI is going to arrest me for this."

"They will not blame you, Miss Pallister," drawls a southern accent. "And there will certainly be no arrests in *my* office."

Septimus steps out of the shadows. Not one of us had noticed him standing next to the large rune-covered cabinet.

"What's going on, Septimus?" asks Mitchell. He's still sitting in front of the safe.

"I need you to listen to me very carefully," replies Septimus. "I require the assistance of all four of you," he adds, looking directly at me, "and we don't have much time. The HBI is in disarray after the unfortunate disemboweling and quartering of Sir Richard, and the Skin-Walkers are a law—or not—unto themselves. I have to remain here to keep Sir calm, but I have a plan. A plan that must fly under the radar, so to speak."

Mitchell, Elinor and Alfarin all gasp as Septimus pulls a piece of purple silk from his pocket. There's something bulky wrapped up inside it.

"Ye had it this whole time?" Elinor asks.

"What's going on, Septimus?" repeats Mitchell, more warily than before.

"It has come to my attention—from a reliable source—that Up There has sent a team of angels to hunt down The Devil's Dreamcatcher," replies Septimus. There is more than a hint of urgency in his voice; the lazy drawl is now gone. "Why angels have become involved, I do not yet know, but the Dreamcatcher belongs back here. It *must* be brought back here. With the exception of Miss Pallister, who I am certain will pick the technique up quickly, you are all learned in the use of the Viciseometer—"

"No way," says Mitchell.

"It is too dangerous," says Alfarin.

"It is an object of evil, Mr. Septimus," says Elinor.

My mouth responds before my brain can stop me.

"I'll take it."

"Thank you, Miss Pallister. I knew you would understand."

"No way," says Mitchell once more. "You can't send Medusa out there with the Viciseometer. The Skin-Walkers and the HBI will be onto her in minutes."

But I know what Septimus wants from me. It was inevitable the second I was hauled in for questioning by the HBI. The only difference is that Septimus is going to do it on his terms. He's not just a fighter, he's a strategic thinker. A chess player. And I'm the pawn.

"You want to use me as bait, don't you?"

Septimus nods in reply to my question. Mitchell and Elinor are now in a total uproar. So much so that they don't notice that Septimus has passed the Viciseometer to me.

So this is what they were talking about. It really is a stopwatch. A strikingly pretty gold stopwatch. It has two sides. One is milky white with golden hands and numerals; the other side is a deep red color with black hands and symbols. A thin gold thread with a red needle hangs from a large button at the top. There are three black buttons on the top left, and three more on the bottom right.

And it's vibrating, like a beating heart. Tiny flames are spitting and sparking from its rim, but even though I can see the delicate fire surrounding it, my skin doesn't burn.

"Give it back to Septimus, Medusa," commands Mitchell. "That thing isn't safe."

"What do you want me to do, Septimus?" I ask, ignoring Mitchell's and Elinor's pleas. Only Alfarin is quiet. At first, I think his red eyes are staring at the Viciseometer, but then I realize he's staring at nothing we can see.

"I will go with Medusa," he announces. "My axe and I will keep her safe, Lord Septimus."

A heavy thud echoes around the accounting chamber: Mitchell has kicked at the wall in response.

"Well, ye are going nowhere without me, Alfarin," says Elinor, folding her arms crossly.

Mitchell sinks down until he's sitting on the floor of the cavernous open safe. He looks utterly defeated.

"I'm sorry, Mitchell, but finding the Dreamcatcher begins with the Unspeakable," says Septimus. His pulsing red eyes are continually flickering to the door of the office. "He wants his life back, and I believe that is exactly where he is headed, and there is no one in Hell who is more versed in Mr. Hunter's life and times than Miss Pallister."

An enormous lump has lodged firmly in my throat. I try to swallow, but I can't. I try to breathe, and I can't do that, either. It feels unnatural, holding my breath for this long, but I do until the swaying stops and the only sensation I feel is the rhythmic beat of the Viciseometer against the palm of my hand.

I'm going to have to face him again, and I know I have no choice. While Rory Hunter is free, I am not. I can't believe it never occurred to me that he was probably in Hell right along with me. If anyone deserved to end up here, it was my stepfather, and now that he's free, I can't exist knowing he's out there. No one—living or dead—is safe from him. There's a place for evil like Rory, and it's with the Skin-Walkers. He has to be returned to them.

"What if the Skin-Walkers track us again, Septimus?" asks Mitchell. I can tell he's pissed off—his pink eyes are narrowed as they stare up at Septimus—but all I care about is the fact that Mitchell said track *us*. That means he's coming with me. They're all coming with me. I won't be alone—at least for a little while longer.

"I am counting on the Skin-Walkers tracking you," replies Septimus. "But they have a solitary goal: to find Mr. Hunter. I need you four to bring back the Dreamcatcher."

"You said a team of angels is also tracking the Dreamcatcher, Lord Septimus," says Alfarin. He is leaning on his axe, and the blade is scratching against the office floor with a screech that sets my teeth on edge.

"Indeed."

"Are they dangerous?"

"They're angels, Alfarin," says Elinor. "Of course they're not dangerous."

But Septimus doesn't confirm Elinor's theory. He walks around the upturned desk and pulls a brown file folder from the floor. I watch him, wondering why he hasn't mentioned the trashed office once.

And then I get it. Septimus hasn't said anything because he was responsible. This was a ruse to make it look as if there had been a break-in. If anyone asks, Septimus can say the Viciseometer was stolen, and it happened when the four of us were seen in and around the dorms and corridors. In one strategic move, Septimus has removed any potential suspicion that Team DEVIL could be at fault for what has happened.

"Details on Team ANGEL, Miss Pallister," says Septimus, handing me the file. "My intelligence source Up There advises that the group consists of four angels led by Private Owen Jones. I have managed to glean some information about them in the time I have been afforded. Read it as quickly as you can. I fear we have just minutes before our meeting will be most unwelcomely interrupted."

I open the file. It contains only two pieces of paper and three photographs.

"'Private Owen Jones, eighteen years old, killed July first, 1916, during the Battle of the Somme. Angela Jackson, seventeen, died of cancer just five years ago in New Zealand,'" I read aloud. "'Johnny—surname redacted—died in 1676 from consumption. Jeanne d'Arc, burned alive in Rouen in 1431, at nineteen.'"

I pick up the three small photographs next. They show a young man with black, slicked-back hair. He's wearing a brown army uniform. Something about him is familiar, but I can't pin down from where. I hand the photo to Elinor.

"That must be Owen Jones," I say. Elinor nods and passes it to Alfarin.

The next photograph is of a really pretty girl with a heart-shaped face. She has blond spiky hair with pink tips.

"Angela?" I ask Septimus.

He nods.

The third photograph is of a girl who is scowling at the camera. Owen looks sad in his image, and Angela looks friendly, but this angel, Jeanne, looks fierce. My first thought is that she would make a good devil. She has light-brown skin and long, wavy black hair that tumbles down over her shoulders.

"'Jeanne d'Arc, burned alive in Rouen in 1431, at nineteen,'" I repeat. "Jeanne d'Arc. Is this Joan of *Arc*? As in, the Maid of Orléans?"

"The very same," replies Septimus.

"I guess she *would* be an angel, huh?" says Mitchell.

"Why isn't there a photograph of the other angel?" I ask, running my finger down the paper in the file. "Johnny."

But Septimus doesn't reply. His bloodred eyes shift from Elinor to Mitchell, who's now looking at the photograph of Private Owen Jones.

Mitchell is leaning forward. A look of deep concentration is etched on his face. He scans the back of the small, glossy picture, as if he's trying to find more information.

"What is it, Mitchell?" I ask.

"Show me the other photos," he replies.

Elinor hands Mitchell the photo of Angela Jackson; I pass over the fierce-looking Jeanne.

Mitchell gasps when he sees the photo of Jeanne.

"I've seen her before!" he exclaims. "Joan of Arc, and she was with this dude!" He brandishes the photos in the air.

"When?" ask Alfarin and Elinor together.

"In the cemetery," says Mitchell, climbing to his feet. "My cemetery. The one in Washington where I'm buried. I saw these two angels just before I saw my mom and M.J."

"Ye did not say anything at the time, Mitchell."

"I know, I…well, everything happened so quickly afterward, I just forgot about it, but I definitely saw them, and they saw me. The girl, this Jeanne, she even called him Owen. She told him to hurry up."

"Are you certain, my friend?" asks Alfarin.

"Definitely. They had this strange glow around them. I knew they were angels right away. What's going on, Septimus?"

"Are you prepared to go back to the land of the living, Mitchell?" asks Septimus, ignoring Mitchell's question. I've never known him to talk so quickly, and his ruby-red eyes are now glued to the main office door.

"No!" snaps Mitchell. "Not without some answers. Why us?"

"Because I am confident you will not use the Viciseometer for purposes other than what I ask," replies Septimus. "You are aware of what I refer to?"

"Ye know we will not change our deaths," says Elinor quietly.

Mitchell walks over to me and lets his hand hover over the Viciseometer. I sense a quickening in its vibration. It feels like it wants to jump off my hand into Mitchell's. I tighten my grip.

"Does it have to be Medusa?" asks Mitchell.

"I am entrusting it to her," replies Septimus. He strides to the door and presses his ear against the rock. Then a cell phone in his suit pocket rings three times.

I know it's an alarm because Septimus makes no move to answer it.

"Now, are all of you ready?" says Septimus. "I would have wished to prepare you better, but the irony is, we are now out of time."

Team DEVIL nods. Elinor is grabbing at the back of her neck again, and Alfarin is spitting on and rubbing the blade of his gleaming silver axe.

"Miss Pallister, you are about to get a crash course on using the Viciseometer," says Septimus. "Quickly, place it on your palm, red face down. I want you to move the golden hands to five o'clock exactly; it would be best if you traveled to the early morning. Then press the three buttons on the bottom left."

I do as Septimus instructs. The stopwatch is vibrating even more desperately now. I think it's excited. The Viciseometer is starting to whistle—my mom had a kettle that made exactly the same noise, only it never stopped because she was usually too drunk to notice.

Mitchell slips his arm around my waist, and I lean into him, not fully, but enough to let him know that I appreciate what he's doing for me. I hear Elinor ask Alfarin to hold on to her.

"Excellent," says Septimus. "Now turn the Viciseometer over. The red face and black hands will take you back to the date where you want to go. So put in this date: June eighteenth, 1967."

A date I know all too well.

"Which hand is which?"

"The shortest is the month; the medium hand is the day; the longest is for the year, and for that you need to move it around all four numbers like you would open up a safe," says Mitchell. "Do you want me to show you?"

I move to hand Mitchell the Viciseometer, but he shakes his head.

"No, it's yours now," he whispers. "I'll just hold the needle."

We lean in even closer to each other. Mitchell smells like bread and chocolate. I watch as he moves the point of the needle quickly around the hands and numbers, which look remarkably like snakes.

They are snakes. They are slithering inside the Viciseometer.

The pitch of the whistling rises, and an electrical current buzzes along my arm. It burrows into my chest. A feeling of warmth spreads through me.

I feel alive.

"I will tell the HBI that I was attacked from behind," says Septimus. "I will keep them off your trail for as long as I can. That should prove easy, as they are incompetent and I am not. You are to track down Mr. Hunter, and more importantly, the Dreamcatcher, using all the means at your disposal. I will be in regular contact with you. You have your cell phone, Mitchell?"

"What if the Unspeakable tries to hurt Medusa?" asks Mitchell.

"This is death, Mitchell. Not life." Septimus hands me a sealed envelope.

"Here is sufficient money to cover your expenses, and, more importantly, details of the Dreamcatcher are in here, too. You *must* return with the Dreamcatcher. I cannot stress enough how important this is. Trust in one another, always. Regardless of what you see or hear."

Septimus takes a step toward me. He closes his still hands over my shaking ones.

"I knew the first time I met you that you were an extraordinary person, Miss Pallister," he says quietly. "It is the biggest tragedy of mankind that some of the young are taken too soon."

Mitchell tightens his grip on my waist. Elinor also slips her arm around me, and I can tell that Alfarin has hold of her because his weight suddenly pushes into all of us, buffeting us forward. Alfarin and Mitchell are holding the backpacks, like we're heading out on some kind of school field trip. None of this feels real. I'm detached from my body. I keep expecting to wake up. In a moment I'll start screaming and see the frightened faces of the girls in my dorm. . . .

Then Septimus's cell rings twice. Whoever's coming is getting closer.

"There is one thing left for you to do before you leave," says Septimus. "Alas, the story that the office was ransacked and I was attacked will not hold water unless there is a body on the floor. So, Prince Alfarin, if you would oblige?"

"Lord Septimus?"

"Your axe, Prince Alfarin. You must hit me with it. I would, of course, prefer the blunt handle and not the blade, if it can be managed."

Mitchell swears as Alfarin steps away from the group, drops his backpack on the floor and, taking a swing like a baseball player, knocks Septimus off his feet with a sickening crack. The most important servant in Hell flies backward over the upturned desk and lands in a motionless heap. The only noise is his cell phone, which emits a solitary ring.

And then several fists bang on the door.

"Hurry, Medusa. Get us out of here!" yells Mitchell. He drops his backpack and lurches forward to grab hold of Alfarin. "You need to see a destination in the face of the Viciseometer."

In my mind I see an old house. My old house. Run-down, with peeling white walls and a broken fence. The thought transfers to the Viciseometer.

"Press down on the large button—*now!*" scream Mitchell and Elinor as the door to the accounting office is thrown open.

There is a rush of flames and wind, and then my existence goes black.

8. June 18, 1967

My body feels like it's been wrapped up in the coils of an enormous invisible snake. I am being squeezed by something I cannot see. I try to keep my eyes open, but the rush of wind has caused my long eyelashes to invert, and they are scratching at my pink irises.

What have we done? Even in 1967 San Francisco, where drugs are everywhere, we're going to stick out as something strange, something unnatural, something evil.

Anything but normal.

The rushing stops, and the four of us land in a heap on the hard ground. The blade of Alfarin's axe slams down and cuts several spiky blond strands from Mitchell's head. Mitchell swears. He's shaking.

No, he isn't. I am.

The Viciseometer is still in my hand. The red face, which had pixelated into an image of my old house, has returned to normal.

Very slowly, I take in our surroundings.

I'm home. I can't believe it. I'm home. The house I lived in for eight years is exactly how I remember it: grubby and tired-looking. The paint is peeling and the weeds in the garden are outgrowing the small patches of grass that haven't died in the heat. I'm so used to the smell of burning, whether it's from the fires of the furnaces or the fires in the kitchen, that my nose feels as if it isn't working properly, because here, there isn't much to smell at all.

A rush of emotion sweeps over me. I want to run inside and find my mom. I want to run away and never look back.

"At least June in San Francisco is an improvement on November in New York," says Mitchell. "I don't feel like a Popsicle this time."

"Are ye all right, M?" whispers Elinor. "Ye look pale."

"I've been dead for half a century, Elinor. I probably look like a ghost."

Am I a ghost?

"Will my mom be able to see me?" I ask, suddenly panicking. Do I want my mom to see me? I don't. Not like this. Not with pink eyes. She'll be scared of me for the rest of my short life, and I couldn't stand that. The living me only has another six months left.

Mitchell pulls me to my feet. "Your mom will be able to see you—this you—so it's really important that you come up with a plan, Medusa. You're still alive in this time. Your mom, your friends, we can't let them see you—the real you. This you." Then he tries to tuck my hair behind my ears. I want Mitchell to help settle my stomach, which I think is still flying in time, but instead his hot fingers make it flutter.

It's dark, but a glimmer of pink is spreading out across the horizon. It's so pretty. I never thought I'd see a sunrise again. I never appreciated the colors of the world before. As the sun starts to rise, the changing palette actually starts to hurt my eyes. I've spent forty years in shadow. It's warm, too, because there's no wind. Just a heavy foreboding in the air that today is going to be a hot one.

Well, I'm used to that.

I look down at the Viciseometer once more. Today is June 18, 1967. In fifteen hours' time, Rory will die. And this is the day I first saw Mitchell, Alfarin and Elinor.

In less than six months, I will die.

"We need to find cover, Medusa," says Alfarin. "We are exposed out here. I sense a malevolent danger coming ever closer."

I look out across the street, past the parked cars, to a litter-strewn playground. Rusty swings stand utterly still. It all looks so surreal, like a painting.

"Over that way, there's a place I sometimes...sorry, there *was* a place I sometimes went to hide...when my mom was out and I was left alone at—"

But I don't want to say it aloud. Why did Septimus make me come back here? This isn't home. It was never home. Home is supposed to be a place where you feel safe.

Elinor takes my hand, and the four of us run across the brittle grass to a small thicket of trees. I look back once. There are two grubby dormer windows on the first floor. The curtains are closed. I saw Team DEVIL from one of those windows. I thought they were angels coming to save me.

We climb over broken branches and discarded car tires. Deep in the trees is a circle. The earth is blackened. There have been several fires here; I lit one of them myself when I was younger. Alfarin and Elinor sit down first and look at me expectantly, but I don't know what Septimus wants me to do. We don't even know if Rory is here.

"I don't know what to do, Mitchell," I whisper. "What does Septimus want from me?"

"We need to think," says Mitchell. "And I can't do that without food."

"Did ye put food in yer backpacks?"

"We did, but we left our backpacks back in the office. I wasn't thinking straight after seeing the office like that, and what with the panic to leave so quickly after Alfarin knocked Septimus down..."

"I concur, my friend," says Alfarin. "The sun is rising, as is my hunger. Breakfast must be our first destination."

Elinor rolls her eyes at me and I smile, but there's something different about her. Even in the weak light, I can tell that her appearance is changing.

"Your eyes, Elinor," I gasp. "You have green eyes now."

"And yours are like pools of chocolate, Medusa," says Alfarin. "Which is doing nothing to vanquish my need for sustenance."

I glance at Mitchell. Pink eyes are cute on a boy, but blue eyes are gorgeous. Alfarin has blue eyes, too, but his are pale, almost gray. Mitchell's are like the Mediterranean Sea.

Get a grip, Medusa.

"Your eyes are really pretty, Medusa," says Mitchell. He smiles at me, and my insides suddenly feel hot and cold. It's weird and nice at the same time.

"Well, are ye two going to find food?" prompts Elinor.

"Your wish is my command, O princess of Valhalla." Alfarin stands up, slaps Mitchell on the back and sends him flying forward into a tree trunk that splinters as Mitchell lands on it.

"My apologies, my friend. I forget that you are built like the women of my Norse ancestors. Let us go forage for sustenance amongst the peasants of this time."

"Ten seconds back and we're already stealing," mutters Mitchell. "My old man would kick my ass if he knew death had turned me into a thief."

Mitchell is still grumbling at Alfarin as they walk off into the dim light of early morning, leaving Elinor and me alone. I peek through the trees for another look at my old house. Everything is so quiet, so still outside.

It's amazing how looks on the outside can betray what goes on inside.

"Why don't ye look in the envelope that Septimus gave ye?" suggests Elinor. "That is, if ye want to."

My fingers reach inside my shorts, but my pockets are empty. The only thing I have on me is the Viciseometer. I pull my pockets out, but they contain nothing except for some crumbs.

"It isn't here!" I cry.

"Did ye tuck it into your shirt?" asks Elinor. She looks horrified as I start patting myself down.

This is a disaster. The brown envelope that Septimus gave me is gone. I run out of the trees, back the way we came. Maybe it fell out as we landed. I jump over the gate, and in the weak light, I search the dirt and threadbare grass with my fingertips for the information on the Dreamcatcher.

All I find are cigarette butts and broken glass. A jagged edge slices through the tip of my index finger, but I don't cry out. I can't let anyone in that house see or hear me.

Elinor is walking across the grass. In her white dress she looks like a ghost. Her long hair catches the light from the sunrise, and it flames with a vivid red glow.

I shake my head at her. "It's not here," I say.

I have to think. I leapfrog back over the gate, grab Elinor's hand and drag her back to the trees.

I must have dropped the envelope in the office after Mitchell grabbed hold of Alfarin. I was so concerned with using the Viciseometer, I wasn't really concentrating on anything else. Now we have nothing to go on at all and no money. We're here to search for something desperately important, but how will we know it if we find it?

Then I hear crying. It's a child. But it's not making the type of wailing that sets your teeth on edge. It's soft. Sad.

"Do ye hear that?" asks Elinor, looking around.

"Yeah. It's a kid. What's a kid doing out here this early in the morning?"

"Hello," calls Elinor gently. "Can ye hear us?"

The crying continues. "Can we help you?" I call out, trying to make my voice just loud enough to be heard by this one child and not the whole street. It's not just my mom in a drunken stupor in that house.

Then we hear a wolf howl. It's long and drawn out and sends shivers up my spine. The hairs on my bare arms rise like the dead. I've heard that exact howl before. Over the loudspeaker system in Hell.

"Oh, my!" exclaims Elinor, grabbing hold of my hand. "Oh, no. They're here already. We need to hide."

But I pull my hand away from Elinor.

"There's no way I'm leaving a little kid out here if there are Skin-Walkers around," I reply. I force my voice to get a little louder. "We won't hurt you. We can help you. We'll take you back to your mommy."

Another howl, only this time it's duplicated. There's more than one Skin-Walker on this street, and my fear turns to panic. Where are Mitchell and Alfarin? Are they safe?

I see the outline of a small child in the distance. It's a little boy. He has a mop of hair so blond it looks like snow. He's walking down the middle of the street, and he's completely alone. His tiny feet are bare, and he's wearing a long T-shirt that comes down to his ankles.

Elinor and I instinctively run toward him. We have to get him away from danger—a danger we caused just by being here. He sees us and holds his arms out to be picked up. His chubby face is clean, but as I get closer I can see tearstains on his deathly-pale skin.

The howling from the Skin-Walkers has picked up. There's a whole pack here. My stomach is twisting and knotting. A sharp pain stabs at the space where my heart once beat. Where are Mitchell and Alfarin? Can't they hear this?

And then *he* steps out from behind my house.

I forget about protecting the boy. Absolute hate and total fear combine to stop me in my tracks. I don't want to look at him, but I am too scared to look away.

Rory Hunter doesn't look the way I remember him. When we were both alive, he had long blond hair and sideburns all the way down to his pointed chin. Now he's bald, and his scalp is crisscrossed with jagged purple scars. His gray-blue eyes are wide—too wide—and he isn't blinking. A few more seconds pass before I realize he has no eyebrows, either.

His chest is bare, and like the little boy, he isn't wearing shoes. Round puncture marks form straight lines from his neck all the way down his arms and torso.

Another two figures appear out of nowhere, and they move to my side. The relief dilutes the fear, just a little. Mitchell has a long piece of wood in his hands; Alfarin's axe is raised, and the blade glints with a silver-pink sheen as the sun slowly continues to rise.

"Stay the Hell away from her, or I swear there'll be nothing left of you by the time we've finished!" yells Mitchell.

But Rory says nothing. His bulging eyes continue to bore into me as he sidesteps across the street toward the little boy. With a beckoning of his bloodied fingers, three of which are missing completely, Rory orders the tearful child to his side.

"No!" I scream at Rory. "*Stay away from him.*"

"I knew you'd come here," he says, but there's something weird about his voice. It isn't the slurred tone I'd come to fear so much. It's deeper and gravelly. It's as if he's learning to talk again. His teeth aren't missing, but they've been broken off. They look like fangs. But that wouldn't explain the sound, would it?

Then I remember what Elinor said about Unspeakables. They have their tongues torn out. They literally can't speak anymore in Hell, presumably to stop their screams. Someone, or something, has reattached Rory's tongue.

Just the thought of it makes me gag.

"Stay away from that little boy. I won't let you hurt him!" I cry.

"You couldn't stop me from hurting you," says Rory. "What makes you think you have the strength now?" Then he laughs and spits blood onto the ground. It sizzles as it makes contact with the pavement.

The little boy holds out his arms to Rory. I start to run toward him, but Mitchell and Alfarin grab hold of me. They're shaking their heads with frantic intensity because they have both been struck dumb by what is slinking out of the shadows. Nine more figures: men with gray-and-white wolf skins. I recognize Perfidious at once, because he's taller than the other eight Skin-Walkers. All have wolf heads on top of their own, but they are no longer howling.

They are whimpering. All, including Perfidious, have bowed their heads in submission.

Rory scoops up the little boy. The child places his head on Rory's bared, scarred shoulder and turns to look at me. His arms reach out once more, and I can still see the tears falling in a thin stream down his face. They're no longer clear. His tears are like tiny red raindrops.

"You have something I want, Melissa," says Rory. "And I have something you want. But now isn't really the best time to discuss this." He glances at the cowering Skin-Walkers with a smug smile before turning back to me. "We'll meet again. But don't think you can find me by chasing me randomly through time. When you do track me down, it will be where and when I *want* to be found."

Rory and the child disappear, leaving red smoke and small pockets of sizzling liquid on the ground.

The Skin-Walkers howl in anger, and it's a terrifying noise with a physical quality that almost knocks me off my feet. All nine throw themselves forward and, on all fours, start running at Team DEVIL. An invisible toxic wave hits us as the stench from the Skin-Walkers returns. It is the smell of hate and blood and pain.

"*Run!*" I scream.

But there's only one place to go.

"Inside—*now!*" I yell as I pull open the screen door of my house. My mother never locks anything. I used to complain to her about it, but I've never been so grateful.

The four of us throw our weight against the inside door, and I pull back the locks. They won't hold for long. We need more time.

"I'll get the back door. You stay and start putting another time into the Viciseometer," says Mitchell.

I don't ask him how he knows where the back door is.

"Get us out of here, Medusa!" bellows Alfarin.

I hear the floorboards creaking above us. I push Alfarin and Elinor into the small room on our left: the good room, with a new television, that Mom keeps perfect for the guests we never have.

I pull the Viciseometer from my pocket. I can still hear the terrible howling outside, and the neighbors starting to shout out of their windows.

Taking a deep breath, I grasp the red needle and change the date to June 15, 1966. The time can stay the same because right now we've run out of it.

Mitchell runs back into the room.

"*Get us out of here, Medusa.*"

"Hold on to someone," I say in a steady voice, which is the complete antithesis of the fear that's rattling my insides. "I'm taking us to Muir Woods."

The deep-red face of the Viciseometer starts to swirl and sing with the high-pitched whistle once more. I zone out of everything around me. The Skin-Walkers, Rory, the little crying boy, and even my mom upstairs become blurred ghosts on the periphery. Every ounce of concentration I have is willed into seeing the giant redwoods standing majestically in a carpet of deep-green ferns.

We are sucked into the darkness once more. There's a faint yellow glow in the distance as the wind tightens around our bodies. Elinor is the only one who lands on her feet. Mitchell is splayed out like a starfish, while Alfarin is lying facedown in a patch of fine green grass.

I am panting heavily, but I feel strangely exhilarated. I did it. I kept calm and got us away from the Skin-Walkers.

Then I remember the little boy and I feel sick. Who is he, and what is Rory planning to do with him? What does Rory want from me? I've got nothing he hasn't already taken.

Mitchell crawls over to me. "Are you okay, Medusa?" he asks simply. He tucks my hair behind my ears again. I feel it pop right back out, and I get the feeling that Mitchell knew that would happen, but it's sweet that he continues to try.

"I lost the envelope Septimus gave me, Mitchell. We're flying blind."

He lies back on a mattress of ferns. It's darker here than it was in San Francisco, probably because the towering redwood trees are blocking out what little light is coming from the sunrise.

"It doesn't matter."

But we all know it does.

"Ye were amazing, M," says Elinor. "Ye kept yer head so well."

Mitchell suddenly bursts out laughing and then quickly apologizes as Alfarin growls unintelligibly at him.

"Sorry," says Mitchell. "Inappropriate humor... what with Elinor saying about you keeping your head..."

But Elinor giggles. "It is okay, Alfarin. I like Mitchell's sense of humor."

"There are some things that are not amusing, my friend," says Alfarin moodily.

I have no idea what they're talking about, but for some reason I suddenly have a cloudy vision of myself standing over a sink, washing blood from Alfarin's axe. I'm a newcomer to Team DEVIL—I've never even touched that weapon—yet the vision seems so real.

"So that scarred man was your stepfather, Medusa?" asks Alfarin, bringing me back.

"Yes, but he's changed. They've mutilated him."

"We won't let him hurt you," says Mitchell. "Not now, not ever."

"What of the boy?" asks Elinor. "Did ye know him?"

I want to say no because I don't know him, but something is nagging away at me. A memory... another image?

No, a nightmare.

I do know that boy.

"I've seen him before! He was in my nightmare, the first night we slept in the accounting office. And two of the angels were there, too. There was blood, and one of the angels, Owen, he was yelling to Jeanne that we couldn't help the boy... oh, shit, *no!*"

The realization—and enormity—of what we have to do hits me. I stumble to my feet, lurch toward a tree trunk that's at least six feet wide and vomit into the bracken surrounding it. For the first time in my existence, I'm glad I can no longer breathe, because I know if I were alive, I wouldn't be able to do it. The hidden evil of Hell has been revealed to me, and I want to scream.

We aren't looking for a willow hoop covered in pretty feathers and beads at all. How could we have been so naïve, so stupid, as to think The Devil would stick to traditions and customs of the living on earth?

That beautiful, sad little boy is what we have to take back to Hell.

Because that child is The Devil's Dreamcatcher.

9. **A Grave Situation**

"M, are ye all right?"

Elinor is the one who asks, but Mitchell's the first one to reach me. He rubs my back as I continue to throw up into the bracken.

"Better out than in," he says in a strained voice. "At least that's what my mom used to say."

"Is Medusa suffering from Osmosis of the Dead?" asks Alfarin. "I thought that only happened to lone time-travelers."

"That's what was written in the book from the library," replies Elinor. "This must be something else."

I wipe my mouth on the back of my hand and straighten, still panting.

"It's the boy," I gasp.

"What's the boy?" asks Mitchell. "You know him?"

I shake my head and stumble back to Alfarin and Elinor. Mitchell now has hold of my hand, but I wish he would let go, because that was the one I used to wipe puke away from my mouth.

"The boy . . . the boy is The Devil's Dreamcatcher."

"Ye cannot be serious," whispers Elinor.

"Not even The Devil would be that nefarious," says Alfarin.

The sun has risen a little more; its pale-golden rays are starting to seep through the gaps in the towering trees.

"He's The Devil, Alfarin," says Mitchell darkly. "If I told you half of the stuff I overhear . . ."

Mitchell leans back against a tree trunk and closes his eyes. His entire body seems to absorb the sunlight, and there's a faint nimbus surrounding him.

"But that means the child, that lovely little boy, is a weapon!" cries Elinor. "Septimus said so back in the office." Her thin, pale hand is covering her mouth, and her startling green eyes are now swimming in tears. "Why would anyone do that?"

"His being the Dreamcatcher would explain the Skin-Walkers' reaction," says Alfarin solemnly. "They would have attacked the deviant, I am certain of it, but they whimpered in fright and backed away once he had the boy in his arms. The boy is a weapon that even the Skin-Walkers are afraid of."

"Then how the Hell are we going to do this?" asks Mitchell. "We left our backpacks in the office, we have no supplies, no money, no nothing. We can't even call Septimus and beg for help because our cell phones are in the backpacks. At least the last time we left Hell I was prepared for it, but Septimus has sent us here to bring back a weapon that made the Skin-Walkers crap their fur."

"Why don't we just go back to San Francisco, five minutes earlier, and grab the Dreamcatcher?" I ask. "Before Rory gets the chance to disappear?"

"We can't," replies Elinor. "Our visit there is now a fixed point in time. We can't change anything that happens in time when we use the Viciseometer."

"We've got to go back to Hell," says Mitchell. "We don't have a choice. We can't do this."

"It's a little boy, Mitchell," I say quietly. "And I am not leaving him with Rory Hunter."

Mitchell and Alfarin both start to protest, but I hold up my hand to silence them. I need to *think*. There *has* to be a way. Septimus never would have sent us out here if he didn't believe in us—believe in me. I think back to our conversation in the accounting office. What else did Septimus say?

I look up into the indigo sky, just visible through the canopy of leaves above us. The few stars I can still see twinkle benignly.

Up There exists…well, up there—somewhere.

I turn to the group. "Septimus said that four angels—Team ANGEL—were also looking for the Dreamcatcher. Why don't we find them, ask them what they know? Eight heads are definitely better than four. They might have provisions and information that we don't."

"That is a fine idea, M, but how do we find angels?" asks Elinor. "We cannot use the Viciseometer to track them without knowing their location, and they could be anywhere."

"Angels will not want to toil with devils," says Alfarin. "They would not trust us as far as they could throw us, and I would like to see any of the winged chosen ones try to throw me."

"What do you think, Mitchell?" I ask. He's still bathed in a sunbeam. He looks ethereal—and very tall. He just needs wings and he could be one of them.

"I think Septimus made you the leader for a reason, Medusa," replies Mitchell slowly. He's staring at the ground. "I don't understand why Septimus couldn't have made this a little bit easier, especially since it's so important, but I trust him, and I'll trust you. If you want to look for the angels, I'm with you."

I'm filled with gratitude. "Thank you." But the words break up in my throat and I don't think they come out properly. Why did I have to die for people to believe in me? It isn't fair. I turn to the others. "Are you all with me? I won't blame anyone for turning back now."

"Team DEVIL stays together," says Elinor. "Always and forever."

"Then let's hunt some angels!" roars Alfarin, swinging his axe onto his shoulder. Several birds swoop into the sky, squawking with fright.

"We are looking for the angels, not hunting them, Alfarin," scolds Elinor. "And remember, they are probably delicate little things and easily frightened."

"That Jeanne didn't look delicate that time I saw her at the cemetery," mumbles Mitchell. "If looks could kill, I would have been dead all over again."

The cemetery.

"Mitchell, you're a genius!" I cry. "That's where we'll find them. Or two of them, at least. Can you remember the date and time you traveled to your grave, the last time you were there?"

"Yeah," says Mitchell, nodding. "I think so."

"But we cannot arrive at the same time," says Elinor. "We cannot meet ourselves."

"A paradox," booms Alfarin. He puffs out his chest with self-importance. "I remember."

He looks so pleased that Mitchell and I can't help laughing. It feels like a huge weight has been lifted from my shoulders. I was so scared of letting Septimus and the others down, but already I have a plan. Whether it works or not is another matter, but it's a start. And there's some comfort to knowing that I will do everything humanly possible to save that little boy from Rory.

I may be a devil, but I will always be a human first.

I pull the Viciseometer out of my pocket. It feels light in my hand, although it looks solid and heavy. The delicate gold chain slips through my fingers as I grasp the red needle. The white face stares up at me, but the Viciseometer vibrates in my hand. It knows it's about to be used.

"Where are you buried?" I ask.

"Washington, DC. In Glenwood Cemetery," replies Mitchell.

"And what time did you arrive when you traveled there last time?" I ask.

"Three o'clock in the afternoon," replies Mitchell immediately.

"Then we should arrive at least thirty minutes before that," I say, manipulating the hands into place. I secure the time of half past two by pressing the three black buttons on the bottom right.

"The date was November twentieth, 2012," says Mitchell.

"You're sure?"

"Positive," replies Mitchell as Alfarin and Elinor move in closer. They're holding hands.

I input the time and then move my hand toward Mitchell. He links his fingers through mine, leaving the Viciseometer clearly visible in the palm of my hand. He knows what to do next. I can't see through his time; only Mitchell can do this part.

A creamy white statue appears in the red face of the watch. It's an angel blowing a trumpet. My thumb is resting against the large button on top of the Viciseometer, and as Mitchell presses down on my thumb, he shouts, "*Now!*"

All four of us land in yet another time, but we're on our feet.

"We're...getting better...at this," I say, looking around, already aware of the abrupt drop in temperature. It's daylight, too, and the sudden increase in sunshine makes my eyes water.

"It will...get better, M," says Elinor, rubbing at her arms. "It is not as bad...as last time. I think our bodies are...getting used to the temperatures...of this world now."

Mitchell and Alfarin have already ducked down behind a tall headstone that has three names carved into it. Green lichen covers the date of death.

"M, get down," whispers Elinor, and she pulls me across the grass to where the boys are.

"What's the problem?" I ask, still shivering. "You three won't be here for another thirty minutes."

"It's not just us we have to avoid," says Mitchell quietly. "My mom is here."

I gasp. "What? But you never said..."

"Mitchell will not do anything silly, will ye, Mitchell?" says Elinor encouragingly. "He has accepted his death."

Mitchell nods, but he's suddenly very interested in picking the petals from a dying collection of flowers on the grave. As they crumble in his hands, I notice gray ash falling from his fingers.

"What's that?"

"It's a flower. Don't ask me what kind, though," replies Mitchell.

"Not the flower, that gray powder."

"It's us," replies Elinor. "We are dead, and therefore we are toxic to the land of the living. We made such a mess of the hotel we stayed in, didn't we?"

Judging by her joking tone, I know Elinor is just trying to make Mitchell feel better, but in doing so, she's just managed to make me feel worse. I never forget I'm dead, but even though I'm in Hell, I've never felt like a monster. I never knew I was toxic until now, and it makes me angry. This is what the Highers bestowed on us: a poisonous existence that never ends.

"What should we do, Medusa?" asks Alfarin. "I volunteer myself and my axe to trap the angel scum by pinning their wings to the ground. You will then be able to interrogate them at will. I suggest plucking their feathers, in the manner of my great-aunt Dagmar, as if she were preparing a chicken for dinner."

"Alfarin!" exclaims Elinor as Mitchell snorts. "Ye are talking about Joan of Arc. Ye must not frighten her, and certainly no plucking."

Thinking of the wingless figures I saw in my dream, I speak up. "I'm not sure plucking is going to be necessary, but thanks anyway, Alfarin," I say, patting him on his upper arm. I withdraw my hand quickly. Jeez, there are some muscles under that tunic.

Out of the corner of my eye, I can see Mitchell trying to flex his pecs. He kinda fails, which I think is cute. Not that Mitchell would ever go for someone like me, with my crazy hair and skinny legs. Besides, he's probably already ridden the train wreck that is Patty Lloyd.

Anyway, none of that matters anymore.

"Is this where you saw the angels last time?" I ask him.

"I saw the army dude here. He was wearing his uniform. And see that white cross over there?" Mitchell points to another towering sculpture, a hundred feet away. "That's where I saw Jeanne. She was wearing an orange dress and a pink cardigan. You won't be able to miss her. She's the hottest girl I've ever seen."

A sudden burst of heat fires through my stomach and chest, and I can feel my cheeks burning. No, I'm clearly not Mitchell's type at all.

"That's what you remember? A hot girl?"

"No," says Mitchell. "I remember a lot of other stuff. I'm just saying she was hot."

I stand up quickly. Too quickly. My head is thumping, and dots appear in front of my eyes.

"Typical boy," I mutter, and I walk away.

I've gone about ten feet before I come to my senses.

And it horrifies me.

Why am I getting so jealous? I barely know Mitchell. We've been through a pretty intense time over the last few days, but that's no reason to get super-clingy, because I'm not like that. I tried to be—with Patty and her friends in Hell, just to fit in—but it was fake. I thought I had a good sense of self, even if it did mean ending up alone. So what's happening to me now?

From behind a headstone, I can hear Mitchell whispering rapidly to Alfarin.

"What did I do? I didn't mean Medusa isn't hot."

"Of course not, my friend."

"Because she *is* hot."

"I understand, my friend."

"Medusa's pissed at me, isn't she?"

"You are out of the fire and into the pan for frying, my friend."

"Honestly, ye boys!" says Elinor. "Stop chattering. Sit here and keep watch. M and I will go up by the cross. Ye said Jeanne was wearing an orange dress, Mitchell?"

"And she is totally not hot," replies Mitchell in an exaggerated, loud voice.

My back is still to him, so he can't see me smile. At least Mitchell's as bad at this as I am.

Elinor slips her arm through mine.

"We will wait up here. Hopefully we can intercept the angels before Alfarin has a chance to remove their wings. If they even have them."

The grass is cushiony beneath my sneakers. Purple storm clouds are gathering in the sky, and they look like huge bruises covering Up There.

"Have you ever seen an angel before, Elinor?"

She shakes her head. "Only devils—but I wouldn't swap, not now."

Elinor looks back fondly at Alfarin, and I look over my shoulder, too. The boys aren't keeping watch at all. They're doing something to Alfarin's axe.

"*Alfarin!*" shouts Elinor. "Will ye refrain from sharpening yer axe on the gravestones? It is disrespectful. Ye could be sharing a dorm in Hell with the person who was buried there."

Mitchell flaps his arms in an attempt to quiet Elinor down. Alfarin hollers back an apology, and Mitchell throws himself backward with exasperation. I try to memorize this strange new happy sensation. I may be on the periphery, but I'm still part of a team who really care about one another. It may be chaos, but it's now *my* chaos. A shared disorder. I know I'll need to keep this feeling close, before the fear of Rory Hunter, and the fate of that little boy, become too much to bear. I quickly scan the gravestones. My stepfather said he would find me. Is he here, watching?

Elinor and I reach the towering white cross. It marks a resting place. I check out the age of the dead person before I read the name, because somehow that seems more important. This person died at eighty-eight years old. That's a good age to die. Not at sixteen like me; I was barely a whisper on the earth. A shadow that few remember.

"How old are you, Elinor?" I ask.

"Nineteen," she replies. "I died on my birthday."

"I'm so sorry, I should never have asked."

"It could have been a lot worse," she replies quietly as her hand clasps the back of her neck. "My death was quick, and for that I will always be thankful."

I don't ask *the* question, but sometimes it takes real restraint not to.

We tuck ourselves in behind the cross. I never do look at the name. I don't feel queasy or disrespectful sitting on the remains of the dead. They won't mind. They're either in Hell or Up There now.

I wonder where I'm buried. I've never really thought about it before.

This graveyard is giving me the creeps. It's dredging up too many thoughts and memories I want to keep locked away.

"Oh, my!" exclaims Elinor suddenly. She is frantically gesturing to Mitchell and Alfarin.

I peer around the cross just in time to see Alfarin throw himself on top of Mitchell, and that has gotta hurt.

Farther along the path is a woman. She's wearing a bright-red trench coat and knee-high black boots. She looks very stylish, but sad. She isn't looking at the graves; she's watching her feet. In her hands is a small bouquet of fresh yellow-and-white flowers.

The color of her hair is familiar, as is the shape of her face and nose.

"Is that Mitchell's mom?"

Elinor nods. "Poor Mitchell," she whispers. "He went to pieces the last time we were here. She must be going to his grave. The last time, we saw her on her way out. It must be so hard to see family and know ye can never speak to them while they are alive."

Does my mom visit my grave? Did they find my body after I fell? Does she know I didn't mean to let go? That my fingers slipped?

"I hate this place," I say. "I hope those angels hurry up."

A strange glimmer of light catches my eye. It's like a flashing torch, and it's coming from a white plinth, some ten rows away from us.

It flashes again, and then I see two people. Even from this distance, I can tell they aren't Owen and Jeanne, although they're definitely male and female.

The girl is dressed in tight white jeans and a pink T-shirt. Her hair is blond, short and spiky with turquoise tips. The boy is tall and gangly, with a shock of red hair.

And they are both surrounded by a full-body halo.

"Elinor!" I cry, pulling on the sleeve of her white dress. "Look, over there. I think there are more angels."

Elinor stands up next to me. The second she does, the boy sees her.

And he starts running straight at us.

10. **Johnny**

His long face is a mask of concentration as his limbs power like pistons toward us. I grab Elinor's hand. I want to shout to Mitchell and Alfarin, but I can't risk drawing attention to them with Mitchell's mom so close by.

"They're angels," I say with more confidence than I feel. "They won't hurt us, and if he tries, well, I work in Hell's kitchens and I know how to pluck a chicken."

The red-haired angel is still running toward us. He reminds me of a gazelle, graceful yet powerful. I wait for wings to sprout out of his back, because I have nothing to go on except legend.

My standard idea disappears as the angel does something no one is expecting.

"*Elinor,*" he shouts. "*Elinor!*"

"Oh, my," whispers Elinor, and she drops to the ground.

The angel reaches Elinor, sinks to his knees and crushes her into an embrace. He's wearing jeans and a pristine white T-shirt. I push him away and he falls backward into the long, damp grass. I am quite prepared to bloody up his clean clothes to protect my friend. He might not need plucking, but I'm handy with my fists all the same.

"Stay away from her if you know what's good for you," I growl as a roar bellows behind us.

Alfarin has seen that Elinor is down.

The gazelle is about to get stomped by the rhino, who's now thundering down the path with his axe clutched between his hands. The fearsome grimace on Alfarin's face is enough to make the angel swear.

"Oh, shit."

Then out of nowhere streaks a flash of blinding golden light. It collides with Alfarin and sends him tumbling into a gray, tablet-shaped gravestone, which splinters with a loud crack.

"Do not touch him, devil."

It's Jeanne. I recognize her immediately from the photograph. She has light-brown skin and black hair that cascades in waves all the way down her back. She's wearing exactly what Mitchell described: a short orange sundress that ends a few inches above her knees, and a pale-pink cardigan that has silver thread running through it. And that isn't all Mitchell was right about, because Jeanne is the most stunning girl I have ever set eyes on. Her skin is flawless and glows without looking sweaty, and her eyes are shaped and colored like milk chocolate almonds.

And she looks as if she would like nothing more than to kick Alfarin's ass from here to the White House.

Mitchell immediately runs over and hauls a disoriented Alfarin to his feet. Mitchell himself looks as if he's in shock. I don't know whether that's because he has just seen his mom again, or because Alfarin is getting beaten up by a girl.

The angel with spiked hair skips over. She is actually skipping, as if she doesn't have a care in the world. The biggest grin I've ever seen lights up her heart-shaped face. Her eyes are turquoise and match the tips of her hair. In the photo she had pink tips, but I like these even more. And perfect skin is clearly a pass into Up There, because this angel is exquisite.

"Move away from her, Johnny," the angel says in an accent that I think is Australian. "You terrified the poor thing, running at her like a madman."

I'm stroking Elinor's face, but the red-haired angel is still trying to reach her. Alfarin roars again, but he seems reluctant to take on Jeanne, who is standing her ground in front of him and Mitchell.

Elinor starts to moan. Her eyes flicker, and then her hand immediately goes to the back of her neck.

"Out of my way, wench!" shouts Alfarin. "I do not hit the daughters of the Valkyrie, but I will make an exception if you do not let me tend to my princess."

"I would like to see you try," snarls Jeanne, calling Alfarin's bluff. Her accent is definitely French.

"I cannot hit a woman," whispers Alfarin to Mitchell. "You must do it, my friend."

"I'm not hitting a woman, either," replies Mitchell. "Especially one I just saw slam-dunk you. And she's Joan of Arc. She's a saint."

"I was not slam-dunked. I slipped on the wet grass."

"She totally owned you, Alfarin."

The angel called Angela bends down over Elinor and strokes her long red hair. Her eyes twinkle with starlight. It's hypnotic.

"She's just as pretty as you said, Johnny," she says warmly. "We thought you would all come here. We've been waiting for ages. Jeanne wanted to leave, of course, but Owen said we had to stay."

Then she leans forward and hugs me.

The angel hugs me! Surprisingly, it's like being wrapped in ice.

"Wow, you're really hot!" she exclaims. "I don't mean hot as in I fancy you, although you are very pretty. Your *skin* is very hot. I'm Angela, by the way—Angela Jackson. Dead five years and counting, thanks to cancer. Seventeen years old forever, although I had cancer from the age of five. Totally sucked. Family trait, unfortunately. The Big C also got my mum and granny."

"M-Medusa," I stutter.

"Where is Owen?" snaps Jeanne. "He needs to know we have found the devil infidels."

"*Jeanne!*" exclaims Angela. "Be nice." The angel called Johnny is still staring at Elinor.

"Hang on," I say, shaking my head, trying to comprehend

everything that has happened in the last couple of minutes. "You just said Elinor was as pretty as *he* said." I point to the angel called Johnny. "But he doesn't know Elinor. They've never met. Elinor's a devil, and she's been dead for hundreds of years. And why were you waiting for *us*? We came here to find *you*. What's going on?"

"Say nothing, Angela," snaps Jeanne. "We were told to trust no one, especially devils."

Angela rolls her eyes at me; she's still stroking Elinor's hair. Static from her fingers is causing the thick red strands to dance like a marionette's limbs.

"Elinor," whispers Johnny. "Wake up, Elinor."

Elinor stirs again. This time her bottle-green eyes open and stay that way. She looks up into Angela's face with wonder, and I see the starlight reflected in Elinor's inky pupils.

"Nice to meet you, Elinor," says Angela. "I'm sorry we scared you. You didn't hurt yourself, did you? That was a pretty impressive drop—very elegant—but I think your brother was rather excited at seeing you again after all this time."

"*Brother?*"

The cacophony of our chorusing voices echoes around the graveyard.

"Our John, is it really ye?"

"Hey, sis. Long time no see."

Elinor scrambles to her feet and throws herself into the angel's arms. Mitchell, Alfarin and I gape at each other with wide-open mouths. I can actually see Alfarin's molars, although I wish I couldn't because they don't look too good. Did Septimus mention at any point in the office that the fourth angel was Elinor's brother? I'm sure he didn't. Now that I think about it, Johnny's last name had been redacted in the information Septimus shared with us about Team ANGEL. Septimus must have done that because Elinor would have said something right away.

First Mitchell, now Elinor. How many more family members are we going to come across? I don't know how to feel about this turn of events. I'm an only child, so I know I don't really get the bond between siblings, but I'm moved almost to tears by the sight of Elinor and Johnny, who are now jumping up and down and laughing. They're so happy to see each other. I'm not jealous, but I do wonder if anyone would ever be that happy to see me.

The look on Mitchell's face isn't jealousy, either. It's worse than that. He looks heartbroken. I'm a poor substitute for family, but I approach him anyway. Jeanne is still standing her ground, and she looks as if she might throttle me.

"Touch me and you'll find out why I'm in Hell," I growl. She steps aside.

Mitchell's head collapses onto my shoulder as I hug him.

"I thought it would be easier seeing my mom this time, but it was worse. It isn't fair, Medusa."

"I know," I whisper, patting his back. His warm hands are on the base of my spine. I can't breathe. I don't breathe. It doesn't matter.

"Alfarin, son of Hlif, son of Dobin," announces Alfarin. He goes down on one knee with his arm across his chest. "It is an honor to meet with the kin of my princess. From this day forth, young John, my axe shall be your trusty comrade in arms, ever ready to hack the ribs from—"

"Alfarin," calls Elinor; her voice is still shaky. "Thank ye kindly, but our John will not be needing yer axe for anything."

"Are ye kidding me?" replies Johnny excitedly. "Are ye a Viking, then? A real one from Valhalla? That is…what's the saying, Angela?"

"Way cool," replies the turquoise-haired angel, with a giggle.

"Way cool," repeats Johnny.

Alfarin strides forward and crushes Johnny into his chest.

"We are now brothers. I shall score our skin for the blood oath."

"This is all very touching," says Jeanne, who doesn't appear touched by any of it whatsoever, "but we must watch for Owen and wait for our orders, since he has been placed in charge of this…mission."

"And aren't you as pissed as anything about that," mutters Angela.

"What did you say?" snaps Jeanne.

"I said that's a great idea, Jeanne," says Angela genially. "Why don't we all go and wait back by the mausoleums over there? Owen said he wouldn't be long."

"He has already been too long," replies Jeanne, with a contemptuous glare at Mitchell and me. "Come, before we attract too much attention. We were meant to be discreet. You are all failing."

"She's a bright bundle of French sunshine, isn't she?" says Mitchell as he pulls away from me. "I'm starting to pity the English who fought her. Maybe something got lost in translation and really *Maid* of Orléans should be *Dictator* of Orléans."

"Sorry about threatening you earlier, Johnny," I say, holding my hand out. "I thought you were going to hurt Elinor."

Elinor has both of her arms wrapped around her brother's waist. He's not as tall as Mitchell—few guys are—but he must be a couple of inches taller than Alfarin. He has a mass of freckles splattered across his face, and his startling green eyes twinkle with the same pulsing stars as Angela's.

"Sorry I scared ye both. I forgot that Elinor hasn't seen me since I was a little lad," replies Johnny, shaking my hand rather limply. "She wouldn't have recognized me. Ye were very brave, standing in front of her like that. It's good to know our Elinor has friends Down There." He lowers his voice. "Alfarin isn't really going to make me do a blood oath, is he?"

"Of course not. He is very gentle, really. Like a big kitten," replies Elinor.

"Can't say I've seen many kittens with an axe," mutters Mitchell, but I think I'm the only one who hears him.

"We'll have to call him Tibbles the Terrible from now on," I whisper back.

"Fluffy the Fart Machine," snickers Mitchell.

"Mufty the Murderous." Mitchell and I are now convulsing with repressed laughter.

"So what age are ye now, our John? When did ye die?" interrupts Elinor loudly.

"Fifteen," replies her brother. "I died from consumption. Sounds like I ate myself to death, doesn't it? Chance would have been a fine thing."

"And our William and Alice? Are they Up There with ye?"

"They sure are. William got to the grand old age of thirty-four before he got trampled by a horse, and our Alice is an old lady. She made it to forty-one."

"Mausoleums—*now!*" demands Jeanne. "You all can play childish games and have happy family reunions when we are out of sight."

Although she is really starting to piss me off, I follow Jeanne to a row of five mausoleums. The bricks are crumbling, the stone is gray. We all squeeze into a gap between the nearest two, and Alfarin only just manages it. All of us are now hiding, with the exception of Mitchell.

"What are you doing?" asks Jeanne.

"I want to see something," he replies. He's looking back at the statue of the white angel blowing a trumpet.

"Is it your fair mother?" asks Alfarin.

Mitchell shakes his head. "It's me—us. I think we're about to walk up the path."

"You what?" asks Angela.

"We have been here on this day before," whispers Elinor. "Mitchell, Alfarin and I. We have been in this moment in time already."

"A double-trouble paradox," says Angela eagerly. "How exciting. I want to see, too."

She clambers over everyone in her white jeans, which are so tight I'm amazed she can move, and takes a stand next to Mitchell. I feel another stab of jealousy as she links her arm through his. I can tell Angela is touchy-feely by nature. I knew people like that back when I was alive. It's a gift that comes with being loved and nurtured. I try so hard, but it's far more difficult when you're used to constantly flinching away. Affectionately touching Mitchell or Elinor is a conscious effort for me. Not so for Angela.

"I cannot move in such a confined space," says Alfarin. He

pushes himself out of the gap, too, and stands by Mitchell and Angela. Next to go are Elinor and Johnny, and before long, we're all standing, watching and waiting, while Jeanne hisses like a snake with venomous words about being seen in a paradox.

A tiny ball of light appears in the distance, next to the angel statue. It hovers several feet off the ground. At first the ball is white, then a brilliant blue. It becomes brown and rapidly expands. The figure of a soldier quickly appears in the light. He is small but muscular. He has fine black hair that is slicked back. Something round and silver is glinting in his hand. The soldier tucks it into his breast pocket without taking his eyes off the angel statue.

It's Owen.

Then we see another version of Alfarin and Elinor approaching, and they walk straight past him with their noses buried in a map. A golden aura surrounds them.

A few yards behind, dragging his feet, is another Mitchell. Just as sad, just as heartbroken as the version I tried to comfort a few minutes ago. This graveyard is clearly toxic for his soul, too.

"Stay here, and do not allow yourselves to be seen," snaps Jeanne. She walks out a little farther. "Owen," she calls in her thick accent.

The soldier looks in her direction, but he quickly realizes when he spots Jeanne that her attention is not aimed at him. After all her hissing about the dangers of being seen, it's Jeanne who gives herself away. Owen follows her line of sight to the other Mitchell, who is surrounded by a halo of light and gaping at them both. I didn't get it wrong that evening when I saw Mitchell, Alfarin and Elinor outside my house. The three of them did look like angels. They were glowing just like Owen and Jeanne and the other Mitchell are now. The brightest one of all was Elinor.

Owen nods to the other Mitchell, and Mitchell reciprocates. Paradox Mitchell then looks away, and in the time it takes for him to look back again, both Owen and Jeanne have become golden streaks of light. Within a split second they are with us, hidden away from the other Mitchell's line of sight.

No one says a word. The exhalations we do not need to make are long and labored and completely fake.

"Thanks for that warning, Jeanne," says Owen in an English accent. He looks at each of us in turn, as if sizing us up. "So this is Team DEVIL. You are aware that some of you are in a paradox right now?" His brown eyes are twinkling with stars as well, but he looks worn out and there are dark shadows, like bruises, under his eyes.

"We know," replies Mitchell.

"Interesting," says Owen quietly. "Both appear to work the same."

Judging by the confused look on Mitchell's face, he doesn't understand Owen's comment, either.

"This is my sister Elinor," says Johnny. "You said she would be here, and she was. Gave her a right old fright, though, because I forgot the last time she saw me I was a young lad. And I remember you, too, Mitchell. You were there when the house caught fire." But Johnny is looking at me and scratching his head. It sounds like something being scraped across sandpaper.

"What?" I ask.

"You look familiar, too. But I can't picture where from. It's like I remember you from a nightmare or something when I was living."

Not a dream, but a nightmare. Way to go, Medusa. I'm actually able to transmit my horrible unconscious thoughts beyond the Underworld.

Owen shakes Elinor's hand and nods to the rest of us. Jeanne has her arms folded across her chest; Angela is smiling away, twirling a turquoise strand of hair around her finger; and now Johnny is pushing Elinor away because she's trying to flatten down his mop of bright-red hair with fingers she has just spat on.

"Which one of you is the leader?" asks Jeanne. She automatically stares at Alfarin, who certainly looks like he should be in charge. He's the only one with a weapon, for a start.

"I was advised Melissa is in charge," says Owen softly.

How the Hell does Owen know my real name? Mitchell seems

to be thinking the same thing, because he says, "You seem to know a lot about us, Owen."

"I was prepared, Mitchell. I once made the mistake of not being prepared, and it cost me my life. You have been sent to recover The Devil's Dreamcatcher, haven't you?" Owen asks me.

I nod. "It was an Unspeakable who took it."

"And would I be correct in assuming that if this involves an Unspeakable, we are also dealing with Skin-Walkers?"

My reply of affirmation is drowned out by cries from the angels.

"We were never informed of this, Owen," says Jeanne. "Why would this be kept from us?"

"Because the Skin-Walkers are not our concern," replies Owen. "We must find the Dreamcatcher. That is all."

"Why were you waiting for us?" I ask. "How did you know we'd be here?"

"When you're dead, you have nothing but time," replies Owen cryptically.

Mitchell rolls his eyes at me.

"So the Dreamcatcher is your quarry, too," says Alfarin. "Meaning Up There desires a weapon?" His eyes are narrowed, and I notice he has tightened his grip on his axe.

Owen shakes his head. He has lines on his forehead and around the edges of his mouth. The soldier looks absolutely exhausted, like he hasn't slept for a hundred years. "I've had enough of weapons to last an eternity, Alfarin," he replies. "And we certainly aren't here to steal the Dreamcatcher, either."

"Then what do ye all want it for, if not a weapon?" asks Elinor.

Owen leans back against one of the mausoleums. I can feel myself being pulled toward him, and it's physical, almost magnetic.

"We don't want to use the Dreamcatcher, Elinor. We want to save it."

11. Two Become One

"You want to save the Dreamcatcher?" I ask incredulously. "But that's *our* job. This doesn't have anything to do with you."

"I knew this was a mistake, colluding with devil scum," says Jeanne. "You should have remained silent, Owen."

"Who are you calling scum?" snaps Mitchell. "Just because you're angels, that doesn't mean you're better than us."

"For Heaven's sake, Jeanne," says Angela, stepping between Mitchell and the French angel. "Could you at least try to be nice? It's not as if they want to hurt the Dreamcatcher."

"Of course we don't," I reply. "We came this close to him an hour ago." I indicate inches with my fingers. "Elinor and I would have grabbed him, given a few more seconds. The last thing we wanted to do is leave it with *him*."

"You've seen the Dreamcatcher?" exclaim Owen and Jeanne together, although her voice is a lot higher and more surprised than Owen's. Even though Owen is the leader of Team ANGEL, it's becoming obvious that it's Jeanne—a former military commander—who *thinks* she's in charge.

I glance at Elinor, and I'm grateful it remains just as easy to catch her eye now that they've changed color. She shakes her head, just a fraction, and I understand immediately. We need to be cautious around these angels, even if one is her brother.

"Where did you see the child, devil?" demands Jeanne.

I ignore her. I've never been a deliberately rude person—dead or alive—but I don't care with Jeanne. She may be a saint, but there are devils in Hell who are more polite than she is. She could give the HBI a run for their money in how to stick your head up your ass and still retain the ability to speak.

"I'm sorry we've gotten off to a bad start," says Owen, and he turns his body, just enough to cut Jeanne out of the picture. "Please forgive us. I truly believe that we can work together on this. It's why I was waiting for you, Melissa."

Even though Medusa is the name I go by now, I don't correct Owen. I don't know why. Maybe there's something about being here on earth again that makes me want to hang on to that part of me that's still Melissa.

"We can all work together, ye know," says Elinor warmly. "We may be devils, but we are very nice."

Angela laughs, and it's like the tinkling of bells.

"You are so sweet, Elinor," she says. "Johnny said you saved his life in the Great Fire of London."

"I helped," mutters Mitchell, and I see Alfarin give him a swift kick to shut him up.

Okay. Team DEVIL clearly didn't stop any of their deaths, but what *did* they do the last time they were here in the land of the living? For every step forward with my new friends, I seem to take two back when it comes to clearing up mysteries about their time travel with the Viciseometer.

I look down at my shorts pocket when a strange heat starts pulsing through the fabric, almost as if the Viciseometer knows that I'm thinking about it. It's getting impatient for something. I look up to see that Owen is getting fidgety, too. His hand keeps going to his breast pocket.

Suddenly I remember that ball of light I saw before Owen materialized in front of the angel statue. It was white at first, then it turned a brilliant blue, and then Owen appeared. He had something round and silver in his hand, which he placed in the same pocket he keeps reaching for now.

Both appear to work the same, he said to Team DEVIL's confusion.

"Do you have a Viciseometer?" I blurt out.

My question takes the angels by surprise, which is enough to confirm to me that they do have another time-traveling device. That's how they got here. Of course. It's so simple.

"What do you know about the Viciseometer?" demands Jeanne. Again, I ignore her.

I look straight into Owen's tired, bloodshot eyes. "Show me."

Owen pulls a silver pocket watch from his breast pocket. He doesn't even try to feign ignorance. The Viciseometer hidden on me is now surging with heat. I take it out and let the red face hover above my open hand. The burnished gold rim is lit up with tiny sparks. Owen's Viciseometer is reacting in the same way, but instead of a red surface surrounded by tiny flames, its face is a deep sapphire blue, and it's surrounded by tiny diamonds glinting away under the darkening November sky.

"Are those stars around the edge?" asks Elinor, inching closer.

"They are," replies Owen. "Melissa, how did you guess we were using a Viciseometer?"

"Because you need to jump through time, just like we do," I reply. "And a Viciseometer was the most obvious way of doing it."

Owen and I are moving closer together, but it isn't intentional. We are being physically pulled by the Viciseometers.

Our hands are inches apart. Both Viciseometers start to rotate clockwise, millimeters above our hands. The flames tickle, but they aren't painful. The watches are mesmerizing, hypnotic. I know I should pull away, but I can't.

Then our fingertips graze.

The red face of my Viciseometer connects to the blue like two magnets pulled together. Our hands join as well; Owen's skin is warm, nowhere near as cold as Angela's was.

Almost immediately, the others start screaming.

"Where did they go?" shouts Mitchell. "What did he do with Medusa?"

"*Owen would do nothing!*" screams Jeanne. "He is a pacifist, not a warrior. That devil woman with snake hair has taken him."

Alfarin is swinging his axe like an inverted pendulum. He narrowly misses Johnny, but Elinor doesn't notice. She's arguing with Angela about where we've gone.

"They can't see us!" I exclaim to Owen. "We've become invisible."

"Did you know this would happen?" Owen asks softly. Our hands are still joined, and the sensation of flame and stars is sending aching spasms through my arm.

"No. I knew about the legend of the Viciseometer, but only because I'd read about it. I hadn't even seen one before today."

Then a hazy thought, like the memory of a nightmare, drifts across my mind. A shadow. I can taste tears and strawberries.

Owen bites down on his bottom lip. His top lip is so thin it's barely visible. My grandmother once told me not to trust men with thin lips.

That turned out to be bullshit. Rory Hunter's lips were like swollen fingers.

"Can you trust me, Melissa?" Owen asks, as if reading my mind.

"That depends," I hedge. "What can you tell me that will *help* me trust you?"

Owen smiles, but he doesn't look happy.

"I can tell you that I was made aware of the Skin-Walkers' involvement in this search before we left Heaven. I didn't tell the others because I didn't want to frighten them—or at least scare Angela and Johnny. I even argued against their coming here. Jeanne and I have seen death in a way most of the dead have not. In my case, I saw men, younger than me, cut down in a hail of machine-gun fire. If they passed quickly, they were fortunate. Death does not always come quickly on the battlefield. I know that Skin-Walkers have no regard for anything but death. They enjoy it. What Jeanne and I have seen would be a feast for them. So I was opposed to bringing two innocents within their grasp, but I was overruled."

"What else do you know about the Skin-Walkers, Owen?" I

ask. "I need to know as much as possible if I'm going to protect the others. They have no connection to the Unspeakable whatsoever. They're here because of me, and I can't—I won't—let anything happen to any of them."

"Apart from their love of death and pain, I know little about the Skin-Walkers. I have heard there are nine in total: one for each circle of Hell, or so I was told. I don't know if this is true. He who rules Heaven is not what you would expect."

I came here for information, for help, and I'm finally getting it, but I don't want to stay invisible like this. The sound of the others yelling is being muffled somehow. We can still see them, but I'm starting to feel like I'm fading away.

"Owen, we should let go," I say.

"Wait. There's something else," adds Owen urgently. "Something you need to know about yourself, Melissa. I know more about your task than you realize, and I want to warn you, because you're being used. The Unspeakable who took the Dreamcatcher is your stepfather, and you're being used as bait to lure him. Those who sent you out here are using you in the same way I was used back in 1916."

"I already know this, Owen. Now please let go."

"Do you? Do you really understand what they are prepared to sacrifice to get the Dreamcatcher back in Hell? Septimus is a Roman general who fought and made sacrifices in some of the bloodiest campaigns in history."

"Septimus *was* a Roman general, but he's worshipped in Hell. He's a good guy."

"I said the same about my commanding officers. I believed the same up until the moment I was hit by a hail of bullets. I thought they would come for me to help, but they didn't. They didn't come to help any of us."

"Septimus is different. Now let go."

"They are all the same, Melissa, but Septimus has given you a gift. You have a Viciseometer. So use it. Run away. Leave the others and go, before it's too late."

Owen's eyes are wide and pleading. The skin around them looks pinched and bruised. Unlike his angel comrades, Owen actually looks dead.

"You think I should desert the others?"

"Yes. You said yourself that you wanted to protect them. By leaving them, you will do that."

"I can't."

"It's because of Mitchell, isn't it? Already I can see that the way you look at him is different from the way you look at Alfarin, or Elinor."

"You know nothing about me, Owen. You've only just met me, and I don't care anymore what information Up There has given you, or what you're keeping from Jeanne, Angela and Johnny...."

But Owen has a fire in him now. I can smell it. It's wood and mud and rain and blood.

"Listen to me. Your name is Melissa Olivia Pallister. You died on the second of December in 1967, at the age of sixteen, after you fell from the Golden Gate Bridge. The Grim Reapers marked you down as a suicide, but you wouldn't sign the form to accept that declaration, so they sent you to Hell for your defiance. But there's another date of death, Melissa, one in June of 1967, that was listed in your records above December second. And then it was crossed out."

"What are you talking about? How have you seen my records?"

"You all trust Septimus. Well, you're fools. You've died twice, Melissa. Did Septimus tell you that?"

"A person can't die twice. Now let go of me."

"Something happened to you. In life and death. You have an entire parallel existence that's been wiped out. I think you're in danger."

With a wrench that almost pulls my arm from my shoulder socket, I drag my hand away from Owen's. Mitchell, Alfarin and Elinor immediately rush toward me, but at the last second, Mitchell veers away and grabs hold of Owen's jacket.

"Do that again and I swear I'll drag you back into Hell with me," he growls.

"It was an accident," replies Owen. "My thumb must have pressed down on the Viciseometer."

The fire in Owen has gone. Did I just imagine all of that? He's telling the rest a blatant lie, and I feel complicit in it, even though it doesn't come from my mouth. My head feels foggy. What was that nonsense he was just spouting about two deaths? I must have hallucinated that. I was probably overwhelmed by the Viciseometers' connection.

"We should remove ourselves from this place," says Jeanne. "Separately."

"Not now, Jeanne," says Johnny. "Please. I've only just found our Elinor."

"We have a task, given to us by the great Lord Septimus," says Alfarin. "We must locate the Unspeakable and reclaim the Dreamcatcher. That is our purpose. However, if we do not find food soon, I will be forced to eat my friend Mitchell, and as you can see, he is but skin and bone. I will choke on him. Food, then foe. Together or separate is of little consequence to my stomach."

"I bet I'd taste pretty good, actually," replies Mitchell. He glances at me and then quickly looks away.

"You can still eat?" asks Angela. "No fair. I never know if what they tell us in Heaven is truth or rumor. Jeez, I'm so jealous. I would die—again—for one last pizza."

"Up There isn't crowded, though," says Elinor. "Ye could not swing a mouse in Hell without hitting another devil."

"But ye get to sleep," says Johnny. "I haven't slept for over three hundred years. I'm bloody knackered—and starving."

They can't eat or sleep Up There? Suddenly it makes sense why Owen looks so tired, and why he talks such incoherent nonsense. I'm beginning to wonder if Up There is as great as we devils have been led to believe.

"What do you think, Melissa?" asks Owen calmly, still acting as if nothing happened. "Do we stay together and pool our resources, or do we part?"

"A meeting of Team DEVIL," I say, and with a jerk of my head, I motion to a mausoleum several yards away. Owen's calmness is unnerving, and my head is hurting. The soldier was just talking utter bullshit and complicating everything. All I want to do is save the Dreamcatcher from Rory. The Skin-Walkers can take *him* back to wherever it is he escaped from, and then I can go back to existing.

The Viciseometer is back in my pocket, but there's no sense of urgency pulsing from it. Like Owen, it seems placid—for now.

The four members of Team DEVIL close into a tight circle against the mausoleum. We're all different shapes and sizes, yet we fit together perfectly. Alfarin swings his left arm over Mitchell's shoulder, and Mitchell wraps his arm around my waist. His skin is hot; I had never noticed just how hot before the ice-cold angels touched me. Elinor is picking at the skin around her fingernails and leaning into Alfarin. She looks really nervous, and I know why. It isn't because of Skin-Walkers or Unspeakables or even crazy French angels.

It's because she thinks we're going to separate her from her brother.

Elinor smiles at me. Her smile is almost pathetic in its sadness. And I know in that instant that we have to stay with the angels, at least for the time being. I can't do to Elinor what we've done to Mitchell by coming here.

"I do not trust Jeanne," says Alfarin. "She would sooner steal my blade and lodge it in my back than assist us."

"I don't trust that Owen dude, either," mutters Mitchell.

"What do ye think, M?" asks Elinor.

I glance back at the angels. "I think they might have information and resources that could help us, but I agree that we need to be careful around them," I reply, trying futilely to tuck my hair behind my ears. "But I'm not going to split Elinor and Johnny up while we're back on earth. We'll stay together, but just be cautious, okay? Especially around Owen and Jeanne."

"Thank ye, M." Elinor hugs me and beams over at the angels. I hear a whoop from Johnny, who has interpreted his sister's smile. We break our huddle and start walking back to the angels.

As we get closer, I see Owen pulling a sheaf of folded papers out of his jacket. The papers are bound with brown leather laces. He beckons us over.

Jeanne has the look of someone sucking a lemon, but at least Angela and Johnny seem happy we're joining forces—for now.

"Do you have money?" asks Owen.

"We have nothing," I reply.

"Then you can have this," says Owen, and from inside the folded sheaf of papers he draws out a thin wad of bills. Mitchell and Angela both make a sound of longing.

"Food!" exclaims Mitchell.

"Shopping," moans Angela.

"This is money, from this time," says Owen. "It will be very similar to what Angela and Mitchell used before they passed over."

"I've changed my mind about these angels," mutters Alfarin. "If we stick with them, we dine like kings."

"Do we stay here in this time and find food, then?" asks Johnny glumly. "Not that I can eat anything."

"No," says Mitchell quickly. "My mom and little brother are here. They can't be allowed to see me."

"I've got an idea," says Angela. "Why don't we travel to New York in the spring? We could head for Central Park and lie on the grass. No one will look twice at us."

"The people will certainly look twice at the beast with the axe," mutters Jeanne.

"And if they hear you talking, they'll look twice because they'll think they're about to be attacked by a swarm of bees," I snap, fed up with this saint who has done nothing but put down my friends since we met her.

"New York?" says Alfarin eagerly. "That is the land of glorious wenches with fried chicken, is it not?"

"Alfarin, ye cannot call the women that!" cries Elinor. "I'm sorry, everyone, but he cannot be trusted in New York. There are just too many large backsides for him to slap."

The hairs on my arms suddenly rise as the bickering continues.

Shadows have started to creep around the walls of the mausoleums. They look like snarling dogs, and the others are so busy talking about food that they haven't noticed.

But I do, because I notice when things are lurking.

We've been tracked.

And we've been found.

12. **Running from Shadows**

Alfarin sees the shadows next; his axe immediately goes into a nine o'clock position. I see a quick glint of silver—so bright it's almost white—to my left. Jeanne has pulled out a small knife with an ivory handle.

"Did you think because I'm an angel I would not be armed?" she says to Mitchell, who is staring bug-eyed at her. "I remember the cruelty of this world only too well."

"What's making those shadows?" asks Angela, her voice breaking with fear as she sees them next.

We all take another four steps back as the shadows continue to stretch out along the white stone. One throws back its head and howls. The black mouth splits apart and the shadowy outline of a man stretches out of it.

We start running.

I still have sneakers on, so my footing is solid, unlike Elinor's and Angela's. They're both slipping and sliding around in ballet flats.

"Leave us behind!" cries Elinor.

"Alfarin, can you carry Elinor?" I shout.

"It would be an honor," he booms. As he shouts, an invisible weight bears down on me and my knees buckle. My head threatens to burst open with a sudden, blinding pain. Then I recall a haunting image, ghostly and pale, of Alfarin sweeping Elinor over his shoulder and the four of us—Team DEVIL—running from a hot wind that comes screaming at us through a cave.

"Medusa, you have to run." Strong hands grab my arms, and I'm pulled to my feet by Mitchell and Owen.

"Which way?" shouts Johnny.

"Put me down, Alfarin," says Elinor. "I will run quicker without shoes on my feet."

I twist around and see the distinct outline of nine Skin-Walkers on the walls of the mausoleums. Are they really here with us, or is this some kind of projection designed to scare the crap out of us? If it's the latter, it's working. Alfarin has dropped Elinor and he's now by my side, sweating. His thick, trunklike legs are bent, ready to launch into battle against enemies we cannot possibly hope to defeat.

"Go with the others, Medusa," he says. "I will hold them back."

I spot the rest of the group running together. If we all had somewhere to hide, I could get us away with the Viciseometer. There must be something more substantial in this sprawling graveyard than headstones and mausoleums, like an office or small visitors' center, but if there is, we're too far away for it to be any use.

Even if we weren't, though, I wouldn't leave Alfarin alone.

"We have to stick together, Alfarin."

Then, as if a light has been switched on above us, the shadows disappear. All nine outlines of the men with the wolf pelts have gone.

The smell hits.

"Oh, shit, oh, shit!" I cry as I spin around. "The Skin-Walkers are here. They're actually here. Where are they? Where are the others?"

Alfarin and I are completely alone.

"*Elinor!*" he cries.

"*Mitchell!*" I yell.

Our voices drop like dead weights. I look down and see that the grass beneath our feet is dying.

"Look, Alfarin," I pant, grabbing his forearm. "The grass has been poisoned just by us being here. We can follow the others' footsteps."

My great plan immediately unravels as we stumble across a large patch of blackened grass that has footprints leading in two different directions. The others have already split up.

"Which one is Team DEVIL and which belongs to the angels?"

Alfarin falls to his knees and spreads his plate-sized hands across the damp grass.

"These are Mitchell's footsteps," he says. "He has feet the size of a longboat. The ones next to them are dainty, the feet of a princess. It is this way, Medusa."

We hurtle down a tightly packed row of crosses and stone tablets. Then I catch a glimpse of blond hair. The head is bobbing and weaving directly ahead of us. It's like an albino hedgehog on steroids.

"There!" I point the way to Alfarin, who is grunting and groaning with every step. The muscles in my neck and shoulders ache as I continue to run while twisting to watch our backs at the same time. I can no longer tell if the shadows around me are cast by some of the ornate gravestones, or whether there is something far more nefarious on our tail.

And all the while, that disgusting stench rolls over us in rotten waves.

"Mitchell!" I cry. "Wait up!"

Immediately the bobbing head stops running and turns around. A gap appears in the headstones, and my stomach drops with a sickening thud.

Mitchell is running with Angela. And they're alone.

"Where's Elinor?" Alfarin and I cry together.

"I thought she was with you two!" shouts Mitchell, looking stricken.

"She must be with her brother," calls Angela. "They went in the opposite direction."

"*Why didn't you go with her?*" bellows Alfarin.

"Because Johnny went in the direction my mom went in, Alfarin!" yells Mitchell. "There's only so much space in my head, and not being seen by my mom and escaping from the Skin-Walkers was all I could think of."

"I am sorry, my friend."

"No, it's my fault, I screwed up." Mitchell is clawing at his short hair.

"Let's just find the others," says Angela, taking Mitchell's hand. "We'll find them."

And Mitchell lets her hold on to him as the four of us run back the way we came. I watch their fingers link, and my throat closes up.

"That smell!" cries Angela. "What in the name of Down There is that smell?"

"It is the worst of Hell," replies Alfarin.

"There's Owen!" shouts Mitchell. "Hey, Owen, wait up."

"Have caution, my friend," says Alfarin. "You cannot let your lady mother hear you."

"Crap."

"She's not here, Mitchell," says Angela. "Medusa and I will keep a lookout, won't we?"

I tear my eyes away from their interlocked fingers, and the heaving sensation in my stomach shifts to my chest.

"Red coat," I whisper. "His mom is wearing a red coat."

But it isn't a red coat we see next. It's red hair. Short, flaming red hair.

It's Johnny, and Elinor isn't with him. Only Owen is.

"Perhaps she's with Jeanne," says Angela hopefully.

"Yeah, because that witch would have waited for a devil," replies Mitchell as Johnny comes racing toward us.

"Elinor isn't with you?" he cries.

"Which way did she go?" demands Alfarin. Mitchell and Owen each place an arm across Alfarin's huge chest, but they are twigs in a tornado and easily brushed aside as Alfarin strides forward and grabs Johnny's T-shirt, lifting his feet clean off the ground.

Suddenly there is a blinding flash. Alfarin is on the ground, and the streak of light that knocked him down is holding a blade to his throat.

"Stop fighting!" screams Angela. *"We have to find Elinor!"*

Her desperation to find Elinor immediately dilutes my jealousy over Mitchell. Locating my friend is all that matters. But the others ignore her and continue shouting at one another. Forget Mitchell's mom and her hearing us—they're making enough noise to wake the dead. Somehow through the din I hear a rustle to my right.

And then I see her. She's next to a stout tree with thick bark that looks like flaking skin. Elinor is motionless; she appears to be floating.

Perfidious steps out from behind her. He's wearing a policeman's uniform, but I know right away it's him because his mouth is too large for his head. He smiles and bares black teeth.

And unlike ours, his irises haven't changed.

"You will come with us, child," he growls in a deep, sonorous voice that stretches with each word. He sniffs at Elinor and then runs his long fingers through her hair. "You will come with us, or you will see your friend devoured by wolves."

13. **A Silent Scream**

I stare at Elinor. She has her eyes closed; I'm not sure she's aware of what's happening. I hope not. I try to take a step toward her, but my legs feel rubbery and unstable. The stench from Perfidious is horrific. It's a mixture of rotten food, sour milk and sweat. He's surrounded by a thin black haze that moves around Elinor's body with thin tendrils that poke and prod her motionless form. The guilt I feel at seeing her like this is drowning me. Elinor is here because she wanted to stay with Alfarin; and he is here because of me.

"Please don't hurt her," I plead, my voice cracking as the syllables gets stuck in my dry throat. "I'll do whatever you want, just don't hurt her."

I glance behind me. I need to warn Alfarin against doing something stupid, like charging at Perfidious with his axe.

But I don't need to, because the blade is lying at his feet. The sight of Elinor trapped by Perfidious has petrified the warrior.

"Slowly walk toward me," growls Perfidious. Each word is elongated and reminds me of someone who is learning a new language for the first time. For the first time, it occurs to me that the Skin-Walkers probably aren't human, and that makes them even more dangerous.

I raise my hands in surrender.

"I will do anything you want, just please, don't hurt Elinor."

Fear makes my feet feel large and clumsy; I might as well be wearing clown shoes instead of sneakers.

Then Mitchell places himself in front of me.

"Take me instead," he says. "Not Medusa. Take me."

A pack of wolves jumps out at us from all directions. I can't help screaming, and I'm not the only one. Two of the beasts bound toward Elinor and then straighten up on either side of her. She jerks violently as they grab her arms. They've morphed into men wearing animal pelts. The black haze surrounding Perfidious stretches out and covers them. When the dense fog evaporates, they're also wearing police uniforms. If anyone were to see this scene, they would assume a large group of delinquents was being arrested for vandalizing graves or something. No one would stop to help us. The Skin-Walkers would probably be cheered and encouraged to take us away.

Jeanne has come back to the group; she's standing next to Owen. He whispers something to her that I don't catch, but she shakes her head in response.

"Mitchell, don't," I say forcefully, pushing against his arm. He grabs my hand, and I hear a choking sob escape from his chest. Winding my fingers around his, I squeeze, but he has to let me go.

"We will tear the girl limb from limb," growls the Skin-Walker to the left of Perfidious. "Do not test us."

"Melissa, the Viciseometer!" shouts Owen.

But I ignore him. Does he really expect me to use the Viciseometer now? I don't run away from problems I've caused—and I'm certainly not running now, when the girl who's the closest thing I've ever had to a friend is in danger. I slowly place one heavy foot in front of the other. My fingers release from Mitchell's, but I'm the one letting go. I'm still a good ten yards away from Elinor. Her thin arms are being pulled to either side by the two Skin-Walkers, and one licks his lips with a forked black tongue.

They are feasting on our fear.

"Melissa," calls Owen again, even more urgently than before. "The Viciseometer. Throw it to me."

Perfidious growls, and the vibration and chill it causes shudder right through me.

"Shut the Hell up, Owen!" I shout, twisting back to glare at him, but the soldier angel is making strange movements with his hands.

Trust me, he mouths. Then he taps his heart and draws a circle with his index finger.

And I understand, or at least I think I do.

My fingers fumble in the pocket of my shorts.

"What are you doing, Medusa?" whispers Mitchell frantically. "Take it with you. Take it with you."

But I throw the Viciseometer to Owen as I take another few steps toward the Skin-Walkers. I'm not trusting the angel for my sake. I'm doing this for Elinor, because it's the only hope we have.

"Let her go," I say.

"*Medusa!*" cries Mitchell. "*No!*"

All of the Skin-Walkers have transformed, and there are now nine policemen surrounding Elinor. Her skin is becoming mottled with purple and green blotches covering her cheeks and neck. What are they doing to her? Her physical form looks like it's rotting. I want to throw up, but the pain of fear is tightening every atom in my soul.

"What did you pass to the angel?" growls Perfidious. His black teeth are bared.

"A Viciseometer. A time-traveling device," I reply. "They will need it to return to Hell. It means I'm unarmed. I have nothing on me at all."

"You will remain in our circle," says Perfidious. "Any attempt to fight and we will attack. Do you understand?"

I nod. My mouth is so dry, my tongue is sticking to my gums. Elinor drops to the ground as the two Skin-Walkers release her arms. She doesn't move. I try to get to her, but the world falls from my feet as I'm lifted up and encircled by the nine Skin-Walkers. Then my ankles turn over with a painful twist as I fall back to the ground.

The second they all close in around me, I feel my ears pop, as if I've been encased in a glass dome. A heavy burning sensation presses down on my chest. The sensation, the longing, to breathe is sucked out of me, and I'm trapped in a vacuum.

But even though the space inside the Skin-Walkers' circle is an airless void, it's filled with the sound of screaming. I can feel invisible hands grabbing at me. I want to cry out, but I can't. I want to run back to Mitchell and Alfarin and Elinor, but I can't do that, either. I have no alternative but to walk with the Skin-Walkers. They are leading me away from my friends.

I trusted Owen. In that split second, I decided to give him a chance to prove that his soul was good.

I hope he proves me right.

For forty years of death I have continued to breathe, even though I know I don't need to. It's a reflex that becomes a part of who you are from the moment you're born. Now, for the first time since I died, I can't do what comes naturally, and the effect is devastating. I claw at my chest and then my throat. The heavy burning pressure forces my mouth open. I can sense invisible fingers inside my mouth that reach down my throat. I gag.

A female mourner is walking toward us. It isn't Mitchell's mom, because this one is too young to be the mother of a seventeen-year-old. She's wearing a short black jacket, and her hair is dyed the same color. She stops suddenly, and her eyes widen at the sight of us. Not with surprise, but with fear. The Skin-Walkers are still dressed like policemen, but the woman doesn't recognize them as men. It's the eyes. There's too much darkness in the eyes.

The woman can't possibly know what they are, but her sixth sense tells her to start walking quickly in the opposite direction. White earphones trail in her wake as she flees from the group striding toward her.

"Down here," growls Perfidious. "Iratol, keep watch behind us. We do not want devil or angel essence tracking us."

The Skin-Walker to my right immediately swings his head

backward. His neck stretches almost one hundred and eighty degrees around without even a shift in his hunched shoulders. I'm in my very own horror movie, and for the first time in my death, I wish there were no Afterlife.

"They have not followed," he replies in a voice that is slightly higher than Perfidious's. It leaves a painful ringing in my ears.

"Forsaken," says Perfidious, and he leers at me with a wide grin. Saliva clings to his blackened teeth like a gauzy drape, and my stomach heaves.

Perfidious leads the group into a small thicket of trees. Twigs snap under my feet, but as I look down, I see what the Skin-Walkers are doing to the earth. They are leaving behind scorched footprints that are far worse than the imprints we left. The ground sinks in where they have stepped, and it steams with putrid-smelling black smoke.

"Release the girl," orders Perfidious.

The Skin-Walkers part and the glass-dome-like atmosphere surrounding me lifts. I choke as the heavy burning sensation in my lungs disappears. I can feel the air in my mouth again, and not invisible fingers. But I'm no less scared. Nine sets of black eyes are now fixed on me. Several of the Skin-Walkers are sniffing me.

"What do you want?" I ask Perfidious. "Septimus told you I know nothing about what happened in Hell."

"Do not speak of Septimus as if you know him, child," growls another Skin-Walker. He reaches out to touch my hair and I flinch, but I have nowhere to go. I simply back into another monster.

"Leave her, Cupidore," snarls Perfidious. "This one is not for us—for now."

Does Septimus know what's happening here? Would he come to help me? I have to believe that he would if the others had gone to him for help. I'm not evil. I'm not like my stepfather.

"We cannot take back that which is ours while it holds the Dreamcatcher in its hands," growls Perfidious. He eyes me, leering again. "We have seen inside the Unspeakable's mind, child, and it is filled with longing for you. You will offer yourself up as a sacrifice. At that time, with what is left of his mind distracted, we will act."

"And what if he decides he doesn't want me?"

"That will not happen. The Unspeakable wants you. And only you can make the Unspeakable leave the Dreamcatcher."

"What if I refuse?"

"You will not."

"What if I can't?"

"So many questions. Let me illuminate your mind, child. If you fail to do as we command, we will tear your lifeless friends apart and make you watch as we feed on their souls, starting with the one who offered himself up," replies Perfidious. "And then, when you think you can bear the pain no longer, we will ravage *you*."

"And if you lay one finger on Miss Pallister, it will be my wrath you have to deal with, Perfidious."

I spin around. Septimus is standing just inches behind the Skin-Walker that tried to touch me. The one called Cupidore.

"You have no power over us, Septimus," snarls Perfidious. Flecks of spit shoot out of his mouth. One of the Skin-Walkers yelps as the saliva hits his face, leaving small red welts on his pockmarked skin.

"And yet you know I am not a devil to cross," replies Septimus, and he steps into the uneven circle and stands by my side. I want to collapse against him with relief. He came. He didn't abandon me.

Then I think back to the last few minutes before I left Hell, when we were all in Septimus's office and he said he was counting on the Skin-Walkers tracking us. Did he mean for this to happen? Has Septimus been waiting for this moment in time?

"You know what I am, Perfidious," drawls Septimus. "What I am capable of."

How can his deep voice be so calm? Septimus could be reading the weather report, he's so collected.

"You are a traitor," replies Perfidious.

"Well, it takes one to know one," says Septimus.

Perfidious laughs. The sickening sound is like a hacking cough.

Then Perfidious's mouth rises at the edges. The cracks in his brown lips widen, revealing throbbing red flesh.

"You sent the child out here as bait, Septimus," says another Skin-Walker. "Do not think you can fool us with your duplicitous words of compassion."

"And Miss Pallister was aware of that, Frausneet," says Septimus. "But that does not mean I intended for her to be offered up as a sacrifice. You can have no claim to her soul, and she and her fellow travelers remain under my protection. And while Perfidious is quite correct in saying I have no power over the Skin-Walkers, need I remind you that Fabulara does?"

Fabulara, the Higher who has control over The Devil and Him, also controls the Skin-Walkers? The effect of that name on the demons around me is instant. The black haze surrounding the Skin-Walkers thickens and starts to swirl like smoke from flames fueled by a gasoline fire. Their appearance is rapidly changing from policemen to their original animal pelts, to the policemen again. I feel nauseous and faint as my vision becomes blurred by the flickering mass surrounding me.

Septimus takes my arm and leads me away from the Skin-Walkers. My legs are shaking so much I have to cling to him with my other arm to stay on my feet.

"Stay here," he whispers, "until I give the word."

"Do not toy with us, Septimus," growls the Skin-Walker called Frausneet. "You will recall the fate of the fool Baumwither."

"And the master is most displeased about it," replies Septimus. "Now listen carefully. Like The Devil himself—and *unlike* Baumwither—I will treat you with all the respect your position in Hell demands, but I reiterate: the minute you touch me, or my charges, it will be Fabulara whom you have to deal with. In fact, it is with her assistance that I am here."

"What do you want, Septimus?" spits Perfidious. The pretense of the policemen is gone. Slowly, one by one, the Skin-Walkers revert permanently to their real forms. Each wolf pelt bristles with anger.

"It is now clear to me that the Dreamcatcher has absorbed much of The Devil's powers, including the ability to leave Hell on a whim," says Septimus. "This explains how your Unspeakable got out of Hell, although it does not explain how he managed to escape all of you in the first place."

At this, several of the Skin-Walkers lunge toward Septimus. The roar from those who stayed in place is like a pride of lions. I scream and jump backward, but Septimus stands his ground.

"You cannot leave the other Unspeakables unguarded in Hell, Perfidious," says Septimus reasonably. "And to have all nine of you roaming the earth looking for the one who has escaped is folly—"

But I don't hear Septimus's next few words because a voice whispers in my ear.

"We're right behind you."

Warm fingers tuck a single strand of hair behind my ear.

I look back to see Perfidious strike two of the Skin-Walkers with the back of his hand. They yelp and retreat behind him.

"Two, you say, Septimus? And why would I take orders from you?" Perfidious growls.

"These are not orders. They are merely a suggestion," replies Septimus. "What say you?"

What have I missed? Two of what? Could Mitchell have picked a worse moment to whisper in my ear? Could he have picked a better moment? I hope Alfarin and Elinor are with him. The thought that Team DEVIL is at my side—albeit invisible—gives me a shot of courage. I had sensed that Owen was giving me a cryptic message about the two Viciseometers, and that was why I threw it to him. Not to take them back to Hell, but to allow them to come with me, unseen by the Skin-Walkers. Owen must have told Mitchell about the effect of the two timepieces: that when they're joined together, the bearer becomes invisible at that moment in time. Only Owen and I proved it works with more than one dead person. All seven devils and angels could be with me right now.

"We will . . . consider," says Perfidious.

"And I will be waiting," replies Septimus, with a slight bow.

"Now forgive me, but I have one last task before I return to my master."

Septimus turns and winks at the space behind me.

"*Now*," he says loudly.

A freezing cold hand grabs mine as a wall of flames erupts around me.

We are traveling through time once more.

14. Septimus's Warning

"Ow, get off me, Johnny."

"I ain't on ye, Angela."

"No, he's on *me*. Jeez, you're as bony as Medusa, Johnny."

"Ye leave my brother alone, Mitchell. He just needs fattening up."

"Unlike the Viking beast crushing my legs."

"*Shut up, Jeanne!*" cries everyone.

We're in darkness. I know by their voices that I have been taken away by Mitchell, Alfarin, Elinor and Team ANGEL. The air is light and crisp on my skin. It smells sweet. That means the Skin-Walkers are no longer here.

A match strikes. The small flame illuminates Owen's tired face.

"Where are we?" I ask.

"Keep your voices down," he warns. "If my grandmother hears us, there'll be trouble."

"You've taken us back to your time in England?" I ask.

Owen nods. "1916, the day I signed up to fight. Septimus told me to take everyone somewhere safe, but I couldn't think of anywhere, so I brought us here. It's the coal shed at the bottom of my grandmother's backyard."

"A coal shed!" exclaims Angela. "I'm wearing white jeans, Owen."

We are plunged into darkness once more as the match burns out.

"Are ye all right, Medusa?" asks Elinor. "They told me what ye did to save me from the Skin-Walkers. Ye are so brave."

"You would have done the same," I reply, although I can't be sure that she would, that any of them would. I don't see condemnation in their eyes when they look at me, but it has to be there, doesn't it? They must blame me for this mess.

I offered myself to the Skin-Walkers because it was the right thing to do. Protecting Elinor was an instinct that I couldn't fight. I didn't want to fight it. Being decent and caring toward another devil felt natural. Empowering. I would do it for any of them.

Mitchell wanted to do it for me. A warm sensation fills my chest as I remember him offering himself in my place. He *did* do the same for me. Or he would have, if the Skin-Walkers had let him.

I can't see where Mitchell is. I need to know he isn't pissed at me for giving the Viciseometer to Owen.

Which reminds me.

"Owen, I need the Viciseometer back."

Another small flame casts a dim tangerine glow over the four devils and four angels squished in the coal shed. Owen holds the match aloft between his thumb and forefinger. He's looking for something.

"Owen," I say more urgently. "My Viciseometer. I want it back."

Mitchell clambers across the coal and plunges his hands into the small hollow where Owen landed. He starts to dig and quickly reveals the two Viciseometers lying inches apart. The miniature flames and stars flickering around each timepiece illuminate the shed better than the temporary light from Owen's matches.

Mitchell throws me the red-faced Viciseometer. I catch it, and immediately a quickening sensation spreads through my whole body. It feels like a pulse, but just as soon as it arrives, it leaves me.

"The Skin-Walkers didn't hurt you, did they?" asks Mitchell. He crawls back over the coal, across Angela's legs, and settles down next to me.

"They threatened to, but then Septimus turned up," I reply. "I couldn't believe it. How did he know? They were on the verge of offering me up as a sacrifice."

Mitchell looks at me sheepishly and pulls his black cell phone from one of the many pockets in his cargo pants.

"I had it the whole time. I thought I left it in my backpack in Hell like you guys. But when the Skin-Walkers took you, I immediately went for it to call the boss—it was just a reflex—and I remembered I changed into these pants before we left. . . ."

"And you realized you'd put your phone in a random pocket," I said, smiling. I'm too relieved to be pissed. Jeanne, however, is not.

"Mitchell betrayed us," she hisses, "and Owen allowed it to happen. Now everyone in Heaven will know that we have joined with the devil infidels."

"No one will know, Jeanne," says Owen wearily, "because no one consequential in Heaven knows we're here."

"That was quick thinking, Owen. Asking for the Viciseometer. It never even occurred to me to become invisible," I say.

"And of course you couldn't have shared that little nugget of information with the rest of us," says Mitchell. I can hear the resentment in his voice. He doesn't know I was going to tell them.

I guess I find it too easy to keep secrets. I don't like to lie, but when I withhold information, is it any different?

"I thought we could track you, but it was Mitchell who went to call Septimus. I think he deserves the credit," replies Owen diplomatically.

"Speaking of Mr. Septimus," says Elinor, "should we wait for him outside? It will get even more crowded in here when he arrives."

"Septimus is coming back?" I ask.

"He told us to wait for his signal, and then to grab you and leave with the Viciseometers," says Mitchell. "He said he would find us. I didn't care about the details. I just wanted to get you—us—out of there. And I'm telling you all now, I am never going back to Washington again. That place has been nothing but trouble since the day I died."

Outside, a cat suddenly shrieks. There's a thud against the shed door, like a boot kicking the wood, and Elinor and Angela both scream. Jeanne jumps to her feet and grabs a small spade that's propped up against the crumbling brick wall. She's joined by Alfarin, who clambers to his feet, squashing both Elinor and Johnny in the process. Mitchell tries to get up as well, but he's jammed into the space between me and the wall. Most of the coal has been dumped here, and it's making movement difficult—and painful.

Three knocks rap in quick succession on the wooden door.

"It must be Septimus," says Mitchell. "We decided the last time that Skin-Walkers wouldn't knock, remember?"

I laugh as if I recall the conversation, but I don't. Maybe it's just that Mitchell has an ironic sense of humor that appeals to me.

"Where's the latch, Owen?" asks Johnny.

"Stand back, young Johnny," says Alfarin. "We need no latch. My axe will make light work of such poor craftsmanship."

But before Alfarin makes a move, the door opens from the outside to reveal Septimus standing there, surrounded by a thin red nimbus.

"I have been on the receiving end of your axe once, Prince Alfarin," he says in his deep drawl. "I would prefer it if we did not repeat the incident."

"Lord Septimus," says Alfarin. He goes down on one knee, knocking Jeanne forward and sending her flying into Septimus's arms.

"I am honored, Mademoiselle d'Arc," says Septimus formally; he bows. "We did not have the time for pleasantries earlier. I have long been a great admirer."

"General Septimus," replies Jeanne, and she takes us all by surprise by reciprocating his bow, although hers is much shorter and quicker. A quick bend of the shoulders and she's upright once more. "Your legend precedes you."

"Private Jones, Miss Jackson and, of course, Mr. Powell. I am always pleased to make the acquaintance of the dead, devil or otherwise," says Septimus, with three nods of the head to the others.

"Private Jones, your quick thinking back in Washington is to your credit. As is yours, Mitchell. I had taken a calculated guess that the Skin-Walkers would track you all. Your immediate action saved Miss Pallister and me a lot of time and, dare I say it, pain."

Septimus beckons to Mitchell and me. "Please forgive my haste, everyone, but I must speak to my two interns in private now. Just so you are aware, Private, I heard a stirring from within the house, and I believe your grandmother may be awake. I am acquainted with Minnie Jones in Hell, and I imagine she is as terrifying in life as she is in death. I suggest the rest of you stay in here and keep quiet while the three of us discuss a few things in a more secluded spot. I will, of course, return both Mitchell and Medusa as soon as possible."

Mitchell and I try to move, but we're still stuck in the coal. Septimus extends his left hand and pulls us both out with a single heave. We close the door of the shed behind us, which barely muffles the protestations from Jeanne.

"That girl is a pain in the ass," mutters Mitchell. He blows in my face and then wipes my cheeks and nose. "Coal dust," he mumbles, before sticking his dirty hands in his pockets.

"Mademoiselle d'Arc was a fearsome warrior in life," replies Septimus softly. "I believe she struggles with existence after death more than most. Yet she could be an important ally. My advice is never to burn any bridges. You never know when you may need assistance from Up There."

"Speaking of assistance from Up There," says Mitchell, "how are you traveling through time, Septimus? Last time you had the Viciseometer from Up There. But the angels have it now."

The Devil's number one servant barks a short laugh. "In Hell, Mitchell, *who* you know is as important as *what* you know," he says cryptically.

"Well, that answers it," says Mitchell sarcastically in my ear. I repress a giggle and elbow him in the ribs to shut him up.

Septimus leads us through a high wooden gate that is built into a brick wall. I look back. All of the houses are tightly compacted together in a row. We turn left and walk down a cobbled alleyway.

The bright moon, larger than I have ever seen it, illuminates us all in a silvery shadow.

Septimus opens another gate, which leads into a small paved backyard.

"The occupants are not home," he whispers. "We will be quite safe here and undisturbed. Now, Miss Pallister, Mitchell, I assume you have many questions, but as usual, time is of the essence. So I must ask you to allow me to direct this conversation in order to make our briefing as short as possible."

Mitchell and I nod dumbly.

"Good. Now, you can probably imagine my distress when the effect of Prince Alfarin's axe wore off and I discovered that the envelope I gave you was left in the accounting chamber, along with your backpacks and belongings. I take full responsibility for the fact that you were not prepared for this mission, and I offer my humblest apologies."

At this, Septimus puts a hand on each of our shoulders.

"I know you've had few resources and very little information to go on as a result, but can you tell me whether you've had any success in tracking the Dreamcatcher?"

"I think so," I reply. "The Dreamcatcher...is it...is it a little boy?"

"I am afraid so," says Septimus gravely. "I do not expect you to accept or understand why this is so, and you would be quite right not to. But that is not your battle to fight. So can I therefore deduce that you have also had at least one encounter with Mr. Hunter?"

"He was outside my house, my old house. But then he picked up the little boy and disappeared."

Septimus drums his fingers on his chin for a thoughtful few seconds. "Listen to me very carefully," he says. "You have done well to join forces with Team ANGEL, and you should know that I was aware that their fourth member was Miss Powell's brother. I did not tell you in Hell because the mission must remain at the fore of your minds, and I was concerned that Elinor's heart would persuade you down a different route."

"What do you mean?" I ask.

Septimus inhales, but nothing comes back out. His shoulders tense up and his bloodred eyes flicker to Mitchell for a split second.

"Do not underestimate the power of love, Miss Pallister. It can blind us all, for better and worse. Miss Powell passed over because she placed the welfare of her brothers ahead of her own. Because you left information about Team ANGEL behind in my office, you had to find the Dreamcatcher first and realize what he was on your own, before tracking down the angels. Miss Powell might have persuaded you to travel differently, to think or act differently, if she had known about her brother, and I could not allow that to happen. The Dreamcatcher remains your number one priority. It must be returned to Hell."

"Would you stop calling the Dreamcatcher *it*, Septimus?" says Mitchell irritably. "The Dreamcatcher is a little boy, and the whole thing is sick."

"I agree," I say. "The angels say they want to save him, and that's why they're here, but I'm not sure I believe them. I'm with Alfarin in thinking they want him for a weapon, especially with Owen and that psycho Jeanne in charge. But I can't return that little boy to Hell, Septimus. I just can't."

Septimus makes a sound like a cough, but more strangled. The sweat on his bald forehead shimmers like tiny crystals in the moonlight.

"You have no choice, Miss Pallister."

"Of course I do."

"Yes, she does, she could just say no," says Mitchell. "Life and death are about choices—you've taught me that, Septimus."

So is this my first test? To see whether I can blindly follow orders? Well, I'm not that kind of devil. I'm sure to be a huge disappointment if Septimus is looking for a capitulating kiss-ass.

"If I don't return with the little boy, I'll lose the intern job, won't I?"

"The end result will be so much worse than that," replies Septimus, "and I see now that I will have to be more open with you both.

I had hoped your loyalty to me would see this through to the end, but your hearts are not as black as mine. I took advantage of you all, and for that, I am so very sorry."

"What do you mean?" I ask, my voice catching.

"There has to be a Dreamcatcher, Miss Pallister. Without it, The Devil's waking hours and dreaming state combine into one continuous toxic loop of terror. His mind is already dangerous, but without a Dreamcatcher to keep those subconscious nightmares away, the effect on the many—both living and dead—will be too horrific to contemplate."

"But why a little boy? I've seen him in my dreams, Septimus. He bleeds tears. It's torture."

"You are seeing the Dreamcatcher in your dreams, Miss Pallister, because of your link to the Unspeakable. The three of you are now bound in death because of the Hell you and the Unspeakable shared in life. And the Dreamcatcher must be a child, because the young are not infected or corrupted with the insidious effects of living," replies Septimus. "The Dreamcatcher is chosen *because* he is young, not in spite of it."

"So if we don't bring back this Dreamcatcher," I cry, horrified, "then you'll simply choose another one?"

"That is how it has been for many millennia, and how it must remain," says Septimus. His voice is becoming more and more detached, like an echo. "A list is drawn up every year, pooled from all under-fives on the earth. One is then claimed for The Devil. They do not…they do not last long because of what they absorb and filter."

"This is sick, absolutely sick…and I won't…I just won't…" Tears start running down my face. I feel so helpless. How can this be right?

It isn't right, I answer myself. Of course it isn't, because this is The Devil and Hell and myths and monsters. And if Hell can exist on earth, where living children are hurt every day, then of course it's going to exist in the Afterlife. This realization makes me feel powerless, and feeling powerless makes me angry.

Is anything ever fair?

"I'm gonna puke," groans Mitchell. "I can't be a part of this, either, Septimus. You should have told us."

"Two of the Skin-Walkers will now be following Team DEVIL and Team ANGEL," says Septimus, ignoring our protests. "I have persuaded the rest to return to Hell. It will be perverse to hear, but to have met them all in the cemetery in Washington so soon into your quest was your good fortune. Skin-Walkers feed off fear. For you to have met all nine in Hell would have been even more dangerous. The terror swirling around Hell over the last day would have been a banquet for them, and I fear they would have lost control. We've been fortunate that Sir Richard Baumwither has been their only victim so far."

"Wow, this just gets better and better!" shouts Mitchell. "Why us, Septimus? We're just *interns*, for Hell's sake. Medusa hasn't even started work yet—"

"You have been drawn into this by powers out of my control, Mitchell," interrupts Septimus. "I wish I could protect you both from this, but I cannot. And so I must try to influence the outcome of these events without anyone realizing my involvement. Miss Pallister is here because of her tragic connection to Mr. Hunter, and you..."

But Septimus trails off. He makes that strangled choking sound again, and suddenly I'm afraid of the words that are trapped in his throat.

"Me? Clearly I'm here because of Medusa and Team DEVIL," says Mitchell.

"Mitchell," Septimus says quietly, "if the Dreamcatcher is not returned to Hell, you will be affected more deeply than you realize."

A few beats of silence follow. I think Mitchell is trying to work out what Septimus is trying to tell him, but I already know. I understand the horrors of death better than most because I had horrors in my life. I know firsthand that twisted people will do twisted things to get what they want. But Mitchell... poor, loved Mitchell...

"You can't let them do it, Septimus!" I cry.

I see that Septimus is silently weeping, too, and that scares me more than anything, even more than Rory Hunter, and more than the Skin-Walkers. It terrifies me because Septimus is the most powerful devil in Hell after The Devil himself, and nothing and no one gets to him.

Except this.

"Mitchell," says Septimus. "The Grim Reapers have already been ordered by The Devil to make up a list of replacements if this Dreamcatcher cannot be located and returned. Their task has been manipulated to ensure that Team DEVIL succeeds."

I grab hold of Mitchell's hands. I want to cover his ears. I can't bear the thought of him hearing what Septimus has to say next.

"I don't understand..." he says uneasily.

"Mitchell, your brother's name has been added to the top of the list," says Septimus. "M.J. will replace the Dreamcatcher if it's not found in time."

15. Immolation

A wall of flame hits Septimus. Only it isn't fire—it's Mitchell.

Melded together, their bodies smack into the opposite wall. Bricks crumble and topple onto them, covering both in dust and stone. They stay entombed for less than a second before an explosion sends a volcanic eruption of debris flying in all directions. I duck and shield my face with my arm, but it isn't enough. A thick, vile, salty liquid fills my mouth, and I know I'm tasting my own dead blood.

The small backyard is on fire. I feel strong, muscular arms around my middle and I'm pulled upward. At first I think it's Alfarin, but then I realize that the person holding me is wearing a suit, because I can feel a vertical line of buttons pressing into my back. I wipe at the blood that's trickling into my eyes and see that Septimus has Mitchell swung over his shoulder.

Mitchell looks dead.

Mitchell is dead.

"What happened?" I groan.

"My intern behaved in a way that was entirely human," replies Septimus. "I should be thankful that his hidden inner rage has only been simmering for four years. Any longer and his untrained anger could have blown apart the entire street."

Septimus has taken us back out into the cobbled alley. I feel his body twist left, right, and then left again.

"I can walk, Septimus," I say. "Please put me down."

"Mitchell received the brunt of my response, Miss Pallister," says Septimus, "but I apologize if you were also hurt. I had no choice but to restrain Mitchell immediately, or he could have combusted. Now tell me, do you still have the Viciseometer?"

Septimus places me back down on the cobbles. My knees buckle, but he catches my arm before I fall. My head is swimming and my vision is foggy. It's still dark, but the explosion in the back street has woken most of the neighbors. We need to get away. Now.

"What about the others?" I say, pulling the Viciseometer out of my pocket.

"You understand now, don't you?" says Septimus. "You understand exactly what is at stake if the Dreamcatcher is not returned to Hell?"

I nod. Salt from my tears mixes with my toxic blood. It seems right somehow. For forty years, I thought vainly, aloofly, that I was too good for Hell. That I wasn't evil.

But I am. Because to save Mitchell's little brother, I will have to send another little boy back into Hell to filter the perverse dreams of The Devil.

"Take Mitchell to a place in your past, Miss Pallister. Someplace that was important to Rory Hunter. Find him and you will find the Dreamcatcher."

"What about the others?" I repeat. "I can't do this without Alfarin and Elinor."

"You do not need to, Medusa," calls a deep voice behind me. "We are coming."

Alfarin, Elinor and the four angels are running along the alley. They are covered in black soot.

"What happened here?" asks Jeanne. "We heard..."

Then she sees the fire, which is spreading rapidly into the unoccupied house. She screams and falls back.

People from neighboring properties are now coming out to look at the commotion. A small old man with a bent back starts yelling. He's quickly joined by another, even older, man, but they aren't shouting about the fire. They want to know why young men are standing in the streets instead of fighting for king and country on foreign fields.

"A place in your past, Miss Pallister," repeats Septimus. He lowers Mitchell onto the ground, and Elinor and I both cry out. Half of Mitchell's face is charred, blackened skin.

Behind me I can hear dry retching. It's Jeanne.

"You said before that two of the Skin-Walkers would be joining us," I say quickly as my fingers start to manipulate the red needle of the Viciseometer around the clock face. I'm stressing out. I need to calm down, but I don't know how. And the thought of Skin-Walkers coming with us isn't helping. This is a nightmare that none of us can escape. And why isn't Mitchell moving? What did Septimus do to him?

"The Skin-Walkers will find you," says Septimus. "Remember, they only want the Unspeakable, and you are the best chance Hell has of finding him. Now hurry."

"Mitchell," says Angela, bending down. "What's wrong with his skin?" She strokes his face, and I am overwhelmed by the urge to punch hers in.

Instead, I smack my head in frustration. Concentrate, Medusa, I tell myself. You need to find Rory. Think. Where in the past would Rory go?

I've already fixed in a generic time: ten o'clock. I will aim for evening. I turn over the red face as the shouts from the neighbors become threats. Several women, armed with brooms, are striding up the alleyway toward us. Other people are yelling for buckets of water. They are torn between wanting to help save their neighbor's house and their desire to kick our asses.

Finally, a response from Mitchell: he groans and rolls over onto his side. The cobbles underneath him are scorched black and coated in a sticky, tarlike substance. Alfarin hauls Mitchell to his feet. Jeanne is still retching, and Owen is shielding Johnny from the stones that are now raining down on us from the neighbors. But just as quickly as the stones appeared, they stop as the neighbors catch sight of us. They're inching back. They're scared.

They've realized we aren't quite right.

Rory Hunter once told me I would never be special. He used to taunt me, saying there was something wrong with me. He even used those words, that I wasn't *quite right*. The memory comes clearly to me as I hear the insults from the terrified people. They want us away from their homes and their lives and their children.

I wasn't *quite right*, Rory said. No one would want me ... except him. It was the first time he ever touched me. A stroke of the face. He waited until I was sixteen; it was my birthday. That touch lasted a second, but the memory has stayed with me for more than forty years. I remember his callused fingertips, and I can still smell the cigarette smoke. It would get worse, a lot worse, but that was the first time my stepfather scared me.

And that's where he'll be now: at the first moment in time when he, a weak and twisted man, became powerful. He'll want to watch it. He probably already has. Rory could be watching it over and over again while he waits for me—this me, the real me—to come to him.

I couldn't stop him then, but I can try to stop him now.

"If you're coming, hold on!" I cry to the group, although it's a question that doesn't have to be asked of Team DEVIL. I look down at the red face of the Viciseometer just as the hands on the timepiece dissolve from the stationary time of February 28, 1967. The face of the Viciseometer starts to swirl with a crimson fire. Tiny particles of flame reach out and caress my skin. I can see the rain coming down, and I shiver. Not with cold, but with dread. We are traveling to Stinson Beach, where Rory will be ready to haunt me once more.

Elinor grabs my spare hand; I see Alfarin and Mitchell on her other side. I feel Team ANGEL's freezing hands grabbing my waist and clutching at the fabric of my shirt. Septimus is shouting something to me, but his voice is smothered by the sound of time rushing around us.

As we travel forward in time, I can feel Jeanne beside me, still shuddering in terror because of our close brush with fire. She buries her face in my neck, and as we hurtle along, all I can sense is her fearful body nestling into mine. I try to comfort her, but time has frozen me.

We land in soft sand. The rain is pelting down. There's no moon, but the sea is reflecting a greenish-silver sheen that gives us just enough light to see one another.

"Ye are bleeding, Medusa," says Johnny. "Yer head is a mess." He spits onto his T-shirt and dabs it at my head.

"That's disgusting, Johnny," says Angela.

"Why here?" whispers Jeanne. "What is this place?"

I look down and see that she's still holding my waist. She quickly lets go.

"This is Stinson Beach. We're just outside San Francisco. The first time Rory Hunter took me and my mom out for a day trip, he took us here. This day in history, in fact." I don't tell them it's my birthday. It's not a day I want to share.

"What makes you think the Unspeakable is here?" asks Alfarin. "And what has happened to Mitchell?"

"Rory will be here—I know he will," I reply. "For the same reason that he was at my old house: because he's haunting me. Remember? He said I'd find him when and where he wants to be found, and I think that means he's going back in time to places that mean something—to him and me. Not in a good way, but in a bad way. And this day is where it all started. It's burned into my memory. It's the next most obvious place he would come to after the house."

Mitchell is groaning; he's kneeling on the sand.

"What if the old you and the old Rory see you now?" he says in a croaking voice. "We'll create a paradox."

"No, we won't," I reply, looking around for Rory. I know he's here. Watching us. Watching me. Every nerve ending I possess is prickling. "When I came here forty years ago, we had left by this time. The alive me is back in my bed in San Francisco, and the alive Rory...he's in the house, too, but the Unspeakable Rory, he'll be here—this date was too important for him to not have come back and waited for us into the evening."

"So are we just going to stand here in the rain until he decides to make himself known?" asks Alfarin. He glances worriedly at Elinor, who looks cold.

"Do you have a better plan, Alfarin?" I reply. "Septimus said we have to find him, and my gut tells me he's here."

"I did not mean to—"

But whatever it is that Alfarin plans to apologize for goes unsaid, because at that moment, two wolves howl in the darkness, and the all-too-familiar smell of the Skin-Walkers quickly envelops us, smothering the salty smell of the beach.

With just a few bounds, the Skin-Walkers are upon us. They straighten up, although the animal heads on top of their own continue to growl.

"You are favored by Septimus, child," says one of the Skin-Walkers slowly. His black eyes bore into mine. "And by the Unspeakable, too. You are wasted in such company."

"You will not take Medusa again!" roars Alfarin, placing himself in front of me. The rain bounces off the blade of his axe with a metallic ping.

That one gesture inspires me, because Alfarin—my friend—is doing exactly what Mitchell tried to do. He's trying to protect me.

But the two Skin-Walkers laugh.

"The Viking prince is not afraid of us, and yet two dogs, two of our mutated kind, sent him to his doom after ripping out his throat," mocks a Skin-Walker. "Yes, we have seen your deaths, all of them," he sneers at a gaping Alfarin. "So be careful, Viking. We are afraid of no man—mortal or otherwise."

"But you're afraid of the Dreamcatcher, aren't you!" I shout back, recognizing this Skin-Walker as Cupidore, the one who tried to touch me in the cemetery. This fuels a fire in my chest, because no one touches me like that anymore. "We saw you cowering and whimpering. You need us way more than we need you."

The two Skin-Walkers fall forward onto all fours. Cupidore stretches his neck back and howls at the moonless sky. The other arches his shoulders, and the pelt on his back ripples. His black, cracked lips curl back over his gums. The rotten stench takes on a metallic edge. It's the smell of blood.

Then we hear crying. My stomach lurches with fear, but there is a triumphant pulse in my chest, too. I knew he was here. I always knew when he was near.

The wind has picked up, but the sound of the child is carried and magnified around us. I push my soaking-wet hair out of my face and cup my hands to my ears. I can't tell which direction the crying is coming from.

"The little boy, the Dreamcatcher, is here," I say. And suddenly the Skin-Walkers are no longer my concern. I already know they're scared of it, and they need me.

"M.J.," groans Mitchell. "Not my brother. I will kill anyone who touches my brother."

He starts shaking. His entire body is convulsing.

"He's burning up!" screams Angela.

"*Not my brother!*"

"No, not again. Not now!" I cry, realizing what is about to happen. "Alfarin, help me get Mitchell into the sea. Septimus said he might combust."

Mitchell is starting to smoke. Both Jeanne and Elinor are screaming, but I don't have the time to worry about them. All I can think about is dragging Mitchell into the freezing ocean before he becomes ash on the wind.

"Stop screaming and see if you can spot the Unspeakable!" I cry. "I'm not alone, I'm not alone," I keep repeating to myself. He can't hurt me.

Alfarin, Owen and I drag Mitchell across the sand and into the sea. Small flames begin to ignite on his body, and they singe my skin as I help guide him into the water. All four of us are suddenly lost in an enormous cloud of steam that is unleashed as we fall into the breaking waves.

"Immolation," I hear Alfarin say through the fog. "I have heard of such an event, but never in all my dark days in Hell have I seen such a thing. Is this what happened when you were with Lord Septimus?"

Mitchell is now on all fours. The surf breaks over his back.

"It's what happened with Septimus, but immolation—that's self-inflicted, isn't it?" I ask. "Are you telling me Mitchell's doing this on purpose?"

"Not on purpose, Melissa," says Owen. "But if Mitchell can do this, just imagine what we all could do under similar circumstances if we learned to control it."

"What are you talking about?" I ask.

"Quiet, *angel*," growls a Skin-Walker from the beach. The two of them are sniffing the air.

"What do you mean, Owen?" I press. The breaking tide is dragging the four of us into the sea. Mitchell is now half submerged. I pull him back to me and whip my head left and right, scanning our surroundings to see if there is another shadowy outline coming closer. But there is nothing, and neither of the Skin-Walkers show any sign of moving.

"Think about it, Melissa," says Owen, and for a split second I think I see a red flare around his irises. "What caused Mitchell to react like this? It was obviously Mitchell who set off that explosion back in my grandmother's street. Septimus said something to you both, didn't he? Something that made Mitchell so angry his rage became fire."

"But why don't more devils in Hell immolate, then? Everyone is angry there," I say as another wave crashes around us.

"Down There, and even in Heaven, the anger we feel at being dead is diluted by other emotions. Worry, fear and sadness are just three off the top of my head," explains Owen. "Mitchell must have experienced pure, absolute rage, and without the confines of Hell to smother it, he unleashed it."

I can no longer hear the crying of the child. It's being suppressed, either by the sound of the rain and sea, or by the residual ringing in my eardrums from the aftermath of Mitchell and Septimus's explosive fight.

The fight. Owen is right. Worry about his little brother caused Mitchell to self-immolate. His rage created a moving wall of fire.

"Can you see the Unspeakable?" I call out to anyone who can hear, but no one replies. He's gone. Why? Was Rory freaked out by what happened with Mitchell? Or did he not expect to see Skin-Walkers here? I know he was out there, somewhere in the darkness.

But instead of being scared, or even disappointed that I couldn't end this here, I'm exhilarated. Septimus trusted me to come up with a plan, and I think I have. The tools to turn this mess around were with us all along; we just needed to find them. Finally, I know how we can defeat Rory Hunter. And it starts with me. I have to stop assuming he has the advantage. I did that in life, and I ended up dead. Now I may not be able to take back my life, but Rory Hunter isn't going to have the advantage over me in death. He won't control me, ever again. He won't control any of us.

I feel powerful all of a sudden, as if I'm meeting a part of myself that I never knew existed. I fall to my knees and sink into the sand as another frothing wave crashes over us. I am submerged for a split second before I rise from the water in triumph.

We aren't just devils anymore. We're weapons.

16. Circles of Hell

I run through the surf toward the beach. The sand gives way beneath my sneakers. I can't locate Elinor or Jeanne in the green glow cast by the Pacific, but I do see Angela and Johnny pass me on their way out to the water. They splash out to where Alfarin and Owen are standing, and together, they each grab a limb and haul a disoriented Mitchell from the cold water.

"Melissa, are you okay?" calls Owen.

"My name is Medusa."

"What?"

"Don't call me Melissa anymore, Owen." I turn to look at the dripping-wet soldier. "The Unspeakable knows me as Melissa, but he doesn't know *me*. The me I am now. He thinks he's baiting the sixteen-year-old girl he tormented forty years ago. He said I have something he wants. He said he'd give up the Dreamcatcher when he gets his life back. I don't know how those things are connected yet, but I do know we have an advantage in that he doesn't know who he's dealing with."

Owen is watching me carefully, and I feel an intensity building in my chest. The powerful feeling that came over me moments ago in the water is coming into sharp focus, and with it comes a strange sensation of relief. It's time to finally shed myself of Melissa, once and for all. Melissa was scared and unprotected. She was friendless and untrusting. When she died, the Grim Reapers at the HalfWay

House inadvertently gave her a clean slate with a new name. Since then I've learned to think on my feet, and to stand up for myself against hurtful people, like misogynistic bosses and mean girls with a pack mentality. It hasn't been easy, and it hasn't been fun. I carried Melissa with me the whole way, and all the self-doubt that came with her. But I did learn how to keep people from taking advantage of me. I learned to control my emotions. And finally, after going it alone for so long, I have friends, real friends, in Mitchell, Alfarin and Elinor.

It's time to let Melissa go. And I need to let something else go, too. From now on, I won't think of my stepfather as anything other than an Unspeakable. Rory Hunter, the man who lived, the monster who destroyed my life and has haunted my nightmares in death, will not be allowed to ruin my new existence as well.

I return Owen's gaze and give him a small, reassuring smile.

"I'm Medusa now, Owen. The girl who fell from the bridge forty years ago is gone. She's dead. The Unspeakable doesn't understand that yet, but he's about to. We're going to learn how to immolate. And then we will rescue that child. When we do, the Skin-Walkers can take the Unspeakable back to Hell, where he will rot."

I try to retain my confidence as Cupidore sidles up next to me. "Septimus knew what he was doing, trusting in you," he sneers. "Yet I smell duplicity in your future. You are not what you seem, child."

"Leave her alone," commands Angela bravely as the Skin-Walker turns to face her.

"Cancer has its own special smell and taste, does it not, Visolentiae?" Cupidore remarks to his partner. His large nostrils sniff the air. "This one is still rank with it."

"Every soul is unique," replies Visolentiae. His black eyes are boring into mine; they're large and round, like the eyes of a dog. The wolf-man doesn't blink once. Then he turns to Elinor and Jeanne. "The two that scream, why, they smell of burning flesh and wood. And the Viking's stench is salt and cold rain and blood."

"You're only here for the Unspeakable!" I shout. "How we smell is no concern of yours."

The Skin-Walkers throw back their heads and howl. For a terrible moment, their perverse laughter obliterates the noise of the wind.

"We cannot help but smell you," growls Cupidore. "But it is true, I am here to track the Unspeakable's stench. It's only fitting, as my quarry is the lustful."

I immediately take several steps back, but the sand is treacherous and I stumble as my heels sink.

"So that legend is also true," whispers Owen. "One Skin-Walker for each mythical circle of Hell."

The circles of Hell...the circles of Hell. I wrack my brains, trying to think back to my literature classes. Dante's poem was called *The Divine Comedy*. I never saw anything divine or comedic in Hell when I was alive, or since, but I know that the poem was split into sections: the circles of Hell, Purgatory and Paradise. The first circle was limbo—everyone remembers that one—and lust was the second one. I can't remember the order of the next three, but gluttony was definitely in there, because my old teacher was obese in the extreme, and we all thought he was heading straight for it when he died. Heresy was next, then violence, then...violence...Visolentiae is the other Skin-Walker's name.

"*Violentiae* is Latin for 'violence,'" I say aloud.

"Clever girl," says Visolentiae. "I knew from the fire in your eyes that you had already worked it out." He takes a step toward me. "So you do not need me to tell you how *I* deal with the Unspeakables that exist in *our* inferno."

I should be sickened, but I'm not. According to Dante, the damned who are trapped in the seventh circle of Hell—the one that represents violence—are continually boiled in blood and fire.

"Dante must have been a time-traveler," I say. "A dead time-traveler. He used a Viciseometer to come back to the land of the living to write that poem. There's no way he could have guessed all of that."

"There are clues to the Afterlife spread throughout the ages and pages of this wretched little world," replies Cupidore. "Only the living are too blind to see what is in front of them."

"Will you give me your word that you will only take the Unspeakable?" I ask. "You won't take anyone else, alive or dead?"

The two Skin-Walkers swap black looks. The edges of their elongated mouths rise just a fraction.

"Perfidious has ordered it so," replies Visolentiae.

He and Cupidore slink away into the shadows. Their stench is diluted slightly by the smell of seawater.

"What was your Septimus thinking, letting them come with us?" asks Angela. "They're evil. I don't feel safe around either of them."

"We aren't safe, Angela," I reply. "And I think that's Septimus's point. We still have no idea how the Unspeakable will use the Dreamcatcher if he doesn't get what he wants. I think we should be thankful that it's only two Skin-Walkers now, instead of nine."

Owen leans into me and whispers in my ear.

"You took Latin in school?"

I nod.

"Perfidious."

"I know," I whisper back. "Tell your team. I'll tell mine."

Perfidia is Latin for 'treachery,' and the treacherous occupy the ninth circle of Hell: there they are encased in ice, and a three-headed Satan bites down on Brutus, Cassius and Judas Iscariot for the rest of eternity.

I don't trust any of the Skin-Walkers, and Perfidious least of all.

We're not safe from them, and neither are the living.

17. **Aotearoa**

We need to start training, but Mitchell is still so out of it, I'm not sure his soul is even conscious right now.

At least I know *how* he self-immolated, though. That's a start.

We can't practice here, that much is obvious. The weather is getting worse. The rain is lashing down even harder, and the wind is approaching gale force. Pockets of fog stretch out in the darkness, lingering like gray blankets, waiting to smother anyone who strays too far out of sight.

I call to Elinor, who, along with Jeanne, has wandered off into one misty patch. Watching Mitchell burn up has clearly resurrected old memories of their deaths for both of them, but neither wants to discuss it—at least with me. Elinor comes over and huddles against Alfarin; Jeanne stands alone with her arms folded tightly across her chest.

"I'm changing the plan," I say, pulling the Viciseometer out of my pocket. "We're not going to let the Unspeakable dictate where and when we meet. I have something he wants, and if it's valuable enough to him, we'll stay ahead of him and let him come to us—to me. We also need to train ourselves to fight, but we need to go somewhere in time where we won't be disturbed. Does anyone have any ideas about where we could go?"

"Definitely not Washington," says Alfarin. "Everything always goes wrong in Washington."

"Not Los Angeles, either," says Angela. "There's so much plastic in that city, we'll melt every actor in Hollywood."

"I also suggest we do not go to New York," says Alfarin. "Indeed, perhaps we should get as far away from North America as possible."

"I cannot do this," whispers Elinor. "I am a failure. Ye should send me back to Hell, M. I can't burn, not again."

"You're going nowhere other than with us," I reply firmly. "We'll need someone to hang back with the Viciseometers. We can't all become raging fireballs. And there's no one I would trust more with our timepiece, Elinor, than you."

She smiles at me gratefully. Why can't all friendships be this easy and natural? Even in the midst of this crazy, Hellish mission, I don't have to work at this. It's so...normal.

"I want to be a raging fireball," says Johnny. "It looks...Angela?"

"Way cool," she prompts.

"Way cool," repeats Johnny. "When do we start?"

"To feel your flesh fall from your body, to endure the most agonizing pain you will ever experience, is not fun or *cool*," says Jeanne. There is no anger in her voice; she sounds terrified.

"I—I d-didn't mean—" stammers Johnny.

"I don't think you'll be able to self-immolate anyway, Johnny," I interrupt as Elinor's brother continues to stutter. "You're an angel. You won't have the same heat inside you that we do. Did you know our bodies build up so much fire in Hell that our eyes change color? Mine and Mitchell's are usually pink, but you should see how red Alfarin and Elinor's eyes are after hundreds of years there. They're ferocious. We're used to fire and heat, we absorb it. You don't."

"Are you saying we won't be able to become weapons in order to fight?" asks Angela.

"We won't know until we try, but you angels have speed. I've seen Jeanne streak across the earth twice now. Once to kick Alfarin's ass—"

"I slipped!"

"—and once to move Owen out of the line of sight of the paradox

Mitchell," I continue. "I don't think your weapon is fire. I think it's the air—wind."

Owen looks thoughtful. He bites down on his thumbnail.

"Fire and wind," he says. "They could be pretty formidable weapons to take on the Unspeakable and rescue the Dreamcatcher."

"*Not my brother!*" roars Mitchell. "*I won't let them!*"

Not again. Just when he starts coming to, Mitchell begins to smoke. This time, instead of dragging him into the surf, I place my hands on either side of his face.

"Look at me, Mitchell!" I shout. "Concentrate on my voice. We will not let anyone hurt your brother."

"I won't let them take him," he groans. I can feel the heat burning through him. His entire body is vibrating under my hands, but I keep hold of him, even though my fingers are starting to blister.

"Listen to me, Mitchell." Instead of shouting even louder, I decide to go the opposite way. If I'm calm, maybe Mitchell will refocus. "Concentrate on my voice. Trust me. We will not let them take M.J."

Mitchell continues to shake, and I can still feel the heat rippling through his body, but it's coming and going in waves.

I soften my voice even further. "Keep the anger, but control it, Mitchell. You can do this."

But he can't, not any longer. Mitchell screams, and I am blown ten feet through the night air as he becomes a fireball once more. Yet this time, it *is* different, because instead of relying on the others to drag him back into the water to extinguish, Mitchell is able to stagger in by himself. The sea sizzles and steams as he falls beneath a breaking wave.

"That was slightly better," offers Owen. "He definitely controlled it for a moment."

"We'll need to practice near water," I say as Mitchell emerges from the surf, lumbering like a smoking Godzilla.

"Can I make a suggestion?" asks Angela. "What about my home country of New Zealand? It's filled with lakes and open spaces. We might scare some sheep, but it isn't populated."

"I thought you were from Australia," I reply, but my mind is suddenly elsewhere, filled with another memory. Something about sheep. And Mitchell. Why are sheep making me think of Mitchell? He doesn't smell like sheep. He smells kind of nice, like fries and chocolate.

Angela rolls her pretty turquoise eyes. "Everyone north of the equator says that, but my accent is nicer. And New Zealand is far more beautiful than Australia. We have volcanoes, and ice-blue lakes with glaciers, and you should see the mountain ranges!"

"Can you think of somewhere specific that we could train?" I ask. "It has to be near water, and nowhere near people. Coming to Stinson Beach was a fortunate coincidence. I can't handle the thought of what would have happened to Mitchell if we had traveled from Owen's time to somewhere where we couldn't put out the fire."

"Sure," replies Angela. "We could head to the South Island and the Mackenzie District. I know it well. The flats of Twizel would be perfect for Jeanne to teach us how to control our speed, and the glacier lakes near Aoraki will put out any flames. If you travel to a time and date in the month of January, it will be summer and not too cold. We could camp out."

"But January is a winter month," says Owen.

"Not in the Southern Hemisphere, dummy," replies Angela. "Oh, please say we can go, Medusa! I want to make a contribution. So far, all I've done is scream a lot and get my white jeans dirty. I want to help. Please."

Tiny particles of sand are spinning around the spitting flames of the Viciseometer. I can feel them flagellating my skin.

"I'll need a date and time, Angela."

"You're the best!" cries Angela, skipping forward. "Right, why don't we travel to the first of January 2015? We should go early in the morning, because the entire country will be hungover from New Year's Eve. No one will be about, not even the tourists."

It sounds like a plan. I don't ask Cupidore or Visolentiae if they're coming. I know they're still here, watching us, watching me, from the shadows. Septimus might want them to accompany us, but

I'm not going to travel in the flames with them, and they don't seem to have any problem time-traveling on their own, anyway.

With the red needle held tightly between my right thumb and forefinger, I manipulate the hands of the milky-white face to lock in the time of seven o'clock. I flip it over and move the three black hands to the day and month and then the four slithering snakes that represent the four digits of 2015. An electrical current ripples up my back. I sense the static in my hair. The year 2015 is far into any future I may have had.

"I'll hold the Viciseometer, Angela," I say. "But you need to be touching it. You need to visualize the place we're going to, and you need to see it in the morning, not evening."

Angela's slim, pale fingers hover over the red, flaming face of Hell's timepiece. She looks nervously at Owen, and he smiles at her.

"Wait," calls Jeanne. "Why do we continue to use the infidel's Viciseometer and not our own? Why should we have to travel with them? Why can it not be the other way? I do not want to see flames anymore. I want to see blue sky and sense the sun on my face, not the destructive force of fire."

I pull my hand away from Angela, but as I do, a sudden charge from the Viciseometer surges through my hand. It travels up my arm and stabs painfully into my chest.

Does it know I'm planning to travel by another Viciseometer? Can this thing sense emotion and betrayal? A sudden thought flickers in my head. Is the Viciseometer a conscious object? I hadn't even considered that before, but the more I think about it, the more it seems possible. This little watch can change anyone's destiny, whether they're living or dead.

"What's wrong, Medusa?" asks Alfarin. His eyebrows are furrowed into a unibrow.

"I just…it just felt…"

I swap looks with Elinor. I'll test out my theory on her, Mitchell and Alfarin later, when we have time away from the angels. We aren't a team of eight; we are two teams of four, and I must never forget that.

"So we travel with our Viciseometer this time?" asks Owen, and once more I see a flash of red in his eyes.

"Are you certain, Medusa?" asks Alfarin. "We will follow your lead."

"Why not?" I reply. I must admit, I'm eager to see what traveling by the blue Viciseometer is like.

I watch Owen input the same coordinates. The red Viciseometer shocks me again as I tuck it back into my pocket, and pinpricks stab at my scalp. Mitchell is propped up between me and Alfarin, and although he's still wobbly, he can at least support his own weight. Elinor holds hands with Alfarin and her brother while Jeanne moves in on my left. She opens her mouth as if to say something, but nothing comes out. There's definitely a hint of a reconciliatory smile, though. She's warming to me, I think. Slowly. Very slowly. Maybe in four hundred years or so, Jeanne will call me by my name and not *infidel*.

"Okay, Angela," says Owen, holding the blue Viciseometer on the flat of his palm. It floats up, just a fraction, until it's hovering above his pale skin. Brilliant white stars twinkle around the silver rim.

"I'm taking us to Lake Pukaki," says Angela. She screws up her heart-shaped face in concentration as her slim fingers touch the Viciseometer.

We all huddle even tighter. Jeanne drops all pretense of being badass and takes my hand. I give it a quick squeeze to show I understand, but I don't look at her. I know what it feels like to *want* to trust people, and the intent right now on her part is good enough for me.

The blue face of the Viciseometer starts to swirl. The blue is becoming lighter and lighter. Instinctively, we all lean in.

Then, just as Angela calls out "*Now*," the stench of rotten meat washes over us, and the sound of the breaking waves is replaced by howls and screams.

Cupidore and Visolentiae are traveling through time with us.

The panic alarm in Hell was bad enough. Hearing the sound of the scream I made as I plummeted toward the Golden Gate Strait, a channel of water that might as well have been concrete considering the force I hit it with, was horrific. But the terror bleeding into our ears now is far worse. With the Skin-Walkers among us, I don't just hear the screams of the tortured in Hell, I can feel them. Their dread, their fear. The spirits flying through time with us now are not just begging for death, they are begging for nothing. A cessation of their existence. Their screams are burrowing into my bones, biting and scratching. Their pain is mine, and it's excruciating.

The terrible sounds continue, but we've stopped flying. I'm lying on my back, staring up into a cloudless blue sky. I want to move, I need to run, but my limbs are like lead. A hand reaches for mine. It's Mitchell. His hand is so hot I fear it will melt away before I can grab it back.

I realize that the moaning and screaming I'm hearing are coming from Team ANGEL. They're in pain.

But angels can't feel pain, can they? I thought that was one of the advantages of getting into Up There.

I manage to raise my aching neck and back off the ground. My arms don't appear to belong to me as I force them back into the ground. It's like manipulating pastry dough.

Angela is the first angel I see. She's sitting, but her legs are drawn up tightly into her body. I can't see her face because she's buried it in her knees, but from the way her shoulders are convulsing, it's clear she's crying.

Johnny is the only dead man standing. He's brushing at his arms, torso and legs, trying to dislodge something that's no longer there.

Jeanne is dry-heaving into the base of a large fir tree. She hollers after every painful retch.

And Owen isn't moving. He's not seeing. He's just lying there. His eyes are wide open and his mouth is a silent scream.

"Medusa," groans Mitchell. "Is everyone . . . here? I can't see."

I crawl closer to him. His burning hand is still touching mine. As gently as I can, I brush the blackened skin on his cheek.

"We're all here, Mitchell."

"How could we hear that?" gasps Mitchell. "The victims of the Skin-Walkers. They have their tongues torn out. So how could we hear them scream? That sound was beyond pain. It was awful."

"I don't know," I reply. "The Skin-Walkers feed off pain. I think what we heard was what those monsters have absorbed, but it's okay now. They're gone. The Skin-Walkers aren't here."

I knew this as soon as we landed because the scent of summer is clean and flowery around us. And while Team ANGEL doesn't sound so hot right now, the spirits and pain of the tortured dead, trapped in the nine circles of Hell, have gone, too. Hell knows where the Skin-Walkers have disappeared to, and I hate the thought of them roaming the land of the living while they wait for the Unspeakable to find me. They gave us their word they wouldn't hurt anyone else, but treachery is in their nature, and I don't know how long they'll have to wait.

Alfarin pulls himself up by his axe, which sinks into the earth. We are surrounded by long yellow grass and dark-green fir trees. Small bushes with tiny thorns are everywhere.

"In all of Valhalla, I have never seen such a sight," says Alfarin. "Come, my princess. The beauty of this place is but matched by your own."

I continue to stroke Mitchell's face. One eyelid is swollen shut; his other eye is open, but bloodshot. I'm so used to pink and red irises, it seems strange seeing that color in the whites of his eyes, but the blue is still there. So deep, so pretty.

"How are we going to do this, Medusa?" he whispers. "This is so sick, so evil, I can't even . . ."

"I know, I know," I say. Already his skin is starting to heal as the burned flesh changes under my fingertips. Scaly black becomes swollen red, and swollen red becomes pale pink before my eyes.

One problem at a time, I decide. We train and then we fight.

"You have a plan, don't you," whispers Mitchell again. It isn't a question.

"What makes you say that?" Our heads are so close, my hair is bouncing on his forehead.

"Because you look…you look…alive."

"You just can't see very well," I whisper back.

My mouth is so close to his now. The smell of burned flesh is gone. Mitchell is whole again, truly whole. I can't understand why he's in Hell. He almost combusted in the rage he felt for a little boy he has never even met.

He's an angel.

My thoughts are interrupted by coughing. Alfarin and Elinor are standing—arm in arm—and staring down at me and Mitchell. I immediately pull away, although I don't want to.

Alfarin pulls us to our feet, and we both gasp at the scene before us.

Angela has taken us to the edge of an enormous lake, surrounded by mountains, the largest of which are covered in snow. I've never seen water like it. The lake shimmers as if it's filled with aquamarines.

"Is this real?" asks Mitchell.

"It reminds me of the home of my fathers," says Alfarin. "I have seen this place in many a book in Hell, never knowing that one day I would witness it with my own eyes. You see that mountain in the distance? That is Aoraki, the son of the Sky Father. This land is Aotearoa, one of the most beautiful places known to man."

"Ye know a lot about other cultures, Alfarin," says Elinor, clearly impressed.

"I am a Viking prince, not a heathen," replies Alfarin, swinging his axe onto his shoulder.

Team DEVIL stands together, drinking in this amazing piece of Up There on earth, and I can think of no better place to prepare for what we're about to do.

18. **Weapons Training**

The angels are still struggling to cope with the fact that they just time-traveled with two of the Skin-Walkers. Team DEVIL has already recovered. I am so proud of my friends' resilience.

My grandmother once told me that strangers were just friends you hadn't met yet. After everything that happened when we moved away from her, I stopped thinking of that sentence in a positive way, but now I get what she meant. Strangers can become friends, and I desperately want to believe that Mitchell, Alfarin and Elinor see me that way now, too.

I'm not sure how friendship works with angels. Angela and Johnny appear to have some kind of bond, but Owen and Jeanne are still in a lonely state of shock. They could take comfort from each other, but they don't.

Death and then an existence in Hell have hardened me up for what we're about to do, but I'm starting to think that maybe we need to cut our losses and break off from Team ANGEL sooner rather than later. I'm not sure they have the nerves for what I'm planning. Not even Jeanne.

Then again, I need that other Viciseometer. It's one thing to become a weapon, but to be invisible is a tool like no other. The Skin-Walkers didn't see or even appear to sense the others when they rescued me in Washington. The only way we have a chance to retrieve the Dreamcatcher from the Unspeakable is if he can't see us as we fight him.

The Viciseometer from Up There puts us at a huge advantage when joined with the timepiece from Hell. So the two teams will have to stay together—for now. There's just no other way.

Angela and Johnny pull Owen to his feet. He's shaking violently. No one goes to Jeanne, and I feel sorry for her because I know what that's like, but when I make an attempt to approach her, she turns away. I'll give her time. I want to believe she's worth the effort I'm trying to put in with her. It may never come to a friendship, but an understanding is possible.

"What did the Skin-Walkers do to us?" whispers Owen. "That noise…it was like…"

"I think we heard the absorbed screams of pain of everyone who's trapped in the nine circles of Hell," I reply. "We should be thankful it was only the two of them that came along for the ride."

"Thankful?" gasps Jeanne.

"There are nine Skin-Walkers, Jeanne," I reply tiredly. "Owen knows. He's going to fill you in on what they all represent."

I know I shouldn't be so harsh, but I won't be the angels' encyclopedia anymore. I'm pretty sure Owen knows far more than he's letting on—even if half of the stuff he's mentioned to me doesn't make sense. I think back to our conversation about my death, when he claimed to have seen my records, to have read that I have two timelines or something. I still think he's crazy—no one can die twice—but that doesn't change the fact that Owen has more information than the other angels.

Which makes me think…I trusted him back in Washington because I had no choice. Now I do have a choice, and I'm going to be wary.

"Angela, I take it you know this place?" I ask.

"Like the back of my hand. My grandpa would bring me and my sister here when we were little. We used to stargaze and make wishes."

Angela stares up into the blue sky.

"They never came true, though," she adds sadly.

"I need you to get supplies, Angela. Owen has money and we still need food." I glance at Alfarin. "Well, we don't *need* it, but we operate much better with full stomachs. We also need sleeping bags or something, because we could be here a couple of days while we train. Devils don't cope well in cold weather."

"You are not our leader," growls Jeanne. Clearly, the warmth she showed me earlier has disappeared after her encounter with the Skin-Walkers.

"Medusa *is* our leader," say Mitchell and Owen together.

"What?" chorus Alfarin and Johnny, staring in amazement at Owen.

"I agree," say Elinor and Angela.

"Never!" shouts Jeanne.

Owen pulls the blue Viciseometer from his pocket and hands it to Angela. "Do as Melissa—Medusa asks. Take Johnny and Elinor. Get everything she requires. Team ANGEL isn't a team, we're just dead souls thrown together. I've seen firsthand what can happen to a team that doesn't work together. Jeanne has been right all along. We need one leader, and I think that should be Medusa."

"You cannot betray us like this!" cries Jeanne. "We were sent on a mission from Heaven. You must see it through!"

"Well, maybe I don't want to—not anymore," replies Owen.

"It was an order."

"I'm sick of orders."

"This is cowardice."

"No, Jeanne. It's self-preservation."

Jeanne is shaking with rage, so much so that her skin is starting to change color. Blinding pockets of brilliant white light seem to be radiating out of her very pores. It's nothing like the flames that erupted out of Mitchell, but instead looks like countless laser beams.

"We must take orders from the devils, Jeanne," says Owen.

And now I see what he's doing: Owen is deliberately baiting Jeanne—and it's working.

"Oh, shit," mutters Mitchell. He grabs my hand and pulls me toward him. "Stay behind me, Medusa. Alfarin, if Jeanne attacks, you know what to do."

"*You are a coward!*" screams Jeanne, and her voice is so deep that the ground beneath her actually rumbles.

"The devils are now in charge, Jeanne. We have no choice but to capitulate," says Owen, standing his ground as he adds extra emphasis to the word *capitulate*. "I hope this works," he adds in a low voice.

Suddenly, Jeanne streaks into the sky. There are no wings and no harp, but finally we see a flying angel.

And it's beautiful.

Jeanne's entire being is golden, surrounded by a crystal nimbus. In the center, I can see the very vague outline of a person: two arms, two legs, a head, but it's like the outline of a body at a crime scene. White stars shoot from Jeanne's form as she speeds into the distance like a firework.

"You did that with deliberate purpose, Owen," says Alfarin. "You are either very brave, or very foolish. Jeanne is as fearsome as my father sister Dagmar, and she would scare the Skin-Walkers."

"Those of us who will train to become weapons will need to have a trigger," says Owen, staring at me. "We know Mitchell's is the thought of something happening to his living brother. I took a guess that Jeanne's would be an angel deferring authority to a devil."

"I'm glad you tried that, Owen, and not me," says Mitchell. "You forget, she's gonna come back at some point, and when she does, I think we'll find out how Joan of Arc kicked so much medieval ass— before she got tied to a stake, of course."

"Do not say that out loud, my friend," says Alfarin. "She may still be able to hear you."

"So what's your trigger, Owen?" I ask. "The immolation is activated by rage. We'll all need that anger for it to work properly—"

"Well, being dead kinda pisses me off," interrupts Angela. "I could think about that."

"It's not enough, Angela," I reply. "We're all angry about being dead, but this goes beyond being pissed off. This is a rage so intense, it changes the physicality of existence."

Angela's heart-shaped face falls. Elinor wraps her arm around the angel's shoulders.

"Ye must not feel sad," she says. "I will not be able to do it, either. I have never felt rage. It just isn't in my nature, although I did once punch Mitchell."

"Yeah, thanks for that reminder, Elinor," says Mitchell, rubbing his jaw.

"And I am still very sorry about it."

"I guess I'll just have to be mother and look after everyone," says Angela.

Jeanne is now a mere speck in the distance. I hope she lands before her rage wears off, because that looks like one awfully long drop.

"What about you, Alfarin?" says Mitchell. "Do you think you'll be able to do it?"

"Find my trigger and watch me burn," says Alfarin proudly, puffing out his chest.

Elinor shakes her head at Mitchell. A deep frown has formed on her pretty freckled face.

"Here goes nothing," says Mitchell, with a resigned shrug of his shoulders.

"Mitchell, what are ye doing?"

"This isn't going to be pretty," mutters Johnny, and he starts taking big steps back.

I'm expecting Mitchell to punch Alfarin, or steal his axe or something, but instead, Mitchell just strolls up to Alfarin and starts whispering in his ear. The Viking's jaw locks, and I can actually hear his back teeth grinding as Mitchell continues to whisper.

"Mitchell," calls Elinor in a warning voice. "Ye had better not be saying what I think ye are saying."

Alfarin's huge frame is starting to shudder. His blue eyes are fixed firmly on the horizon.

"He's making him relive something," says Owen quietly. "But what?"

"His death?" I ask, with a glance at Elinor.

"Not *his* death, no," she replies, tugging at the back of her neck. Elinor is getting more and more distressed as Mitchell continues to whisper.

Alfarin's immolation is immediately triggered when a sob breaks from Elinor's chest. Mitchell and Owen are thrown thirty feet into the air as Alfarin explodes into a mushroom cloud of crimson fire.

"Holy shit!" screams Angela as an invisible heat wave knocks the rest of us off our feet, with a blast of burning air that reminds me of the enormous ovens in Hell's kitchens.

"We have to put him out!" cries Elinor. "There will be nothing left of him."

Mitchell and I start crawling through the thorny grass toward the burning Alfarin. I had completely forgotten what Septimus said about combustion, and Alfarin, who died a thousand years ago, has enough heat in him to take out half of New Zealand.

"What did you say to him?"

"Elinor's death is his trigger," pants Mitchell. "I just...I just made it worse."

Suddenly a golden streak zooms over our heads. It lifts the Alfarin fireball and flies it at high speed through the sky like a blazing comet—and then we hear his elongated cry as he's dropped into the aquamarine lake.

The water explodes as a cloud of steam and spray gushes upward like a geyser.

"*Alfarin!*" screams Elinor.

"Holy shit!" cries Angela again.

Mitchell and I are already running toward the pebble-lined shore. A steaming Alfarin emerges from its depths; his beloved axe is still in his hand.

"The French wench is strong," is all he says before falling forward, flat on his face.

"What was Jeanne thinking?" yells Mitchell. He skids into the stones and tries to haul Alfarin out of the water. He doesn't get very far with such a dead weight.

"She was the only one who *was* thinking," I reply. "Alfarin can't possibly control his immolation yet. He would have combusted if Jeanne hadn't dropped him into the water so quickly."

Jeanne lands next to us on the shore. The blinding light fades like the filament in a bulb.

"Thank ye, Jeanne!" cries Elinor. "Thank ye."

Alfarin starts to stir at the sound of Elinor's voice. He pulls himself onto his haunches and shakes his long blond hair and beard like a dog.

"I will need to practice," he croaks, "but I will be victorious once I have food in my belly."

"Did it hurt, Jeanne?" I ask.

"Of course it hurt, but I have known worse."

"Will you be able to train Owen?"

"If he will listen."

That's good enough for me.

"Okay, I think I have the first stage of a plan ready," I say when Elinor and the guys finally manage to drag Alfarin out of the water. "Mitchell, Alfarin, Owen and Jeanne will train to control their immolation. Elinor, Angela and Johnny are responsible for keeping a lookout and getting supplies. Angela will have the Viciseometer from Up There, and I will keep hold of the other one. Even though Angela and Johnny will be keeping watch, we all need to be alert for the Skin-Walkers. That should be easy because we'll smell them before we see them. But even more importantly, we need to be alert for the Unspeakable and the Dreamcatcher. He's coming after me, and I'm happy to be the bait. When the time comes, we, as weapons, will attack the Unspeakable and I will rescue the Dreamcatcher. I'm going to need both Viciseometers for that, Angela, so you'll need to be ready to hand it over when I ask. The Skin-Walkers will take the Unspeakable back to Hell, and we'll have the boy."

"And what then?" asks Jeanne.

"Then comes stage two."

"Which is what, Medusa?" asks Mitchell, and I know what he fears.

"We're going to change the culture of Hell, Mitchell, because no more children will be used as Dreamcatchers. Not ever."

19. **Mother Love**

Elinor, Angela and Johnny disappear in search of food. Owen is happy to entrust Angela with their Viciseometer, and I know I can count on Elinor. Jeanne complains, but not for long. She has a purpose now, which is to train the guys for their immolation. She's a natural, and my intuition is telling me it's something she's done before. Not just at the graveyard when she slam-dunked Alfarin, or the time she took Owen away from the paradox Mitchell, but other times, too. She's just too good at it.

I think back to the information Septimus showed us before we left Hell. Jeanne d'Arc was burned alive by the English in Rouen in 1431. That's a long time to exist Up There with so much anger. I'm guessing she's been here before, back in the land of the living. I'd like to ask her if she's immolated before, but there's no point; Jeanne wouldn't answer. When I was alive, there were always stories about people having visions of saints. If Jeanne really did come back, something tells me this mission is already entirely different from her previous visits. I think her rage may turn out to be the most powerful weapon we have. Plus, she's a leader, a strategic thinker. She led entire armies when she was alive.

And don't Mitchell, Alfarin and Owen know it.

Now she has them standing in a straight line, and she's pacing up and down in front of them like an army general issuing orders. Owen appears to be quite passive, but the looks on Mitchell's and

Alfarin's faces are priceless. Mitchell's mouth is open in shock, practically catching flies. Alfarin's bushy eyebrows have imploded into the creases in his forehead. They keep swapping glances, but both of them are too scared of Jeanne to do anything other than listen.

Mitchell catches my eye, and I have to stuff my knuckles into my mouth to keep from giggling. I don't want to piss her off, either. "Keep your friends close and angels with a vicious temper even closer" is another motto I'm going to exist by.

I leave Jeanne to her training and walk up from the shoreline to a long bank of pine trees. We're well hidden here, and the entire landscape is unspoiled by the living. I just hope that by the end of this, it will be unspoiled by the dead, too. Elinor said that we're toxic and that we leave traces. I remember watching those flower petals crumple to gray ash in Mitchell's fingers at the cemetery. I would hate to ruin such a beautiful place as this.

It's a shame I had to be dead to see it, but even though we traveled a lot when I was young, I never really saw anything other than the inside of one neglected house after another. Muir Woods and Stinson Beach were the nearest I got to nature, but even those memories are corrupted by evil.

I start thinking it'd be a lot of fun to go play in those white-capped mountains and make snow angels. Yeah, right. Nice thought, Medusa. You'd probably melt them and cause an avalanche or something.

Suddenly, I'm blown off my feet. My back hits the trunk of a tree, and a shower of pine needles falls on my head. I swear aloud. Not because my back is hurting—which it is—but because I'm never going to get all of those needles out of my hair. When she gets back with the supplies, Elinor will have to deneedle me like a monkey delousing a buddy.

Then I see that Alfarin has immolated again, and pine needles in my hair don't seem so important anymore.

A caustic, ammonia-like smell hits my senses. The Skin-Walker called Visolentiae steps out from behind another tree, just a few yards away.

"The Viking has unveiled much hatred in his dead soul," growls Visolentiae appreciatively. "That much fire, that much power..."

"You stay away from Alfarin," I hiss. "You stay the Hell away from all of us. You should be hunting the Unspeakable."

"He is already ours no matter where he runs, and there is little left of him to consume," replies Visolentiae. His black tongue slides over his sharp teeth. "And as you've already deduced, we do not need to hunt him, for we are with you, and eventually, he will seek you out." He regards me with a sinister smile. "You must know why, child. You must know by now what he wants. He wants *you*. Your soul. And we will be waiting. Yes, little one, we can smell it when a flesh soul is aroused by nefarious thoughts and deeds. A new chase is what we desire—it is what we always desire. This world with its hate and its violence—"

"Stop it!" I cry. "Stay away from me. You're no better than the souls you take away."

Visolentiae laughs, and the chill in his voice turns my skin to ice.

"Why, isn't that what the living's so-called justice serves to ensure? They execute the evil in the name of the law, never realizing that by deliberately taking a life, they become ours in death. The righteous are the most enjoyable, little one. Once they realize what their actions in life have condemned them to in death..." Visolentiae licks his teeth and his cracked, weeping lips again, and the stench of rotting souls makes me gag.

When I look up, the Skin-Walker is gone. He was simply here to bait me, to snack on my fear.

"I'm coming...Medusa," groans a voice from the shore. "Medusa...I'm...coming."

Crawling through the long, prickly grass is Mitchell. Gray smoke is billowing from his body, but at least he's conscious.

"Don't move, Mitchell," I call, and I run down toward him. He's immolated again, but he's recovered far more quickly than the other times he's done it, and his skin is reddened like a sunburn, not flaking in blackened layers.

It seems perverse to call such a sight an improvement, but it is. Jeanne is good. Really good.

"You're doing so well, Mitchell," I say, touching him gently on his burned face. "Do you need to take a break?"

"Only the weak rest," calls Jeanne. "Get back here, Mitchell. You are a soldier, not a coward."

"I swear that angel was never human in the first place," groans Mitchell as he lifts himself up onto his knees. "What did that Skin-Walker say to you, Medusa? Did he touch you? I swear I will immolate on his wolf-head—"

"He's gone," I interrupt. "And I'm fine, honestly."

"Why aren't he and that other freak tracking down your stepfather?"

"Because there's no fun in that for them. Visolentiae just told me there's little left in him for them to enjoy. They're going to wait for him to come to me, but then, I knew that."

"Jeez, they're sick. . . . What do you think their story is? Who created them?"

"The Highers, I imagine. Or maybe The Devil." I give him a shaky laugh. "It's comforting to know there's a class system in Hell, as well as on earth. The good, the bad, the ugly and the downright evil."

"Medusa, was that a joke?"

"Poor taste. Sorry."

"It wasn't bad, actually," says Mitchell, finally pulling himself upright. Already the flaming red burns on his body have healed to a pinkish tinge.

"Mitchell, get over here now!" shouts Jeanne. "You are stalling."

Mitchell is biting down on his lip; his eyes are closed.

"I would say take deep breaths and keep calm," I whisper. "But seeing as you don't need to breathe, that probably won't help."

"Joke number two," replies Mitchell. "I'm impressed."

Our gentle teasing is brought to a sudden end as Owen erupts into a bright white ball and shoots into the sky.

"What was his trigger?" calls Mitchell.

"A battle," replies Alfarin. "I do not understand how something so glorious could be the cause of such rage. I believe Private Jones must have carried an affliction of the head with him onto the other side."

"Owen does not see war as a necessary means to an end, Alfarin," says Jeanne. "He sees it as wanton destruction of life."

Mitchell nudges me. "I think those two are bonding," he whispers.

I nudge him back, but I don't know my own strength, or the sharpness of my own elbows, because Mitchell yelps in pain.

"I have known women in childbirth to make less noise!" cries Jeanne. "Now get in line, Mitchell."

Reluctantly, Mitchell trudges back to the shoreline for more immolation training. I don't know how Jeanne is making them control the fire and flight, but whatever her tactics are, they're working.

Do the others think I'm a coward for not trying? If so, they aren't wrong. I *am* a coward. But if I unleash the fire in me, if I let the rage consume me, I'm afraid there will be nothing left. Embracing Medusa and letting Melissa go doesn't mean my pain and anger and memories will automatically disappear. My nightmares may stay with me forever. And right now, I don't want to risk being overcome by fury before the Unmentionable finds me.

Where is he now? Is he already here? Watching, waiting? We would hear crying, surely? That poor little boy. My soul aches for him. In Hell we still feel pain and emotion, and I know now that it's real. Because if this experience has taught me anything, it's that we do more than just exist in the Afterlife.

I'd like to clear my head, but I know I can't risk going off alone again in case the Unspeakable is here and I just haven't been able to detect him. Also, I'm not wild about the possibility of running into Visolentiae again.

The thought of that vile Skin-Walker reminds me of our conversation. Visolentiae said the Unspeakable wanted my soul. And the message the Unspeakable left in blood in The Devil's bedroom said he wanted his life back in exchange for the Dreamcatcher. But I'm not sure how he could get at my soul *without* the powers of the Dreamcatcher. It's all so confusing, and I desperately need to talk to someone who understands. Someone who might have answers.

I realize with a start that there is someone here who could possibly help me; I'm just not sure I want to hear what he has to say. But sometimes we have no choice. I keep pushing him away, telling him he's wrong. . . . But what if he isn't?

"Owen," I call. "Owen, could you come here for a minute?"

Jeanne turns around and scowls at me for interrupting her training session. I ignore her. At the very least, Owen might know more about the Dreamcatcher than we do—which wouldn't be too hard, seeing as we know practically nothing.

"What is it, Medusa?" replies Owen. He straightens his brown army uniform and stands at attention in front of me.

"Tell me everything you know about the Dreamcatcher," I say. "Don't leave anything out. We left Hell in a hurry and didn't have time to read up, and Septimus didn't end up filling us in all that well. But I know you were briefed. What powers does that little boy have?"

"My information may not be veritable fact, Medusa," replies Owen. "Rumor and misinformation are as prevalent in Heaven as they are Down There. What I tell you could hinder as much as help."

"Let me rephrase the question, then. What have you been told, or read, or heard whispered in the clouds about The Devil's Dreamcatcher, Owen? I would rather be prepared for a rumor than prepared for nothing at all."

Owen flattens down a patch of long grass with his boot and sits. He pats the ground next to him, and I make myself comfortable. I'm so tired I could lie down and sleep for a month.

"It is my understanding that the Dreamcatcher is used as a trap," says Owen carefully. "Whenever The Devil has dreams—or nightmares, depending on how one views these things—the Dreamcatcher will absorb the toxicity of the thoughts into its own consciousness."

"And what happens to those thoughts once they're in the Dreamcatcher?"

"The Devil isn't human, Medusa. He allegedly has powers that the rest of us normal people couldn't possibly comprehend. He can move about through time and space without the need of a device, and he could unleash Hell on earth, or in Heaven, if he wanted to. This is just my own opinion, but from what you have told me, and from what I've overheard, I think the Dreamcatcher has the same powers as The Devil, because they are one and the same. I believe your stepfather, the Unspeakable, is going to use the Dreamcatcher to give himself back some kind of mortal form."

"How?"

Owen opens his mouth and then quickly shuts it. He won't look me in the eye. I know that face too well. I perfected it.

"Owen, how?"

"The Unspeakable is after you, Medusa."

"I know, but I'm dead. He can't get his life back through me."

"His soul and existence are mutilated. What if the Dream-catcher had the power to restore life by using someone else's soul? I think the Unspeakable just has to learn how to tap into those powers...."

"You think he wants my...my body for something?"

"I think he wants *your* soul in *his* body. It'll be mixed with what's left of his own. It will make him stronger," says Owen. "Look, it's just a theory."

"He plans to destroy me."

"There's something special about you, Medusa," whispers Owen. "And your stepfather knows it. That knowledge indicates to me that he can't be acting alone. He would have needed help from someone to escape from the Skin-Walkers, and that same someone could have told him about you."

"But I'm not special."

"You are. You have no idea how special you are. You changed time. Do you know how few people have done that? You died twice."

Up until now, Owen's insight has been frightening and intriguing. But bringing up my death is exactly what I wanted to avoid. "Stop it, Owen. Just stop it!" I cry. "No one can die twice. Isn't it bad enough we die once?"

A dark shadow looms over us. Mitchell and Alfarin are glaring at Owen. Mitchell's knuckles are pure white as he clenches them tightly. The morning sun glints off the blade of Alfarin's axe and reflects into his pale-blue eyes, making them look as if they're ringed with silver.

"What do you think you're doing, Owen?" growls Mitchell. "I hope you're not trying to trigger Medusa, because if you are—"

But Owen jumps to his feet and pushes past Mitchell. Jeanne has immolated and is speeding into the sky.

And I can see from here what her trigger is this time.

Walking along the shoreline are four people: Elinor, Angela, Johnny and a woman with long blond hair.

"What has Angela done?" groans Owen, half running, half stumbling toward her.

Mitchell and Alfarin both turn around. Alfarin's axe handle hits my hip bone, but I am too dumbstruck to cry out.

"Who's that woman?" says Mitchell. "Alfarin, get rid of your axe."

"In the name of the goddess Freya, what is going on?" booms Alfarin. "Angela has deceived us."

Even though they're still some distance away, it's clear that Elinor, Angela and Johnny are all happy to be in the woman's presence. Elinor and her brother are beaming, and Angela has her arm wrapped around the woman's slim waist.

I jog toward them. Angela has a smile that looks as if warm chocolate is sliding down her throat.

"Medusa, Owen, I've got someone I want you all to meet," she calls.

The three boys aren't being choosy about the curses they're now uttering, but I keep my mouth shut, because the closer I get, the more obvious it becomes just who the woman is. She has the same turquoise eyes, the same smile. Even her dimples are in the same place.

Angela has brought us her mother.

20. **Don't Follow the Crowd**

"You must be Medusa," says the woman with a wide smile. Her arm is outstretched and her thin hand, covered in glittering rings of every gemstone, takes mine. He skin is beyond cold, colder than the angels'. I pull my hand away for fear that I'll stick to it if I hold it for much longer.

"Angela and Elinor have told me all about you," adds the woman in a voice that's an exact copy of Angela's. She peers around my shoulder. "The young men don't seem to be as welcoming as you are, but give them time."

"But I thought...Angela said...aren't you dead?" I splutter.

Internal brain slap. What did you say that for? Could you be any ruder?

But Angela's mom laughs. It sounds strange, like an out-of-tune musical instrument.

"Of course I'm dead, dear Medusa. Did you think two angels and a devil would just turn up at my house if I weren't?"

Mitchell's swearing has now gone up to a whole different level. I think he's actually making new words up. Either that or he's fluent in Swedish.

"You went to see your dead mother?" I say faintly to Angela. "You were supposed to be getting food and sleeping bags."

"But we did get food, M," replies Elinor. She slips a bag off her shoulder and walks to Mitchell and Alfarin, who dive straight into it. The smell of bacon wafts over to me.

Mitchell and Alfarin stop swearing and start stuffing their faces with crusty round rolls of white bread, stacked high with sausages and bacon.

But Owen doesn't eat, which means he can carry on where Mitchell and Alfarin left off.

"What have you done, Angela?" he cries. "We were expressly told not to have anything to do with anyone back in the land of the living."

"But my mother isn't living, Owen," replies Angela, placing her hands on her hips, "and so I haven't broken any rules and laws by seeing her, have I? And before you start shouting and pouting, you should know that I've told her all about our mission, and she and Granny are very proud of us."

I'm going to throw up. I want to put my head between my knees, but I'm distracted by Alfarin, who's performing the Heimlich on Mitchell because he's choking—an uncomfortable situation even when you don't have to breathe.

"There's...a...granny?" gasps Mitchell as Alfarin continues to shake him up and down.

"Ye are taking this as well as I expected," mutters Johnny sarcastically. "I knew Jeanne would do her head in, but I thought ye all would see what Angela and our Elinor are trying to do."

"Ye aren't angry with us, are ye, M?" asks Elinor, taking my hand. "We were just trying to help."

"But we don't need help, Elinor. And certainly not from...not from..."

"Nonsense, of course you do," says Angela's mother. "You poor devils can't even eat without choking."

She pushes Alfarin away from Mitchell and wraps her arms around Mitchell's chest, and with her hands clasped in a tight ball, she expels half a sausage from his open mouth.

"Chew your food properly, young man," she says, slapping him on the back for good measure. "You may be dead, but that's no excuse for laziness and poor manners."

"Angela," implores Owen. "Please explain."

"I don't mean to be nasty," says Angela crossly, "but not one of you has given the end of this mission any real thought, have you? Owen and Jeanne, the two of you can only see the fight to get the Dreamcatcher back. Mitchell and Alfarin can't see past their next meal, and Medusa, I think you're truly awesome, I really do, but you have to deal with that awful Unspeakable, as well as the Skin-Walkers...."

"What about me?" asks Johnny.

"Johnny, sweetie, you're so out of your depth here I can't understand for the death of me why you were even asked to come along," replies Angela. "The fact is, only Elinor and I have picked up on something that you all seem to have forgotten."

"Which is what?" I ask, not bothering to hide how pissed off I am at Angela for doing something so serious behind my back. If there was one angel I thought I might be able to trust, it was her. But she's just another Patty Lloyd: pretty, flirty and dumb as shit.

"Medusa, what happens to the Dreamcatcher once we have him back?" replies Angela. "Say we're successful, and the Skin-Walkers take that disgusting monster back into the circles of Hell. What then? The Dreamcatcher is a little boy. He'll need someone to care for him, because he can't be taken back Down There, and I don't think he'll be safe if we take him with us."

"B-but..." stammers Owen.

"But nothing, Owen. We all exist in the Afterlife. The Dreamcatcher won't be safe. Heaven and Down There won't be safe if he's as dangerous as we think. He'll need supporting, and nurturing. He needs normal. A dead kind of normal."

Angela's mother smiles at me, and at that moment I understand exactly what they've done, and more importantly, why.

And it breaks me.

I've been able to manipulate the fear and rage in our two teams, albeit for the greater good. I've even fooled myself into thinking we can change time and stop the need for a child Dreamcatcher at all, but Angela's right, I hadn't really given a second thought to what we would actually do with that little boy once we had him. It's not as if we could take him back to his living parents; he's dead. And he's too young to be left to fend for himself.

It came so naturally to Elinor and Angela. So why not me? What's wrong with me? Am I really that hard?

"Medusa?" asks Owen. "What are they talking about?"

"The Dreamcatcher, Owen," I whisper. "Didn't you hear a word she said? While I've been plotting, and you've all been training to control your immolation, Elinor and Angela were the only ones who gave any thought to what we do with the little boy once we've rescued him."

"Which is what?"

"I will care for him," replies Angela's mom. "I can't have my Angela back, but I can do the next-best thing and protect that little boy."

"But you're dead!" yells Mitchell. "And sorry, Angela, but how did your mom and granny die and get to stay on earth in the first place? The last time I checked, the HalfWay House didn't have an exit."

"You must be Mitchell," replies Angela's mom. "Process of elimination, because that handsome young man next to you is surely Prince Alfarin?" She checks with Elinor that she got it right, and Elinor nods.

"Alfarin, son of Hlif, son of Dobin" replies Alfarin, going down on bended knee. "It is an honor to meet the lady mother of such a graceful, beautiful angel. From this day forth, my axe—"

"*Shut up, Alfarin,*" echoes a chorus of voices, mine included.

"I could use an axe like that to cut down firewood in the winter, Alfarin," says Angela's mom. "I'm afraid I tend to rot the wooden handles of mine a little too often."

"Sorry, but you didn't answer Mitchell's question," I say, interrupting what is clearly about to become a two-way rapture about weapons. "Dead people go to Hell, or Up There. I've never heard of dead people being allowed to exist back in the land of the living."

"That's because it isn't allowed, Medusa," replies Angela's mom.

"There are a few of us, here in secret. It's a nomadic existence, for we would draw too much attention to ourselves eventually if we stayed in any one place for too long. You must be aware of the traces you are all leaving back in the land of the living already."

Like flowers turning to gray ash. I nod.

"But how?" asks Mitchell. "Everyone who dies is processed at the HalfWay House. I've seen babies ripped from mothers' arms. I've heard the screams as new devils are dragged into Hell...."

Mitchell's voice fades away in my head and is replaced by a faint ghostly echo of a young mother screaming to keep her baby.... I've heard those screams, too, in my nightmares. It's not just my own cries that haunt me.

"Oh, Mitchell!" exclaims Angela's mother. "Human beings are so conditioned and accustomed to doing what they are told that even in death, they follow each other like sheep. When you arrived at the HalfWay House, what was the first thing you all did?"

"But with esteem and respect, Angela's lady mother," asks Alfarin, "what does that have to do with how you stayed here?"

"What did you all do when you arrived at the HalfWay House?" repeats Mrs. Jackson patiently.

"I went where everyone else was going," replies Johnny. "When I died, the HalfWay House was a grand palace, like Versailles, they said. I thought they would look after me."

"It wasn't like that when I died," replies Mitchell. "It was the same glass-fronted building it is now. I went inside because some dude was about to kick my ass. Everyone kept asking me how I died, and I was looking for a way out. But before I knew it, my photograph was being taken and I was told I was going to Hell. I just thought they were insulting me. I didn't have time to process that I was dead."

"And you, Prince Alfarin?" asks Angela's mother.

"I went searching for Valhalla," says Alfarin proudly, puffing out his enormous chest. "They told me it was in Hell, so there I went to be reunited with my brethren. I ran into the mouth of Hell before the Grim Reaper had finished speaking, and I have never regretted my haste."

"What about you, Medusa?"

But suddenly I don't remember.

"M?"

I don't remember.

"Medusa, are you all right?"

"I don't... I don't remember."

Owen coughs, but not because he needs to. He does it to get my attention, and he is successful.

"Why can't I remember?"

"Ye were probably traumatized, M," says Elinor, slipping her arm around my shoulders. "Death isn't easy, unless ye are Alfarin."

But it has nothing to do with trauma. I'm dead because I fell from the Golden Gate Bridge on December 2, 1967. I know the Grim Reapers got my name wrong and marked me down as a suicide, but I can't remember arriving at the HalfWay House.

I remember slipping. The horrible lurch in my stomach. I can still taste the fear, and when I sleep, I can still feel the wind whipping my skin. The cold rush. I couldn't breathe.

Then darkness and a split second of the most intense pain I have ever experienced. My brain, exploding into fragments within my skull.

And what then?

I can't remember being told I was going to Hell. All I can recall is seeing a cadaverous hand writing the word *Medusa* on a sheet of paper. I can't remember that first time waking up in an overcrowded dorm. I know I worked in the law office, and I remember the interview for the trainee patisserie chef position.

Paris, and fountains, and strawberries on my tongue. More ghostly images start to blur into one flickering gray mass in my shattered brain. I'm being haunted by a past I'm not even sure I own.

I'm going crazy. How can a person forget being told they're dead?

"I followed," says Owen softly. "I followed men onto the field, and I followed them into the HalfWay House. I just followed."

Mrs. Jackson takes my hand. It's neither hot nor cold. It's just pressure on my skin. A ghostly imprint.

"Well, I didn't follow. And neither did my mother before me," she says. "Angela has probably told you that cancer has an unfortunate habit of attacking the women in our family. Because of that, I had time to plan and time to think. I've never been much of a follower, you see, Owen. Always striking out on my own, that was me. I thought if I lived my life differently, perhaps the cancer would leave me alone. Unfortunately, it doesn't discriminate. My mother—Angela's granny—found me again, just before it was my time. Because she was family, I could see her, but I was in so much pain, I thought I was hallucinating. She told me not to follow. Then I appeared to Angela just before her time to tell her the same thing, but she decided on her own path."

"So you aren't dead?"

"Oh, I'm certainly dead, Mitchell. Indeed, I am deader than any of you. The traits of human existence that you are allowed to keep in your immortal domains do not work on me. I do not sleep, I do not eat. I feel no pain, which at first was a blessing, but I feel no empathy, either. I am a true ghost haunting the landscape of the earth. Others can see you, and you are all surrounded by a thin nimbus of light. The living see me and I am white vapor. The living would not fear you, even if they thought you were different. But they fear me and those like me."

"But you're holding my hand," I whisper. "You can't hold my hand if you're vapor. And you do have empathy in your soul, because you want to look after the Dreamcatcher."

"I'm holding your hand, Medusa, because that is what I know I should do, not because I want to. And I'm corporeal to all of you, choking devils included, because we are all dead."

"So you don't actually *want* to look after that little boy?" I ask. "Then why would we give him to you?"

"What choice do you have?" replies Mrs. Jackson. "The ghosts upon the earth are aware of the tradition of The Devil's

Dreamcatcher. We see and hear what happens to those who have served their usefulness. They are returned here, and the destructive force of their little bodies is used to terrible effect by The Devil and his servants, the Reapers. Earthquakes, hurricanes…they are the remnants of each Dreamcatcher—"

"My brother is next on the list," interrupts Mitchell. I tense up, waiting for his body to immolate, but although I can smell burning, Mitchell doesn't burst into flames. I think he realizes that what he has to say is too important now.

"Your brother?"

"Septimus—he's the top servant in Hell—he told me my little brother is next on the list. Septimus wants the Dreamcatcher taken back to Hell, and if we do that, then M.J.—my brother—will probably be too old to be picked when the time comes again. But Medusa has a better plan. We're going to stop The Devil from ever needing a child Dreamcatcher."

"How?" asks Mrs. Jackson, her eyes widening.

"I think we'd all like to know that," says Owen.

"I have a plan," I reply. "That's all you need to know for now."

And I do. But I can't tell the others. They'll only try to stop me. Even Mitchell, with everything he has at stake. The Devil's dreams can't be worse than my nightmares, and I've been existing with those for a long, long time.

Which is why, when we get back to Hell, I'm going to offer myself to The Devil as his next Dreamcatcher.

21. **An Existing Paradox**

Mrs. Jackson offers us the use of her home while we're training; she says we can stay as long as we like. This isn't a field trip, though, so we remain where we are.

Mitchell and Alfarin continue to work on their immolation. Alfarin is proving to be an absolute natural, although it takes another three attempts before he can turn himself on and off at will. It appears Elinor's death is his trigger, but she's also his trigger to stop. All she has to do is call out to him and his flames vanish in an instant.

Mitchell is still struggling, though. His immolation isn't as intense as Alfarin's—who explodes like a bomb—but it takes Mitchell longer to get it under control. As a result, he burns for a lingering period, and his form takes longer to recover. Mitchell's clearly in a world of pain, but he doesn't complain once. His bravery astounds me. Mitchell isn't an in-your-face warrior like Alfarin, but I don't think he appreciates how much we—I—admire him.

Jeanne is already an expert at flying, and as she continues to teach Owen, it becomes clear that she knows how to control the air around her. She does this so well that she can hover just above the ground, with a faint nimbus of stars surrounding her. The Maid of Orléans looks so beautiful and serene, and precisely the image of what people who are living think angels should look like. I'm sure of it now: she's definitely done this before, but when I finally dare to mention her immolation she refuses to talk about it.

Owen's transformation gets him from A to B—eventually—but he has little control. Jeanne gives him a target: a snow-covered ridge on one of the mountain peaks, but he overshoots it by miles. He's starting to get frustrated, and I notice that when he hovers, his movements affect the pinecones and needles on the ground. They whizz around his army boots, as if caught in a funnel of wind. The effect of flying is also changing Owen's appearance. After every flight, his skin is paler, so much so that by the time we call it a day, his face looks like white marble.

Jeanne's light-brown skin is unchanged, and I add that to the list of questions I know she'll never answer.

I think we'll be ready after one more day of training. Our moment in time, right now, is January 1, 2015, but when the time comes to confront the Unspeakable, I think we'll have to be back to the date we left Hell. We just can't run the risk that another child will be chosen to be the Dreamcatcher in the time that has elapsed. We haven't slept since we left Septimus's office in such a rush, and although we've been to moments in time in San Francisco, Washington, the UK, and now New Zealand, I think in true terms, we've only been gone from Hell for a day or two at the most.

One more day, and this could be over for the others.

And then everything will be over for me.

When it's time to call it a day, Angela wants to go back with her mom. But when the rest of us elect to stay on the shores of Lake Pukaki, she reluctantly decides to stay as well. Owen takes Mrs. Jackson home and reappears a minute later. He says he won't let Angela do it because he's still mad at her for using the Viciseometer to involve her mom in the first place. Secretly I think he's angry at himself. I think Owen's scared he's losing his humanity because he never thought of the Dreamcatcher's future, either. For a while I was mad at myself for this, too, but I've been doing some thinking, and

I've decided my true humanity disappeared the second my fingers slipped from the bridge. I'm an echo of my living self. And I have to wonder, if I stopped the behaviors that the Highers left us devils with—like the desire to eat and sleep and breathe—would it make any difference at all?

In the back of my mind, I hear my conscience telling me that I'm only saying these things to harden myself up for the battles to come. Taking back the Dreamcatcher is only part of the war. The real horror comes after.

And I'm scared.

Night falls, and the eight of us make camp beneath a canopy of towering pine trees. We light a fire, but we keep it small because we don't want to be seen. My body is telling me I should sleep, but I'm fighting the sensation and winning. I've never seen a night sky like this, and I want to remember it. Millions and millions of stars gaze down at us, like glitter sprinkled over a black blanket. There is a huge cluster directly above, which Mitchell says is the Milky Way. He starts pointing out constellations and the different swirling galaxies that make up the universe.

"Are ye making these names up, Mitchell?" asks Elinor as Mitchell maps out the sky with his index finger. "Because that is the strangest bull I've ever seen. It has only two legs and no head, for one thing."

"No, I'm not making it up," Mitchell replies indignantly. "And I'm telling you, that constellation is called Taurus. I wanted to be an astronaut when I was little. My mom and dad used to buy me space books. They said those were the only things I would read."

"Tell us about Orion the Hunter again, Mitchell," says Alfarin. "To be placed in the stars is a great honor. I would like to hunt bulls and giant crabs. Tell me, do the heavens also have winged beasts and monsters from the deep? My brethren and I would wage war against them all, and it would be bloody and savage and glorious."

"I think that cluster, the one near that red star, should be named after you, Alfarin," says Angela. Johnny is lying across her legs, and she's absentmindedly twirling his red hair through her fingers. "It looks like there's an axe right in the center of it."

"That red star is Mars, which is actually the nearest planet to ours," says Mitchell. "And Alfarin deserves to have a whole galaxy named after him."

"My friend, that is the nicest thing you have ever said about me," replies Alfarin, and even in the moonlight I can see he is a little misty-eyed. "You, too, shall be immortalized in the stars. I name those three stars in a row after you, as they remind me of the sticklike form you possess. Indeed, I shall find stars for all of Team DEVIL."

"Do you call yourselves that because you're devils, or does it actually stand for something?" asks Angela.

"Dead but not Evil Vanguard In Life," replies Elinor. "Mitchell thought of it."

"Only smart thing I did the last time," mutters Mitchell.

"What about Team ANGEL?" asks Alfarin. "It is not as majestic as our glorious name, but I am interested to hear what name you gave yourselves as you prepared for battle. Wars have been won and lost on the fear of a name alone."

"We weren't preparing for a battle, Alfarin," replies Owen. "But we did name ourselves before we left Up There."

"And?" asks Elinor. "What is it?"

"It is ridiculous," mutters Jeanne.

"No, it isn't," replies Angela defensively. "And Team DEVIL did exactly the same thing."

"Which merely proves my point," says Jeanne, rolling her eyes.

"ANGEL stands for Armored Ninjas Going to Emancipate Life," says Angela triumphantly. "I thought of it."

"I like it," I reply, not because I do, but because Mitchell and Alfarin have burst out laughing and now Angela looks a bit hurt.

"My point is proven again," mutters Jeanne, but everyone ignores her.

"Armored Ninjas," says Mitchell, still laughing. "That's awesome."

"I like the word *emancipate*," adds Elinor.

"Well, He approved," says Owen diplomatically. "And for angels, Up There's approval is all that matters."

"Can ye see Up There from down here, Owen?" asks Elinor. "Is it on one of the stars or clouds?"

"Heaven is an immortal domain, Elinor," replies the soldier. "We aren't in the skies, the same as devils are not trapped below the earth."

Mitchell sits upright. "What do you mean? Hell's in the center of the earth, isn't it?"

Owen shakes his head. "We all exist in another realm. When we die, our forms move on, so while you might think you have been sent Down There, the truth is you exist in a different place altogether. One I believe the Highers created, just for the dead."

"That cannot be true," says Alfarin. "I have read many books in Hell's library, more than most devils combined, as has Elinor. We have never heard of such a thing."

"It isn't broadcast, Alfarin," says Owen wearily. "There are so many secrets. Some are kept quiet for the greater good, and some . . ." Owen trails off.

"But Hell feels the tectonic plates of the earth shift," I reply. "We have to be in the center of the world."

"Such arrogance," mutters Jeanne. "You are devils, and yet you still believe yourselves to be at the heart of it all."

"Shut up, Jeanne," says Angela. "That's not what Medusa meant at all, and you know it." She's clearly still pissed at Jeanne for mocking her team name, but regardless, I'm really starting to like Angela. She reminds me of a modern-day Elinor. Her heart may not beat, but it's definitely in the right place.

And she's stopped being so touchy-feely with Mitchell.

Jeanne rises into the air and hovers several feet off the ground. The nimbus surrounding her is even more pronounced in the darkness, and she glimmers with a golden sheen.

"You know nothing of life and nothing of death," she snarls. "You are all so wrapped up in your sorrow and self-pity. There are millions of the dead who would glory in the opportunities that have been afforded to you by General Septimus, and yet you are totally ignorant about your existence and the domain where you dwell. Knowledge is power, and you fail to use it."

"Knowledge is power?" I reply. "Are you kidding me? You came out on this mission with Owen knowing absolutely nothing. You didn't know about the Skin-Walkers, for a start. Owen is the only one of you angels who knows a damn thing."

"Hey, don't get pissy with us," says Johnny loudly. "And I'm getting a bit fed up with everyone making me out to be stupid."

The tranquillity of the stars is broken as the two teams descend into trading insults. Even Elinor starts in on Jeanne for causing trouble; Jeanne in turn yells at Alfarin for one thousand years of ignorance.

"Why did you say that, Medusa?" asks Owen.

"Don't get high and mighty with me, Owen. I'm sick of you and Jeanne always trying to pick a fight, but at least she's obvious about it. This is your fault. You and your superior I've-read-your-file-Medusa-and-you've-died-twice garbage. You've been insinuating that you know secrets about us since we joined forces."

"What did you say?" asks Mitchell suddenly.

"All I wanted was to enjoy one final moment of peace, before everything goes to shit," I continue. "But no, the angels have to start fighting with us—again. We went looking for you, hoping you could help us save a little boy, but it was just too much to ask, wasn't it?"

"What did you mean about Owen reading your file and you dying twice?" Mitchell demands.

"It's nothing, Mitchell," I say, shooting Owen a look. "Just some nonsense that Owen keeps going on about. In fact, I take it back, because Owen doesn't know a damn thing, either. I'm starting to suspect that no one here has any knowledge and not one of us has any power. Every one of us is a pawn, and we have been since the day we died. Knowledge isn't power, not when you're dead."

If I was expecting some sort of divine intervention or confirmation of my tirade, it doesn't come. The mad rantings of a mad girl with mad hair evaporate in the air. They float up into the star-filled sky and disappear into the cosmos with every other word that has been whispered, spoken or shouted since the Highers created the living, because I'm irrelevant, and I have been since the day I was born.

"Owen, what did you mean when you said Medusa has died twice?" asks Mitchell for a second time.

Once again I see a flash of red around Owen's pupils, and curiosity supplants my rage. Why do his eyes keep doing that? It doesn't happen to Angela or Johnny, or even Jeanne, who is more devil than Team DEVIL combined. Does it happen when he's angry, or scared?

Or does it mean he's manipulating us? I'm suddenly struck by the thought that maybe Private Owen Jones isn't an angel at all.

"Have you ever read Medusa's personnel file, Mitchell?" asks Owen, stepping away from me.

"Most of it, but some of it was marked *personal*. And I didn't read that, because it's private."

"It's *personnel*, not personal. And seeing as you've just interviewed her for a role in the accounting office, I would have thought that the first thing you would have done is check the details on her records. If you had, you would have seen that Medusa, or Melissa Olivia Pallister, has had two dates of death recorded."

"How do you know I've just interviewed Medusa?"

"Septimus has his spies in Heaven, and Heaven has its spies Down There, Mitchell."

"Ignore him, Mitchell," I say. "This is all just another war game to you, isn't it, Owen?"

"No war is a game. But the winner is the one with the best strategy, all the same," says Owen. "I'm not trying to scare you, or disarm you. I've said all along that you're special, Medusa."

He reaches out to touch me, but Mitchell gets there first. Owen reels back as Mitchell lands a right hook on his jaw. Jeanne drops down to intercept, but with a speed that betrays his huge form, Alfarin grapples the French warrior from behind, pinning her arms to her sides as she thrashes to release herself. She tries to fly away, but Alfarin sinks his heels into the ground and holds on.

"I will not hurt you, French wench," he booms, "but you will not attack my friend."

"*Stop it!*" scream Elinor and Angela as Owen picks himself off the floor and launches himself at Mitchell. Johnny looks completely torn as to which side he should be fighting on. Instead, he tries to become a peacemaker by forcing himself between Mitchell and Owen, but Mitchell is taller and Owen is broader, and the three of them are soon rolling around on the ground. Fists are flying, and I don't think any one of them has any idea who they're connecting with.

"Stop messing…with Medusa's…head!" yells Mitchell. He extricates himself from the two angels and staggers to his feet. The second Owen stands up, Mitchell punches him again.

"You…know…I'm…speaking…the…truth," groans Owen. "You all know."

"Why am I feeling pain?" calls Johnny, rubbing his ribs. "I'm an angel, we aren't supposed to feel pain."

"It'll be the Skin-Walkers," sobs Angela. "They've done something to us."

"To Hell with the Skin-Walkers!" cries Elinor. "M, what is Owen talking about? Does this have something to do with why we were outside yer house in San Francisco?"

"I can't remember."

"Have ye died twice?"

"I don't know. I don't know why you were outside my house that night. I don't know, okay? I just don't know."

I start running. I was always good at long distances at school, and somehow I feel as conditioned in death as I did in life.

It feels strange not breathing as I power along the shoreline, but I want to defy this entire existence that was forced on me. I won't breathe, I won't breathe, I repeat in my head as I reach a narrow pathway, cleaved through the undergrowth that leads away from the lake. There are a million stars above, but without the moon and the small fire we lit by the shore, there is no light to guide me. I'm running blind, away from whatever this truth is that the others seem to know about me, and the lies I don't want to say.

But then hot hands grab me and I tumble into the prickly bushes. Mitchell scoops me up and pulls me around the thick trunk of a tree. He puts his hand over my mouth as two figures crash past us, but Owen and Johnny can't see us in the darkness.

A solitary shooting star flies high above.

"It's Jeanne," whispers Mitchell. His mouth is so close to my earlobe I can feel the soft fuzz on his face against my skin. "Alfarin is staying with Elinor and Angela, but Elinor is freaking out, Medusa. You need to come back."

"I'm not right, Mitchell," I whisper back. My hands have grabbed hold of his T-shirt and he is pressing against me. "There's something wrong with me—there always has been."

"San Francisco doesn't matter, not anymore," he whispers. "The only things that matter are the Unspeakable and the Dreamcatcher."

"But if I've died twice, how do I know what's real anymore? I could be an existing paradox."

"You're here, with me and Alfarin and Elinor. That's what's real now."

Mitchell's mouth moves a fraction so his lips are brushing my cheek.

"What's wrong with me, Mitchell? Why don't I exist properly?"

His lips graze my jaw. Mitchell's doing this deliberately; I can feel the slight bend in his back as he lowers toward my mouth. I let go of his T-shirt, only to slide my hands underneath it. His skin is blistering hot. I spread my fingers, trying to touch as much of him as possible. My mouth finds his, and it's so gentle on mine, but his fingers are desperate, clawing into my hair as we fall back even harder against the tree. One of his legs moves into the space between mine and he leans into me fully, from head to toe. With my arms now around his neck, we continue to kiss as if our existences depend on it. I can taste strawberries on his mouth. My stomach is flipping and fighting, and for one glorious instant, my night under the stars is the most perfect moment ever. The past and the future are forgotten as Mitchell and I are cocooned against the universe.

Then the cries of a child break through my shield.

22. The Red Mist Descends

A sensation of intense cold washes over me. The hairs on the back of my neck stand at attention, as if an electrical current has been fired through every nerve ending in my scalp. For once, any self-conscious thoughts I have about my hair are gone. Nothing matters, except that little boy.

But the two teams are now two fractured groups. Owen and Johnny have run off into the darkness, and Jeanne is flying in the heavens. Alfarin is with Elinor and Angela, but what if the Unspeakable is near them now?

Mitchell and I break apart. "This is it, Medusa," he gasps. "Shit, we're not ready."

"Go back to Alfarin!" I cry, pushing Mitchell away. "If the Unspeakable's here, the Skin-Walkers will be here, too. You have to look after Elinor and Angela."

"What about you? I'm not leaving you." Mitchell grabs for me, but I push him away again. Harder, so he knows I mean it. For a few seconds, I experienced something wonderful, and now the Unspeakable has contaminated that, too.

The Unspeakable. My anger surges through me. In life, in death, that...that...*thing* has haunted me.

Now I am going to end him.

"I'm going to find Owen," I explain. "I need that other Viciseometer."

Neither Mitchell nor I want to part, but we do. He heads off in pursuit of Alfarin; I go in the other direction. My feet stumble through the undergrowth. Twice I fall, head over ass, as my Converse sneakers catch in roots and broken branches. My hands sting violently as thorns and other objects I cannot see pierce my skin.

Dare I call out to Owen? I can still hear the cries of the Dreamcatcher, but they're higher-pitched than before. It sounds like he's hurting, and I feel it, too, deep in the pit of my stomach, because I know what it's like to be scared and alone and in pain.

Now I hear shouting that seems to be coming from several directions in the dark. After a moment of careful listening, I think they're actually concentrated on the shoreline, but in this impenetrable darkness, under a canopy of thick fir branches, I can't see enough to confirm it.

I have no choice—I have to call for Owen and Johnny. They need to find me, because I know I won't be able to find them.

Just as I'm about to holler for them, a heavy weight tackles me to the ground. It pushes down on my body and I feel the fabric of my shirt tear. Hands are grasping at my skin, and I'm paralyzed by a fear I haven't felt in over forty years.

"You're coming with me."

The rasping voice is not the one that has haunted my nightmares, but I know it's him because of the smell: oil and beer and salt. My stepfather is pinning me down, and the bravery I thought I possessed is gone. To the Skin-Walkers he's an Unspeakable: a person who inflicted such incredible cruelty on earth that he's forced to endure an existence of unbearable torture in the nine circles of Hell.

But he's so much more than that to me. He's the monster my mother brought into our lives.

And he destroyed them both.

I thought I could dismiss him. That he wasn't worth naming. But I realize that Rory Hunter can never be an Unspeakable to me. I am who I am because of him.

And I hate him.

I hate him.

I hate him. I hate him. I hate him.

My body starts to shake uncontrollably. I know what's about to happen, and I release myself to the inevitability of fire. In real time, it could be seconds, but as I immolate, the last fifty years of life and death flash before my eyes. I can see my mother's proud smile as she brings home a handsome young man; the smile turns to a frown as she puts down a telephone; she sobs into her hands; then I see my grandmother with open arms, reaching for me....

...water droplets on an orange steel structure; my feet, slipping...

...Alfarin with snarling wolfhounds at his throat; Elinor in a burning building...

Rory screams and the fire in front of my eyes is extinguished. I did it. I immolated and I'm still here, lying supine on the forest floor. I'm too shocked to move. What were those other visions? I remember my living memories well enough, but those images with Alfarin and Elinor weren't real, were they? It felt as if I had experienced them, beyond knowing about them from just words.

Scalding hands reach for my throat, and my arms are no longer pinned by my side. Self-preservation kicks in, and my fists start pummeling every part of Rory I can reach. I hear a whimper, and I realize that he has the Dreamcatcher on his back, and the little boy's arms are wrapped around his scarred neck.

"Bitch." My cheek burns as his spittle sprays my face. Then Rory slaps me.

The explosion from my next immolation throws my stepfather into the dark. He could be six or sixty yards away; I just can't tell.

...a tree with branches shaped like tusks...

...splashing with Team DEVIL in a shallow pool...

"*Medusa!*" cries an English voice, and the flames are vanquished. The voice is quickly followed by a streak of golden light that illuminates the entire area.

Owen and Johnny crash through the trees, but momentum has them both and they trip and roll down the bank toward the rock-strewn shore.

I see Rory. He's about twenty feet away from me, and now he has the Dreamcatcher tucked underneath one of his arms like a sack of potatoes. The boy isn't struggling at all. His arms hang limply toward the ground.

Why doesn't my immolation last as long as Mitchell's and Alfarin's? And why do those visions seem so familiar to me?

Rory is inching toward me now. "He told me it would be you," he says in a cold, rasping voice. He heaves the little boy up toward his armpit to get a better grip. "You've been betrayed, you stupid bitch, and you never had a clue. Now come with me, or I will use the kid, I fucking swear it."

I don't know what to say to him. Who betrayed me? I want to scream and tear his head off. I want to run away and never see his face ever again. I feel so dirty and ashamed and sick of everything that Rory Hunter was, and still is.

I hear rustling in the surrounding foliage. "Stay back, all of you," growls Rory. He yanks the Dreamcatcher up in front of his scarred body like a human shield. The little boy is conscious, with wide-open eyes, but he's no longer crying. Long dark stains have left a trail down his T-shirt.

Stepping through the undergrowth are Mitchell, Alfarin, Elinor, Owen, Angela and Johnny. Jeanne is still high above, illuminating the scene like a searchlight. Rory is surrounded by a heptagon of devils and angels. Alfarin is the only one who's armed, but the others are shadowed with a fierce determination. I don't think Rory understands, but every time he repositions the Dreamcatcher in front of him, he only increases our resolve to rescue the boy.

Two fractured teams have finally become an army.

"Put the boy down," booms Alfarin. "This will not end well for you, deviant."

"Don't test me... I'll use it. I'll destroy you all with it. He told me how to use it, and I will. I'll fucking destroy all of you."

Angela's hand reaches out to me, and at first I think it's just because she's scared, but then I see a flash of silver in the light afforded by Jeanne.

It's the other Viciseometer.

Rory starts to whisper to the little boy. Suddenly, a red mist starts to creep around our legs. It's coming from the child, who is now crying silent streams of blood again.

"What is this devilry?" yells Alfarin. He raises his axe above his head as the mist winds its smoky crimson tendrils around our legs. It's burning hot.

Elinor and Angela scream out, and so does Johnny, as the mist snakes higher and higher around our bodies.

The ground splits apart with an earth-shattering roar. I throw myself forward and grab hold of a hanging root as the dirt beneath me starts to crumble into a deep fissure in the ground. Towering pines are uprooted, and I can only watch them plummet into the newly formed hole, which is at least the length of a tennis court. Red mist is now pouring out of the Dreamcatcher's hands, and the screams of pain are getting louder.

In the smoking crimson mass, I can just make out Alfarin and Elinor on my left; I can't see Mitchell, Owen or Johnny at all.

"Medusa…Medusa…help me…I'm slipping!" cries Angela. She is also hanging by a root, but hers is thinner than mine, and I can see that it's coming away, dropping Angela farther and farther into the chasm. The red mist is winding its way around Angela's bare arms, and although the light from Jeanne is dimming, I can see that Angela's arms are starting to blister with yellow pustulating sores.

I'm still holding on to the angels' Viciseometer, and without thinking, I tuck it straight into my pocket and make to grab Angela. But as I snatch at her T-shirt, two things happen simultaneously: Angela screams, a high-pitched, primal shriek that jolts me back into the memory of my own death, and I feel the two Viciseometers connecting.

"I've got you," I whisper, thinking I've scared her because I've become invisible.

"The mist…the mist…" sobs Angela. "It's got Johnny."

Then Elinor screams, and I watch helplessly as a shadowy figure falls through the mist into the chasm below us.

"*Elinor!*" roars Alfarin, and another, much bulkier figure drops down after her.

An explosion from the deep throws me clear of the fissure. Angela lands next to me, and I hear a dull snap. A fireball explodes out of the hole as a blinding flash of lightning spears the earth. My friends down there are immolating.

And all the while, the red mist is burning into our skin. The pain from the boils now erupting over my bare legs is agonizing.

"Where's Medusa?" groans a loud voice. "Did she fall? I can't see…I can't see."

Rory's voice rises above the din. "*Give me Melissa Pallister or there will be nothing left of any of you.*"

Every instinct I possess is pushing at me to help Angela, who is lying in a heap on the ground with one leg bent at a strange angle. The mist is sliding all over her body, tearing at her skin. She's an angel and not supposed to feel pain, but she can feel this. They all can.

I'm invisible, and I have a choice: do I show myself to Rory by helping the others, or do I try to take back the Dreamcatcher and end this now?

"I am *Medusa*," I hiss quietly.

And I start running in the direction of his voice.

23. Manifestation of Evil

The red mist has covered everything and everyone, but the strange bubble that enclosed Owen and me the first time the two Viciseometers joined together is back. It distorts my view of everything around me, but I can also see the black outline of a lightning-shaped crack in the ground. Deep inside it is a golden glow. It isn't fire, yet I can't exactly make out the source of its light. But because I can see the fissure that Rory created with the Dreamcatcher, it means I can dodge around the edges without falling in.

I can't see or hear any of the others anymore, and it terrifies me. How deep is that hole, and what will happen to anyone who has fallen into it? They can't die again, so it isn't that which frightens me; it's the thought of what will happen if the earth closes back up with devils and angels still trapped down there.

The reality that the Dreamcatcher is finally being used as a weapon truly hits me as the sores spreading across my legs and arms reach my neck. The pain has been dulled a little by the pressure in the invisibility bubble, but my neck burns and itches and I can't stop scratching. I only stop when I feel my skin peeling away, in thick strips that smell like bleach under my blunt fingernails.

A concentrated patch of red mist appears in front of me, and I momentarily stumble because it's shaped like The Devil. For one hideous second, I think he's here with us, but then it implodes on itself before taking the outline of the master of Hell once more.

It's Rory and the Dreamcatcher. It seems that the evil they have unleashed on us is manifesting itself in the shape of the being that created the dreams in the first place.

Sprinting now, I try to block out the pain radiating from my wrecked body. Ahead I see Rory crouching over the Dreamcatcher. My forehead connects with Rory's temple as I head-butt him as hard as I can. My fingers clasp the slippery hot skin of his face, and I stick one thumb into his eye with all the strength I have. He screams a terrible long shriek, almost like a wolf's howl, and he claws in the direction of my face with his spare hand. But it doesn't have the same effect as my attack on him because he has several fingers missing. The rough stumps feel as if they have been hacked off and left to rot, and the jagged skin scapes across my cheek.

"Where are you, bitch?" he snarls, reaching for me, and I move my arms to his waist. I feel physically sick being this close to him, touching him, but the fact that the Dreamcatcher is still in his other arm helps keep my mind fixed on what I have to do.

I'm going to drag Rory to the edge. He'll have to drop the boy if he wants to hold on.

Unfortunately, we're still some distance from the chasm.

Just then a familiar fireball slams into all three of us.

"Not my brother!" Mitchell hollers.

He must have been thrown clear when Alfarin exploded inside the fissure. Mitchell's immolation has engulfed Rory, the boy and me. The pain I'm now in is a world away from anything I've ever gone through before. It's beyond endurance—it's not human.

Then again, I'm not human, not anymore. But it's hard to forget when you can smell your flesh melting.

"Let go of the boy!" I cry.

"He betrayed me!" screams Rory. "He let me out and betrayed me."

I don't have time to try to figure out what—or who—he's talking about. My nose and throat are too filled with smoke and the scent of burning flesh. I loosen my hold from Rory's waist and pull on his free arm, trying to drag him toward the crater's edge.

The little boy is completely untouched by the red mist and

Mitchell's fire. I can see him, staring up at me, from his position underneath Rory's arm. He stretches his arms out to me, but as he does, the blood from his eyes starts weeping again.

"*Help us!*" I scream. "If anyone can hear me, *help us.*"

Several bolts of lightning hit the fissure again, but something strange is happening. It takes me a moment to realize that the rays of light are not shooting down from the sky, but are rising up from the ground.

The streaks of light are quickly joined by another enormous fireball that throws me at least thirty feet into the air. Alfarin, Elinor, Owen, Jeanne, Angela and Johnny somersault past me before I land with a steaming splash in Lake Pukaki. Everything is now in slow motion. Fire and light and screams and smoke. It's all so unreal.

Someone drops into the water next to me. I think it's Elinor, but as I kick my way toward the body, I see a white T-shirt, stained with blood. It's bubbling up like a flotation device.

Rory has let go of the Dreamcatcher.

I have him. I have the little boy.

24. The Voice of The Devil

With a strong front crawl, I swim toward the Dreamcatcher, who is floating on his back with his eyes closed. An orange glow illuminates the aquamarine water, making it look brown and dirty. Contaminated. I'm not sure if the fire on the shore is the small one we lit earlier, or whether devils are still immolating, but it calls to me like a beacon showing me the way to safety.

"I've got you," I say, gently levering my right arm underneath his tiny body. He isn't moving at all and doesn't register hearing my voice.

I quickly scan the water and see someone else, about twenty feet from me, splashing and flailing. Long red hair confirms it's Elinor.

"I can't swim!" she cries. "M, help me, I can't swim."

A scream echoes into the night, followed by the excited howls of wolves.

"Hang on, Elinor," I call. "I'm coming."

More screams from the shoreline, and terrified shouts of "No, no, no!" The pitch of the wolves' cries is rising. I can still only make out two distinct howls, but the noise coming from them is so rapid, it sounds like they're hyperventilating.

The wolves are excited. That can mean only one thing. They have someone.

The little boy is a lightweight, and he barely slows me down as I swim on my side with him toward Elinor. I make a grab for her dress, but she's panicking so much that all three of us are suddenly dragged under the water.

"Elinor!" I shout as I surface. I'm forced to let go of her. "Stop thrashing! I can get you out, but you have to stay calm and trust me."

Different noises are now coming from the shore. Along with the screams and cries, I hear a wet tearing sound, like something is being shredded. Torn apart.

"He's not to be trusted," says a high-pitched voice next to me.

Now it's Elinor's and my turn to scream. I've heard that voice before—moments before my interview for the other intern job.

The Dreamcatcher is speaking with The Devil's voice.

"M, that was The Devil! What's happening?" cries Elinor.

The three of us go under the water again. The Dreamcatcher repeats the same sentence, but because we are under the lake, the voice sounds deeper and even more menacing.

I kick to the surface and tread water as I try to stabilize Elinor on her back. The Dreamcatcher is still underneath, and I can see the bubbles—which clearly aren't air—floating up to the surface as he continues to talk. Each bubble breaks as it reaches the top and disperses into bloody ripples.

The awful sounds from the shoreline, the ice cold of the water, and the sight of blood rising from the Dreamcatcher's words are too much. I push the red slick away, and the sight of my blistered arms, covered in yellow sores, is the last straw. I start to gag. The sound of that is enough to make Elinor gag, and then she starts to panic again and she goes back down under the water.

"*Why me, Septimus?*" I scream. "*Why us?*"

The Dreamcatcher rises up and I grab his T-shirt. I no longer care about being gentle; I'm going to get him and Elinor to the shore if it's the last thing I do.

"He's not to be trusted," says the Dreamcatcher again, his eyes still closed.

"I know," I sob. "He was my stepfather. I know all about him."

"Not the Unspeakable," he replies, continuing to speak with the same voice as the overlord of Hell. "The Devil is a bad man."

"I'm scared, M!" cries Elinor. "And it hurts."

"I know, Elinor," I reply, pulling her and the boy onto their backs again. "I'm hurting, too, but this will be over soon. We've got the Dreamcatcher. We can take him to Angela's mom and…and…"

I stop supporting Elinor and, in a blind panic, plunge my blistering arm into the lake toward my shorts pocket. The Viciseometers are gone. The fact that I'm visible to Elinor has only just registered.

Where are the two time-traveling devices? We can't get the Dreamcatcher away if we don't have them. He'll be taken back to Hell.

My strength is failing fast. I can barely keep the three of us afloat as my exhausted legs feebly kick us back to the shore. I'm shocked when my feet touch the stony bottom of the lake. Inch by inch, I carry and drag Elinor and the little boy out of the water. Elinor collapses on the ground, but the little boy, now wide awake, wraps his tiny fingers around my wrist.

"He meant for this to happen," he says. "I'm sorry."

I have no idea what he's talking about, but I don't have time to find out. I have to find the Viciseometers. They must have fallen out of my pocket as I was thrown into the lake.

I lead the Dreamcatcher behind a large bush. "Stay here," I tell him. "Don't let anyone see you. I'll come back for you soon."

He nods, and I start running toward the dark pine trees. I've gone about fifty yards when I'm stopped short by the sight of Mitchell and Alfarin, who are lying on the ground, groaning. Alfarin's axe is several yards away from him, but he isn't even making the effort to reach for it.

Then, as I get closer, I see why. Their skin is splitting apart with weeping boils that are pulsing with bloodstained pus. Their sores are a thousand times worse than mine and Elinor's.

The lake must have diluted some of the effect the red mist had on us. But we were the only ones who got cleansed. Everyone else stayed out here.

I have to get Team DEVIL back to Hell, but I can't do that without the Viciseometer.

"You are wasted with Septimus, child."

I know that voice. Visolentiae the Skin-Walker is suddenly at my side. Blood is smeared all across his mouth and down his chest. The wolf head on top of his is licking its bared, sharp teeth with a black tongue. The stench from his body hasn't changed.

"You have the Unspeakable!" I cry. "Go back to Hell and tell Septimus we need him."

"And why should we help you?" asks Cupidore, stepping out from behind Visolentiae. He is covered in even more blood than his partner. It's dripping from his hands. I start swaying.

"Mitchell and Alfarin have to get treatment; they've been infected with something. It's destroying them. Please...we helped you get the Unspeakable."

"And what a treat he was," says Cupidore; he starts sucking and licking his fingers. "It's always better when they fight, but he was a fool to trust him. The Unspeakable was the conduit. He was never going to get his life back, although what a vessel you would have been."

Mitchell and Alfarin have stopped groaning. I kneel down beside them and take their swollen hands in mine. Tears are streaming down my face, and the salt stings my sores.

The Skin-Walkers are enjoying this verbal torture. I don't care what they've done to Rory, but they said they wouldn't hurt any of us.

Then the Skin-Walkers' laughter suddenly stops short. I look up to see them lowering their bodies to the ground; their heads are so low, the wolf snouts are almost touching the grass. They look exactly like cowering dogs.

"Wh—" I start to say, and then I feel the sweet touch of the Dreamcatcher as he wraps his fingers around my wrist again.

"You were supposed to stay put," I say.

"The angels," he says in the voice he's absorbed from The Devil. "He meant to hurt the angels. All of them."

"I don't understand."

The Dreamcatcher lets go and drops down beside Mitchell. He

slips his little hand into Mitchell's pocket and pulls out a black cell phone.

"You can call Septimus with this," says the Dreamcatcher.

Cupidore and Visolentiae are whimpering like pathetic dogs. Their bodies are lurching, as if they're trying to move back. But they can't, and they don't like it one bit.

"We will get Septimus," whimpers Visolentiae. "Just take the weapon away."

"Bullshit," I spit harshly.

"He's not to be trusted," says the little boy. He holds his arms up to me, as if he wants to be held, but I lower myself to his height and take his hands in mine.

"You can't be seen by Septimus," I say. "You need to run and hide again, and stay where you are this time. I mean it. I'll find you, I promise. But if anyone else sees you, they'll take you back. You have to hide."

I kiss his head and gently push him away. I know that the moment the distance is far enough, the spell on the Skin-Walkers will break and I will be at their nonexistent mercy, but there's nothing else I can do. I have no Viciseometer, and Mitchell, Alfarin and Elinor need to get to Hell's sick bay—fast.

But the Dreamcatcher isn't running and hiding. He won't move. I push him again, but he shakes his head.

"You have to hide. Otherwise Septimus will take you back," I plead. "Please, run away."

The little boy is pointing over my shoulder. I turn around to see what it is he won't run from, and my blistered legs give way.

Septimus is standing right behind me.

25. The Devil's Betrayal

After living for sixteen years, I thought I knew what anger looked like. After existing in Hell for forty years, I believed I had seen pure hatred.

But I was wrong. What is radiating out of Septimus right now is beyond any of those emotions.

It's his eyes that give him away. It's always the eyes. The Devil and the Skin-Walkers have black, inky pupils, like pools of shimmering tar. Septimus's eyes are crimson red in Hell, but here, back in the land of the living, his anger has turned his eyes into pools of fire. I can see the flames licking at the whites, and in the darkness, they're terrifying, because he doesn't look like he was ever human. He's a monster, a god, something you should never, ever betray.

And he's just heard every word I said.

Septimus is tall and thin, just like Mitchell, but he's looming over us in such a way that his body looks twice as large. Everything about him seems enormous, from the golden hoops in his earlobes to the knot in his black silk tie.

"Where are the angels?" asks Septimus. He surveys the area, and as he turns his dark head from left to right, I hear his neck crack. It's an unsettling sound.

"I don't know," I whisper. "But Mitchell, Alfarin and Elinor have been infected with something, Septimus. I know you're angry with me, but please, help them first. And I'll take his place. Take me instead of the—"

But Septimus raises his hand, and I immediately fall silent.

"We have little time. We have all been betrayed, Miss Pallister. The other domain, too."

Septimus sweeps past me and goes straight to Mitchell and Alfarin. He bends down and pulls back one of Mitchell's closed eyelids. As it opens, yellow pus oozes out.

"Oh, Mitchell," says Septimus softly. "I am so sorry."

"Elinor is infected as well. She's down by the lake."

"Miss Pallister, where is the Viciseometer?" asks Septimus.

"I don't know. I lost them, I lost them both."

"Use the Dreamcatcher to find them. He'll be able to see. I must get Team DEVIL back to Hell and into quarantine before this manifests itself too deeply."

"Septimus—"

"Later, Miss Pallister. We must prioritize, and the safety of my charges is number one. Alas, I will have to take the angels as well. I wish there were another way, but there is not."

"But the boy—"

"Not now, Miss Pallister," booms Septimus. "Cupidore, Visolentiae, it disgusts me to even consider this, but you must each take two of the angels. Transport them into quarantine area number seven."

"Our job here is done," replies Cupidore with a sneer. "We have the Unspeakable, and soon he will be back in chains, once we have regurgitated his worthless remains back into the circles of Hell."

The two Skin-Walkers howl with laughter, but Septimus is in no mood for fun. He steps forward and grabs Cupidore's pelt. The wolf head snaps and growls as Septimus drags him to a tree and shoves him against it.

"*Do not test me*," roars Septimus. "You will each take an angel, or Fabulara will be informed of how you defied her edict on the handling of devils."

"We have done no such thing," spits Cupidore.

"Your word against mine, and you know whom she'll believe."

"Septimus, please," I beg. "Just take Mitchell, Alfarin and Elinor. I'll stay here and search for the Viciseometers. The angels can be taken back Up There once I've found their device."

But Septimus ignores me. The two Skin-Walkers slink off into the darkness; I can hear them sniffing. Elinor is still lying on the shore, but I can't go to her yet, and the thought of leaving her there alone, even for a minute, is destroying me.

Septimus grabs hold of Alfarin and, to my absolute amazement, hauls him over his shoulder. Then he does the same to Mitchell. I don't know how Septimus can carry Alfarin, let alone Mitchell as well, but he does without breaking a sweat. His fire-filled eyes turn to me.

"I will return for Miss Powell shortly and then come back here. Do not move from this place in time in my absence, Miss Pallister. I know what you're concocting in your head, but you cannot possibly hope to achieve it alone."

And then he's gone and it's just me and the little boy. The Dreamcatcher leans into me and wraps his little arms around my swollen legs. It hurts so much, but I can't push him away again.

"Do you know what a Viciseometer looks like?" I say softly, stroking his strawlike hair.

The Dreamcatcher nods and answers, "Yes," in The Devil's voice.

"There are two of them here, somewhere. Do you think you can help me find them?"

"I know where they are," replies the Dreamcatcher. "I know where both of them are, because I saw them fall out of your pocket. You tried to help me." He hugs me tighter.

I'm trying so hard not to scream. Everything hurts, inside and out. My arms and legs are blistering badly now, and I can't see properly. The world is starting to double up and swim around in my peripheral vision. The only thing that doesn't move is the Dreamcatcher, but I don't want to look at him because I know I've failed. I thought I could save him. In my arrogance I thought I could change Hell and deceive not only Septimus, but The Devil as well.

All I managed to do was unleash a toxic cloud of poison that is eating away at my friends.

"Don't be upset," says the Dreamcatcher, and when I look down, I see that his tears of blood are falling, too. "The pretty watches are just over there."

He's pointing to the edge of the fissure that he helped create. It's closed up a little now, but it's still dangerous. I have no idea in this darkness how far down it goes. It must go some way, because Jeanne flew into it to save the others who had fallen.

It's probably a shortcut to Hell, I think.

"It is," says the Dreamcatcher.

"What? How did you—"

"I can see inside your head. Are you always so sad?"

Now my nose is running and my eyes are blistering and it feels like there are great chunks of grit rubbing against my retinas. It all hurts so much.

"I haven't met anyone like you before," says the Dreamcatcher. "Your head is jumbled up."

"What do you mean?" I ask, sobbing so hard now my chest is rattling.

"The others, like that man with the yellow beard and the girl with red hair, I saw into their heads and they only had one, but you have two."

"Two of what?"

"Memories."

"I don't understand."

"You've died twice," says the Dreamcatcher. "But they made your first death disappear by changing time. So you had to die again."

"Who made my death disappear?"

"The devils. The dead people who love you. The ones Septimus took away," replies the Dreamcatcher. "Is Septimus going to take me away, too? Is he going to take me back? I don't want to go. The Devil is a bad man—he has bad dreams that he makes me keep in my head."

I pick the boy up and hold him tightly against my chest. So Owen was right. This is as close to the truth about my existence as I have ever come. I think of all those details that are held in personnel records, but because most of us don't read the damn things, no one knows.

But Owen knew about me, and so does the Dreamcatcher. And I would bet everything that Septimus does as well.

"Please show me where the Viciseometers are," I whisper. "And tell me exactly what you see in my head. I'll get you to safety, I promise."

"And how will you do that, Miss Pallister?" drawls Septimus. He's back already. I slowly turn to face him. "Without Private Jones or Miss Jackson," he continues, "you will be unable to find the wandering ghost that is Miss Jackson's mother."

Instinctively, I back away from him, shielding the Dreamcatcher as I move. I won't hand over this little boy. I won't, not without a fight. I don't care if there's nothing left of me by the end, but I have to save him.

"Stay away from us, Septimus!" I cry. "You're not taking him."

"I have no intention of taking the Dreamcatcher back to Hell, Miss Pallister," replies Septimus softly. "Not anymore."

"I'm offering myself in his place, Septimus." I take several steps farther back as the pressure from two little arms around my neck increases. "I'll be The Devil's Dreamcatcher."

"I've told you before that you are an exceptional person, Miss Pallister," replies Septimus. "Your willingness to sacrifice yourself to such a fate is further proof. But this is not a matter we can discuss right now.

"As we speak, Mitchell, Prince Alfarin and Miss Powell are being treated in Hell's quarantine section, as are the four young angels. I fear the angels' predicament will be the most grievous of all, and no doubt they'd prefer to be Up There, but I had no choice." I cringe at the thought of Team ANGEL in Hell. "Their timeline is now in sync with the time that you all left my office," continues Septimus. "And I'm relieved to report that the Unspeakable is back with the Skin-Walkers. Right now, you and I must transport the Dream-catcher to the protection of the ghost of Mrs. Jackson, and then I need to return you to Hell for treatment." He looks at me sadly. "You are not doing as poorly as the others, but you will get worse without proper care."

I'm still digesting his words about the Dreamcatcher. "You mean you won't take him back to Hell and The Devil?"

Septimus takes several long strides toward me until he's only a couple of feet away. For the first time, I notice a big lump on his forehead. It's shaped like an egg.

"I was deceived, Miss Pallister. There are times I forget—foolishly—about the true nature of the office for which I work. But not even I thought..." Septimus trails off and looks across the shimmering lake. Starlight is reflecting off the surface, now that the fires of Hell are gone.

My thoughts drift back to the accounting office, where this all started. Something falls into place. "That red mist, the smoke that hurt us," I say. "It's the weapon that you spoke about in the office, isn't it?"

Septimus raises his hand, as if to touch the Dreamcatcher, but pulls away before making contact. I see the Dreamcatcher as a little boy, but Septimus still sees him as something else. Something worse.

"So much sacrifice," mutters Septimus. "And nothing ever changes."

The Dreamcatcher is pulling at my hair, or maybe he's trying to push it away. Either way, he's got my attention.

"The pretty watches are over there," he says. "Put me down. I can show you."

I gently lower him to the ground, and he immediately takes my hand in his and starts to pull me over to the end of the fissure. Faint smoke, not red but gray, is snaking up from it. I can hear voices coming from inside. Shouting, crying, screaming and howling.

"There are people down there. Are you sure you got everyone away, Septimus? I think someone's still down there."

"Team DEVIL and Team ANGEL are all accounted for," he replies. "The voices you hear are the dead. It is a portal to the true Underworld."

"To Hell?"

"Not the Hell you and I know, Miss Pallister. This is a portal to the nine circles. The domain of the Skin-Walkers. What you can hear is the inner essence of the Skin-Walkers, much like what you experienced when two of them decided to travel through time with you."

"But Alfarin fell down there, and I think Johnny did, too."

"As did Private Jones and Miss Powell," replies Septimus. "They were saved by Mademoiselle d'Arc. This makes her fate even more repulsive to me."

I'm about to ask him what he means, when the Dreamcatcher suddenly runs ahead with an excited squeal. He crouches down, then straightens and runs back to me. In each of his hands is a Viciseometer: the red one from Hell, and the blue watch from Up There.

"Take the Viciseometers, Miss Pallister," instructs Septimus. "We must not change the date. You have crossed one timeline with the ghost of Mrs. Jackson, and therefore must remain in that stream so as not to confuse her. I will determine her whereabouts in the timepiece."

I pick up the boy and balance him on my hip. Owen used the Viciseometer from Up There to take Angela's mom home, and I decide that will be the one I use now. I look up at Septimus for affirmation, and he nods. I don't ask Septimus how he knows what we've done, because I know he won't tell me. But he's been keeping an eye on us, somehow, this whole time.

I move the time forward by five minutes, just to allow a big enough gap between the time when Owen left Mrs. Jackson's house and when Septimus is about to show up.

We're ready, but there's one thing I do want to ask him before we go. "Who deceived you, Septimus?" I ask. Yet as soon as the words are out of my mouth, I realize I already know the answer. The one person powerful enough to deceive Septimus is also the only person powerful enough to release my stepfather from the nine circles of hell. There was only ever one person it could have been.

"I don't want to go back to him," says the Dreamcatcher.

"You are not the only one, child," replies Septimus darkly.

"I want my mommy."

The face of the blue Viciseometer starts to swirl. Ice-cold stars bounce around the palm of my hand and between my fingers, like fireworks.

"I will place one finger on the Viciseometer, Miss Pallister, as I visualize the final resting place of the child," says Septimus.

A blanket of azure blue rises up in front of us, but while the view of traveling with Up There's Viciseometer is serene, the sensations I feel are not. It's nothing like traveling with the Skin-Walkers this time, but it's unsettling all the same. I feel nothing. I can't smell, I can't taste. The sense of pain I had before has been replaced by nothingness. This is what it must feel like to be an angel, and I don't like it. There is no sense of self at all.

The pain returns as soon as we land. The Dreamcatcher falls from my hip as my legs give way and I sink into red gravel.

"Hold on, Miss Pallister," says Septimus. "I will leave the boy. Just hold on."

I'm lying in a shallow, stone-filled hole. I try to raise my head, but I can't. I want to say good-bye to the Dreamcatcher, but my throat is now so swollen, nothing comes out. He looks back at me once as he follows Septimus through a line of trees. The Devil's accountant still won't touch him, and I'm overwhelmed by the feeling that if I could speak, I wouldn't be saying good-bye to him, I would be telling him to run.

The world is dissolving into time and space. The images I'm now seeing, haunting me before my eyes, don't make sense. I can see the HalfWay House, glinting under a rainbow, but that dissolves into an image of Elinor throwing a young boy out of a burning building.

So much fire. I'm burning up. No wonder Jeanne was so scared of the flames.

Alfarin is on fire, too, but not through immolation. Instead, he's lying on a longboat in choppy water.

I've changed my mind. I want to be an angel. I don't want to feel this pain anymore. I don't want to feel anything anymore.

But I have offered myself up as the next Dreamcatcher, and I know that soon, I will never feel anything but pain.

"Don't let me go, don't let me go."

The words are in my head, but they aren't mine. They belong to another Medusa. The one who disappeared from time?

"Don't let me go."

Septimus is back. We disappear on the wind.

26. The Sacrifice

When I wake up, I'm lying supine on a rock-hard bed. It's comfortably warm. I blink several times as tiny red spotlights shine down on me.

Where am I?

There's a slight whiff of antiseptic in the air, and something else, too. I think it's lavender, because it reminds me of the flowers my grandmother used to have in huge clumps in her garden.

"Don't try to move," says a bored-sounding voice over an intercom. "You won't get very far if you try."

So, of course, I do—and quickly find out that I can't. There are thick straps holding down my arms and legs. I raise my head, just a fraction, and see wires and tubes of various colors, pumping liquid into my limbs.

"What's going on?" I ask. "Where are the others? Where are Mitchell, Alfarin and Elinor?"

"You really need to stay still, you know," replies the voice, completely ignoring my question. "The antiserum takes far longer to work if the...patient...is resisting."

"Antiserum...what are you putting in me?" I cry. "Where's Mitchell? Where's Septimus?"

There's a crackle, and then another voice—with a deep southern accent—drawls throughout the room.

"You are in quarantine, Miss Pallister," says Septimus. "As is the remainder of Team DEVIL."

"What happened? Where are you? I can't see where you are."

"Healer Travis, could you leave us for one moment?" asks Septimus. "Miss Pallister needs to be debriefed, and as I am still unable to enter her decontamination chamber, I will have to do it over the speaker system."

"Can't do that, General Septimus. Orders from The Devil. All eight are to be kept under observation."

My neck is aching, so I lie flat once more, trying to take in my surroundings. The room looks small, only fifteen square feet at the most, and it's windowless. I know I'm back in Hell when I note the black stone walls, but unlike the rest of Hell, they don't drip with moisture. There aren't any shadows, either, even with the red lights above glaring down.

I'm naked underneath a white sheet. There's no sensation of pain anymore. The only part of me that I can really see is my hands, and they are a pale orange. There's a drip with three red prongs inserted into the middle three fingers on my right hand. On the left, there's a thick yellow tube dispensing liquid into my wrist. My skin is actually bubbling up as the mixture pumps through my body.

The next sound I hear is a dull thump, quickly followed by the clatter of several metal implements falling onto the rock floor.

"Miss Pallister?" says Septimus over the intercom.

"Septimus, what's going on?"

"Healer Travis has just—accidentally—fallen onto my fist. It is ironic just how many times these days I find myself saying these next words, but we do not have long."

"The little boy?"

"Is gone. The official report is that he was destroyed when the Unspeakable unleashed him as a weapon. You and I are the only ones who know the truth, but the lie has been accepted and the truth will stay with us. There is to be a meeting in the next twenty-four hours, when the next Dreamcatcher is chosen."

"Not Mitchell's brother."

"He was the next name on the list. A threat to ensure that Team DEVIL did not fail. This is not a situation of my choosing, but I am running out of options, Miss Pallister."

"You have to get me out of here, Septimus."

"You need to think this through very carefully, Miss Pallister. Your intentions, while very brave and noble, could unlock a chain of events over which you will have no control. I strongly counsel you against this course of action."

"Septimus, get me the Hell out of these straps. I won't let them take any more children."

I hear a groan, an exclamation, and then another dull thud. The intercom crackles once more.

"Healer Travis appears to have fallen onto my fist again," says Septimus. "Never mind, he will have a story to tell in the medics' quarters tonight."

The room shudders and dark-blue light smothers the red, creating a dirty brown haze. "Hm. Evidently I *am* able to enter the decontamination room." Warm hands release the bonds on my arms.

"I will leave you to unstrap the remainder, Miss Powell. You will find some clothes on the ledge underneath your bed."

Septimus slips out of the room, and the rock door closes again. With fumbling hands, I slide my fingers across my chest, my thighs and finally my ankles and release the straps that held me to the bed. My skin, once smooth, is rippled with lumps: scars from the red mist infection.

I stand on the hot stone floor, completely naked, and so dizzy it's a wonder I'm standing at all. Before I put clothes on, I have to remove the IVs from each hand. I don't like blood—and I *really* don't like dead blood—but Travis the healer won't stay out of it for long and I have to act fast. With a high-pitched squeal, I pull the thicker tube out first. Yellow liquid, which looks like pus, throbs out of the end of the tube and onto my skin. I dry-heave at the sight and wipe my hand over the white sheet. The liquid immediately burns a hole in the fabric.

"What the…" I swear aloud.

Now I have to take the three prongs out of my right hand. The only thing that motivates me is my fear that Septimus, or Travis, will walk into the decontamination chamber while I'm standing here butt-naked.

The skin around the puncture points wrinkles as I slide the three prongs out of my hand. Two of the thin needles are dispensing bloodred liquid; the center needle is releasing red vapor that smells like coffee.

Finally free, I bend down and search for the clothes Septimus mentioned. I pull out a plastic bag and find navy cotton shorts, underwear and a bra, and a white V-neck T-shirt sealed inside. They fit perfectly.

"I'm ready, Septimus," I call, and the room shakes once more as the rock door opens. Septimus is standing in the entrance, framed by blue light, and Mitchell, Alfarin and Elinor are standing directly behind him.

I want to run toward them, but my legs now feel as if they're ten times too big for my body. Everything is disjointed and new.

"Ye will get used to it, M," says Elinor. She slips past Septimus and takes my arm. "Ye should see Alfarin trying to walk. It's like watching an elephant on a tightrope."

"Where are your brother and the other angels?" I ask. "Are they okay? Septimus said they were here."

"They will not let me see our John," replies Elinor. She bites down on her bottom lip.

"We know they are here, though," says Alfarin darkly. "We could hear Jeanne screaming." He tries to push past Septimus and accidentally sends him flying into an alcove. "My apologies, Lord Septimus. My legs still don't belong to my masculine form."

"Why haven't the angels been returned to Up There?" I ask. "The little boy—the Dreamcatcher—he found their Viciseometer."

"Oh, M," whispers Elinor. "It's so unfair."

"We will debrief you on the way to level 1, Miss Pallister," says Septimus. "But I believe Healer Travis will be awakening soon, and

I would truly hate for him to make accidental contact with my fist for a third time today."

Walking is as awkward as a three-legged race. We stumble forward on shaky legs until we eventually reach an express elevator. For the first time in Hell, I'm not crushed by the dead, because the corridors are deserted on this level and eerily silent.

Why isn't Mitchell speaking to me?

His face is a mess of scarred lumps and burned skin, and his scalp is bald in several small patches. He winces with every step, but his teeth are clenched together so rigidly that his jaw is jutting to the side.

"Septimus," I say quietly. "Can devils immolate in Hell?"

My new boss leans forward and presses a black button with the raised outline of The Devil stamped in the center.

"One cannot immolate in Hell, Miss Pallister. Our immortal domain produces too many emotions in a person for that to occur. A devil may sense they are feeling true rage, but never underestimate the subconscious and the dilution of the senses that this can cause. A devil has never immolated in Hell before because our confines are too claustrophobic. Indeed, the vast majority of devils have never even heard of immolation, let alone managed it."

We enter the elevator with difficulty. Mitchell still won't look at anyone; his restored pink eyes are burning through the floor. It's as if he's staring into the very pit of Hell.

The nine circles of Hell are here, somewhere. The Skin-Walkers and the Unspeakables could be right under our feet.

It's Rory Hunter who's on my mind as we stumble along the level 1 corridor toward the accounting chamber. I can sense my body absorbing the heat of Hell once more, but I'm shaking, and my skin feels cold, as if there's an icy breath blowing on me.

I know The Devil was the one who let Rory out. I know he tricked Septimus and the HBI and everyone by letting Rory take the Dreamcatcher back to the land of the living.

But why?

"Medusa, what's wrong?" asks Elinor.

The others have reached the door to the accounting chamber, but I've stopped walking without realizing. There are a million thoughts racing through my head, and none of it makes any sense.

The enormity of what I'm about to do is paralyzing. I can't tell Elinor what's wrong, because that means I'll have to say good-bye.

Good-bye... Oh, no.

With a flash of understanding, I realize why Mitchell isn't speaking to me—to any of us.

He's saying good-bye to us by saying nothing at all. Mitchell Johnson is going to offer himself to The Devil, too.

I suddenly find the strength to move.

"Mitchell," I say, grabbing his arm.

"Drop it, Medusa. He's *my* brother."

"But—"

"I said drop it."

"You—"

"Did you think I wouldn't guess your plan, Medusa? You're the most selfless person I've ever met, but what right do you have to offer yourself? Did you seriously think I would stand by and let someone else—let you—sacrifice yourself?"

"I am confused," interrupts Alfarin. "I thought we were here to return the Viciseometer after another marauding in the land of the living. What in the name of the gods are we sacrificing, and to whom?"

"Mitchell and Miss Pallister are both prepared to offer themselves as a replacement for the Dreamcatcher," says Septimus solemnly. "They do not want the next device to be a mortal child."

"What?" cries Elinor. "Ye cannot allow this. Ye mustn't, Septimus."

"It is not my choice, Miss Powell," replies Septimus. "I do not want this, and if there were any other way, I would gladly take it."

"So ye will sacrifice one of yer interns?" she screams. "Ye mustn't!"

"There must be something else that can be used as a

Dreamcatcher," says Alfarin. But whatever Septimus is about to say remains unspoken, because the doors to the Oval Office have opened, and a little woman has walked out.

She's old. I think she must have died when she was at least eighty. Her hair is gray but is swept up into a severe bun that stretches back the skin around her eyes. It makes them look catlike. She can't have been dead for long, because her pupils are pink. The old lady is wearing a black skirt and a pink twinset with a pearl brooch.

"Keep the noise down, Septimus," she scolds in an Italian accent. "The master is going through his official papers, and you know he cannot concentrate if there is noise."

"I apologize, Lucretia," says Septimus.

The little Italian lady takes a long, hard gaze at each of us in turn.

"You should not have brought children up here," she replies. "The master isn't sleeping, and if he were to see one of them—"

"We aren't children," interrupts Mitchell.

"Again, my apologies, Lucretia. We will come back later. I wasn't thinking."

"Well, I don't care what The Devil's doing," announces Mitchell. "He's not taking my brother."

And he forces his way through the doors, quickly followed by Alfarin and Elinor.

"Septimus, you have to stop him," I beg.

I run after Mitchell into a large oval room. Long drapes hang along the walls, each topped off with elaborate tasseled pelmets. The entire room is a riot of color; I can sense a nosebleed coming on just looking at it. One side has pink curtains made from plush velvet. The other is covered in gold-and-green fabric imprinted with shapes that are actually moving in a hypnotic cycle.

And directly ahead, sitting behind a large mahogany desk, is The Devil.

The Devil himself. A mythical entity who is, in fact, very real. And I'm actually standing in his office. I swap looks with Alfarin and

Elinor, and they are as dumbstruck as I am. Elinor is, in turn, grabbing at her neck and then wringing her hands.

The Devil hasn't seen any of us. We could back away now.

But Mitchell won't—and neither will I, regardless of how terrified the mere aura of this office is making me feel.

"Lucretia, I can't decipher Hannibal's writing," The Devil wails. He is bent over a document lying on the desk in front of him. His face is so close, the swirl at the end of his goatee is touching the paper.

"Sir, you have visitors," announces Lucretia.

"Not the French delegation again," sighs The Devil dramatically. "How many times do I have to tell them? I'm allergic to cheese. Brings out the worst boils on my—"

Then he looks up and sees Team DEVIL, pockmarked and battle-weary, from a fight that he sent us into. Completely unprepared. Completely in the dark. It might have been Septimus who gave the orders, but it was The Devil pulling the strings. He released my stepfather from the circles of Hell; he told Rory how to unleash whatever toxin was stored in the Dreamcatcher. I wouldn't be surprised if it turned out to be The Devil's blood that was used to write that message.

"Interesting," says The Devil, with a smile that bares his pointed teeth. "So this is Team DEVIL. They appear to have recovered better than the other lot. Speaking of which, how is the other lot doing, Septimus?"

"The effect was the same for all, Sir," replies Septimus, but I'm shocked by how cold his voice sounds. The Devil picks up on it immediately.

"Oh, come now, Septimus. You were taking too long. Sometimes the bull has to be taken by the horns. It was only a test."

Alfarin and Elinor are swapping confused looks, but Mitchell has nerves of steel, because he's looking The Devil squarely in the face with a ferocious glare.

"Operation H," Mitchell says. "This whole thing was a setup to release Operation H, wasn't it?"

"Clever boy," says The Devil. "Septimus speaks very highly of you, Mitchell. And this must be Medusa. What a fabulous name. I do love snakes, you know. My favorite drapes are the ones in the ballroom—"

"We don't give a crap about your curtains. That's not why we're here. I'm offering myself as your next Dreamcatcher," interrupts Mitchell. "My little brother, my living brother, is next on the list. I'm offering myself in his place."

But I run forward and place myself in front of Mitchell.

"Don't take Mitchell, take me!" I shout at The Devil. "I have nightmares that can't be worse than your dreams. I can take it."

"Back off, Medusa."

"You don't know what you're doing, Mitchell. You don't know what it's like to be truly haunted. I do."

The Devil stands up and walks around the desk. His long fingers stroke the goatee on his pointed chin.

"Well, this is fun, and I must say that both you interns would make fine additions to my intimate staff, but alas, neither of you could be a Dreamcatcher. You've both been corrupted."

Behind me, I hear the sound of Septimus whispering furiously to Elinor. From what I can tell, he wants her to leave the room, but she's refusing to go without me and Mitchell. Then The Devil giggles, and I want to retch at the sound.

"You're going soft on me, Septimus," he says with a smirk.

"Miss Powell, leave now," orders Septimus loudly.

"What do you mean, corrupted?" I ask, with a nervous glance toward Elinor. Both of her hands are on the back of her neck.

"A Dreamcatcher needs to be pure of heart, innocent in body and spirit," replies The Devil. His shoes tap across the floor as he starts walking toward us. "Medusa, my dear, you have been corrupted by filth. The fact that it was not of your doing or acceptance is irrelevant. And Mitchell is a young man, and as I know all too well, all young men have minds as dirty as the squalid beings from the Dark Ages. Neither of you is capable of being a vessel for my glorious dreams."

"Miss Powell, *leave now*," orders Septimus. "Sir, we will find an alternative—"

"But we have one," says The Devil quickly. "And how rare to find one of such beauty and maturity." He raises his high-pitched voice, and it's like nails down a blackboard. "*Restrain the others!*" he screeches.

Guards, completely camouflaged within the drapes, rush forward and grab Mitchell, Alfarin and me. The Viking tries to fight them off, but they overpower him with a metallic mesh net that sparkles like diamonds in sunlight. I'm screaming words, but I have no comprehension of what they are. Powerful hands are wrestling Mitchell and me to the floor. The only part of me that I can move is my eyes, and they are being dragged like magnets to Elinor. We're all yelling at her to run, to fight, but we know full well she can't. I'm retching and howling as Septimus's protests fall silent.

"It's your lucky day, Elinor Powell," says The Devil.

Elinor is paralyzed with fear as The Devil runs his fingers through her long red hair. The guards are still coming out of the walls in droves.

"My next Dreamcatcher will be you or young M.J.," continues The Devil. "Choose wisely, Elinor Powell, for I don't need to remind you that I have access to your own brother in my laboratory, and, as He well knows, I do like to hear angels scream."

27. **The Nightmare Begins**

Mitchell, Alfarin and I are swept out of the Oval Office on a tide of gaudy-looking guards. We are thrown into the level 1 corridor, and the doors shut with a solid thump. The guards' colors shift once more and they become glistening black. They dissolve into the walls of the central business district and are gone.

"*Elinor!*" roars Alfarin. "*Elinor!*"

He pounds the door with his huge fists, but it makes little difference. Mitchell joins him and the two boys throw themselves, again and again and again, at the doors, trying to force them open.

Suddenly I remember there's another way in: through the accounting chamber. I run into Septimus's office and grab the door handle. It sizzles against my skin and burns an imprint of The Devil's smiling face onto my palm. It's locked, and my smoldering skin is the notice.

"*Septimus!*" I cry. "*Get El out of there.*"

I fall back as a strange sense of déjà vu takes hold of me once more. I've never called her El before, but it also feels as if I've called her that for years.

"Stand back, Medusa!" cries Alfarin. He rushes into the room with his axe raised high. His pale-blue tunic is torn from the shoulder to his waist. The skin beneath it is red and raw from where he was slamming his weight into the doors of the Oval Office.

He starts swinging the axe at the large oak door, but it just bounces off.

"Septimus will stop him," says Mitchell. "Septimus will save Elinor."

But the brief glance he and I exchange at his words lets us know neither of us believes it. Elinor is trapped in a locked room with the master of Hell: a maniac who released an Unspeakable and tricked him into taking a toxic virus to the land of the living with the sole intent of testing its effect on angels.

"What have I done?" I cry, ignoring my spitting and sizzling palms as I pull at the door handle again. "This is my fault. I thought I could reason with him."

"*Elinor, Elinor!*" Alfarin continues to wail. He's thrown his beloved axe aside and is now beating on the door like he's beating a drum.

"I just wanted to save my brother," sobs Mitchell. "I didn't want this."

He falls back onto the floor and crawls on his hands and knees to the rune-covered cabinet.

My stomach is heaving. Every part of me has gone into uncontrollable spasms. The pain in my chest is worse than anything I felt when I was alive; it's worse than the burning from the toxic red mist. Something is eating me from the inside out, but while it chomps with a heavy gnawing, it speaks to me in my own voice. Its mocks me for being so arrogant as to think I could take on The Devil and win.

We've lost. Lost horribly.

We've lost Elinor, and for no other reason than she was the best of us all.

Days have passed. I've begun having that same nightmare over and over, night after night, again and again and again. There's a small child, the boy again, with a thick mop of blond hair that looks like straw. Tears are silently streaming down his pink cheeks. When I see his ruby-red eyes, the tears are no longer clear. He's crying blood. He holds his arms out, as if he wants to be picked up. Mitchell is holding Alfarin back. I can't see Elinor, but there are two other people in the nightmare with a halo of light surrounding them. One is a young guy with bright-red hair. The other is also male, late teens, and he's dressed in an old brown army uniform.

"Johnny, you can't help her," calls the soldier.

Then the screaming starts.

I turn around, and the little boy is no longer there. It's Elinor, and she's bleeding torrents of thick blood from her eyes into a pool around her bare feet. Someone has written on the walls in blood. The words read: *You can never have her back.*

Mitchell and I have no choice but to return to work. We don't know where Alfarin is. His cousin, Thomason, said he got arrested after smashing up his dorm, but when Mitchell and I ask the HBI, they plead ignorance.

We barely see Septimus, either, and I know Mitchell is as worried about that as he is about Alfarin going missing. Without Septimus's presence to influence The Devil, we can't bear to think about all of the horrible things The Devil is thinking, and that just makes Elinor's imprisonment even worse. Septimus knew Mitchell and I could never be Dreamcatchers, and that was why he allowed us to try, to make us feel better. He just didn't realize until it was too late that Elinor could.

"*I hate him!*" yells Mitchell on the fourth day. He throws his calculator across the room, where it smashes into the opposite wall, breaking into several pieces. I know he's trying to immolate. We both are—but we can't.

We're back in Hell, and it's mocking us.

I don't know what to say, so I keep quiet. I want to ask questions, but I don't know who will give me the answers. Mitchell, Alfarin and even Septimus are dealing with their grief and guilt by turning away from me.

Then the door opens, and Septimus walks in. His red eyes look unnaturally bloody and much larger than normal. He's lost his swagger. In fact, he's walking differently. More heavily. He has the weight of the Underworld on his shoulders.

"The master has instructed me to invoice Up There for the cost of the medical treatment Team ANGEL is receiving," says Septimus. There's no intonation in his voice—it's even lost some of its southern twang.

"I hate him," repeats Mitchell. "I hate him." It's all he says these days.

"Medusa, would you prepare the invoice?" asks Septimus. He stopped calling me Miss Pallister on my first day in the office. I nod. If I open my mouth to reply, I'll start screaming, and I'm afraid I won't be able to stop.

"Private Jones has been released from the quarantine unit," continues Septimus. "I understand from Healer Travis that Miss Jackson will have her final assessment today. I have suggested to the housing section that they be moved into segregated quarters for their own safety until they have acclimatized."

Mitchell and I swap looks, but he moves his gaze from mine first. Sometimes I want to kiss him like I kissed him on the shores of Lake Pukaki. Not with passion, but because I think it will revive me from this death. I know Septimus wants us to feel compassion toward the angels, and I do, but it's hard to feel sorry for them when Elinor is trapped in a nightmare that has no end.

Still, the cruelty that has been forced on Owen, Jeanne, Angela and Johnny is desperately unfair. They were sent out to "save" the Dreamcatcher, too, and like Team DEVIL, they were duped. The authorities Up There knew the Dreamcatcher could be used as a weapon, and they wanted to capture it to use against Hell.

But the search party ended up getting infected, and because of that, Up There won't take them back. Owen and Angela have apparently taken the news better than Jeanne, who screams in a nonstop fit for twenty-four hours a day. And as for Johnny, the moment he found out that Elinor had replaced the original Dreamcatcher, he fell into a catatonic state and hasn't moved. He refuses to talk. I haven't seen him—no one is allowed to see him—but Septimus has spoken to the healers, and they say Johnny's in shock.

No shit. How the Hell did they expect him to react to the news that the sister he's only just found is being perpetually tortured by The Devil? The idiots in this place make me sick. They're just vessels. There's no soul or humanity in anything anymore.

I can't concentrate. The figures and words written on this invoice just swirl into one amorphous mass. I pick at the toxic scabs on my arms and make them bleed, just to see the lumpy red gravy that is dead blood, because—for a second—it makes me feel like I'm sharing Elinor's fate.

We have to get her out of there. There must be another way, but I'm out of ideas. Which leads me to realize that I'm going to have to do some research.

In the vast arena of books that make up Hell's library, there just might be a tome that will give us enough information to figure out how to get Elinor back. But I'll need help to find it, and unfortunately, the only person I know who works in the library is Patty Lloyd. She won't help me—but she might help Mitchell.

I shake my head and manage to print up the final invoice. I leave it in Septimus's in-box for approval and clearance. Mitchell is watching me, and his eyes look so fierce with contempt, it's a wonder the paper doesn't burst into flames.

"Wanna go for a walk?" I ask him.

He shakes his head.

"What's the point?"

"I want to go to the library."

"I hate that place. It makes me feel stupid. And I used to ask Elinor to get books from there for me, so being there will just remind me…"

He trails off, but before he can turn away, I grab his fingers, which are sweaty and covered in ink. I don't care. Interlocking them in a cradle, I pull until they crack.

"I can't sit here thinking," I whisper. "I have to do something, anything."

"If Septimus can't get her out of there, what hope do we have?"

"That's no reason not to try."

If Septimus overhears us, he doesn't say. He appears to be absorbed in his work. Lately, when The Devil's accountant is at his desk, he just types and types, but the spreadsheets don't make sense.

Mitchell told me that the first time he took the Viciseometer, he was worried that Septimus was about to start a celestial war against Up There because of the horrendous overcrowding in Hell. But now I think Septimus has a bigger target. He's been duped and lied to by The Devil—made to look a fool. Even the HBI is mocking Septimus—albeit behind his back.

I'm pretty sure Septimus is plotting something, and as a senior devil who's been in Hell for over two thousand years, that doesn't bode well for the person he's plotting against.

There's a knock at the door, and in walks Aegidius. He's still wearing a toga, and his horrible hairy feet still squelch on the ground. Some things don't change around here.

"General Septimus, this just arrived," says Aegidius. He hands over a black envelope that is gently smoking with pale puffs of gray steam.

"About time," mutters Septimus. "Thank you, Aegidius. I take it the protocols I instigated were observed?"

"They were."

"And if any more arrive?"

"The same routine, General. I am overseeing it myself."

"Thank you, Aegidius. I won't forget this."

Without another word, Aegidius turns about and squelches out of the office, leaving sweaty footprints on the ground behind him.

"What's that, boss?" asks Mitchell. "Interdepartmental letters don't usually smoke."

"I will let you and Medusa know when the time is right, Mitchell," replies Septimus. "Now I need you both to do something important."

"What?" I ask.

"Find Prince Alfarin," says Septimus, and his bloodred eyes

flash quickly, as if someone has flicked a light on and off behind his irises. He rises from his seat, tucks the black envelope into the inside pocket of his pinstripe suit and enters the Oval Office through the side door.

The handle doesn't burn his skin with an imprint of The Devil, but Mitchell and I have been scalded so many times in the last few days, I doubt the scars will ever heal.

The Devil didn't just take our friend. He's branded us with a permanent reminder that we were stupid for thinking we could stop him.

"I can't work in this place anymore," says Mitchell. "I don't care what they do to me. All I can think about is Elinor, and I hate myself, because while she's in there"—Mitchell jerks his thumb toward the connecting door to the Oval Office—"it means M.J. is safe. So what kind of sicko does that make me? This place is turning me into a monster. We've lost everything, Medusa. Everything."

"Then help me," I plead. "I think The Devil took Elinor because she was the easy option. We—I—handed her to him on a plate, Mitchell. There has to be another way. What did The Devil use to catch his dreams before children? There must have been something, and we need to find out what, because that's our best chance. That's why I want to go to the library. There has to be a book, or records, or something that will help us save Elinor. Sitting here feeling sick and sorry and angry isn't going to help her. We need to get Alfarin like Septimus said, and the angels, and we need to tear that library apart."

The truth is, I'm prepared to do much more than that. I will tear Hell apart if that's what it takes to get Elinor back.

28. **Secrets in the Labyrinth**

Mitchell and I head out of the accounting office. Before we leave level 1, we press our ears up against the large doors to the Oval Office. It's habit now. We're listening for signs of Elinor, but what would we do if we heard her? We can't get in there.

So for a split second, I'm grateful for the quiet, because the thought of hearing her in pain terrifies me. And then I feel guilt and shame for wanting that silence.

I take Mitchell's hand in mine as we push through the crowds toward the library. He crushes my fingers, but he doesn't speak or even look at me. We still haven't discussed what happened down by the lake. Maybe that's because kissing Mitchell became the prelude to a nightmare.

But sometimes, when I'm falling asleep, I think about it, hoping it might save me from the visions of a bleeding Elinor. And sometimes I think about it when we're alone in the office together, and I see him looking as sad as I feel.

I'll admit it: I liked kissing Mitchell. But after everything that's happened, I have to wonder if it's wrong for me to even be thinking about it. Because I should only be thinking about Elinor, shouldn't I? Why can't I manage to do that?

I never deserved what Rory Hunter did to me, but maybe he was onto something when he said I'm *not quite right*.

"Medusa."

"What?"

Mitchell raises our interlocked fingers. His have swollen to the size of sausages because I've been squeezing them so tightly.

I let go. We've reached the library, anyway.

"Do you have any idea where we should start looking?" asks Mitchell, massaging his fingers.

The library in Hell is gigantic, even bigger, apparently, than the room where The Devil's annual Masquerade Ball is held. Millions and millions of books line the shelves, and the dark, musty rows are patrolled by teams of librarians, some armed with whips.

I don't understand the filing system—I don't think anyone does—but if you dare put a book back in the wrong place, you walk out of the library with welts on the back of your legs.

"You need Patty Lloyd," I reply. "We have to find the section that deals with the history of Hell, and she'll be able to help us— or rather, you. I'll hide behind the shelves while you talk to her, because if she sees me, she's less likely to help."

"And how do I find her? There are thousands of devils in here."

I snort. "Trust me, we won't need to. From what I hear, she has finely tuned Mitchell radar, fully primed. She'll find you."

I duck behind some nearby bookcases, and sure enough, it isn't long before Little Miss Wet T-shirt is sashaying toward Mitchell. She's barely managed to squeeze her breasts into her tiny top, which I'm betting was left over from when the cherubs departed Hell without their belongings.

"Mitchell," she says, sticking her hands in her back pockets, just to stick her boobs out even farther. "Fancy seeing you here. Bored with that crazy-haired Medusa Pallister already?"

She laughs, and I repress the desire to give her a close-up of my hair—via a head-butt. I need to stay back, hidden from sight. The sooner we get to the books we need, the sooner we can start making plans to save Elinor.

"Actually, I need your help, Patty," mumbles Mitchell.

Her pink eyes light up and she steps in closer to Mitchell. Too close.

"What do you want?" she asks.

"Can you show me where the section on the history of the immortal domains is?"

"I'll take you there personally," she whispers, and from my position behind a small bookcase, I see her hand move out and sweep across Mitchell's stomach. At least I think it was his stomach, because he has his back to me.

The library is packed with devils, although most of them aren't reading. Several are rocking to and fro, muttering wildly to themselves. Others are asking for the way out, and I'm pretty sure they aren't talking about the exit from the library. I keep my distance from Mitchell and Patty as they wind their way through the rows of dusty books. Thankfully, Mitchell is tall, and with his blond spiky hair, he's easy to keep in my line of sight.

The deeper into the library we walk, the darker the rows become. More than once it crosses my mind that Patty isn't taking Mitchell where he wants to go at all, but I don't say anything. Not even when some jerk with deep-pink eyes sidles up to me and puts his arm around my waist. I know what devils come down here for—and it isn't books. It's why Patty Lloyd and her friends are so at home here.

I shove the devil with wandering hands into a shelf filled with rolled-up scrolls. No one touches me without permission. As he makes contact, a cloud of dust mushrooms into the air, and I hear the angry shouts of an elderly librarian. The cracking whip and screams fade behind us as Mitchell and Patty go deeper into the labyrinthine library.

I stick close by, but I'm running out of devils to conceal me. They're thinning out. On the other hand, the place is now so dark that I don't think Mitchell and Patty would see me if I stood on their toes.

Where the Hell is she taking him?

Left, right, left again. My overactive imagination, which has experienced the absolute worse that Hell has to offer now, is waiting for the Minotaur to come roaring out of a passageway. We are so far into the depths of the library that the dust on the shelves is worse than the layers of flour in the kitchens.

Finally, Patty stops. She pulls out some matches, and her hourglass figure is illuminated in an orange flare as she lights a torch that's hanging from an iron bracket on the wall. Thankfully, Patty doesn't see me crouching down nearby. Suddenly, she pushes Mitchell backward into a bookcase. He's so surprised he falls onto his ass. Patty immediately straddles him.

"What the . . ." swears Mitchell.

"Don't pretend, Mitchell baby," says Patty, kissing his neck. "I know why you really wanted to come down this way."

"I want the history section, Patty!" cries Mitchell, and his voice is so high I imagine the Skin-Walkers and their wolf heads can probably hear him.

"No one comes down this way," murmurs Patty. She slides her hands up his T-shirt eagerly but then gasps as she feels the lumps and scars left by the toxic virus unleashed by Rory Hunter and the Dreamcatcher.

"What's wrong with your skin?"

I seize my chance and jump out from my hiding place.

"The Devil Pox," I call out. "It's really contagious, apparently. The effect in female devils isn't known yet, but for guys, it makes parts of their bodies shrivel up and fall off."

"What?" exclaims Mitchell.

"What are *you* doing here?" snarls Patty. She's already clambering away from Mitchell.

"Septimus asked me to see where you were, Mitchell," I reply. "He really needs us to go through those history books as soon as possible, but he was worried the itching and the *you-know-what* on your *you-know-what* might distract you. But don't worry, the healers have found a cream that might help it grow back again."

"*What?*"

"Help what grow back again?" Patty asks worriedly.

"So, those books, Patty. A history of Hell and anything on the

Highers are a good place to start. And also anything of the personal history of The Devil, because...because it's his birthday soon and we want to check...we want to check on his past gifts, because we don't want to replicate anything."

"Are you telling me you really did want a book?"

"Yes!" cries Mitchell.

For the first time since coming back to Hell, I actually smile.

Patty, still in shock, is staring blankly at Mitchell.

"Patty, the books?" he prompts.

She removes the flaming torch from its bracket and uses it to indicate a hallway beyond us.

"Keep walking until you get to the rock with seven heads. The historical documents are down the third aisle."

"That's way too vague. We need you to show us," I say. "It's important, Patty."

"And why should I help *you*?"

"Because that's your job," replies Mitchell, standing. "I do shit every day that I don't like doing, Patty, but I get on and do it. Now I'm asking you—no, I'm *telling* you, I don't want to get laid, I want a damn book."

"My friend, you seriously have me doubting your sex at times," booms a deep voice from the dark.

And out of the shadows steps Alfarin.

"Where the Hell have you been?" cries Mitchell. "We've been going out of our minds. We thought the HBI had locked you up!"

I'm so relieved I can't speak. Instead, I just run forward and hug Alfarin. He pats me awkwardly on the back.

"I am sorry, my friends. Losing my princess has been a blow to my soul. It is as if a barbarian has taken my axe and my manhood. I needed time alone, to grieve, to think."

"So you've been hiding out here?" I ask.

"Hiding? I am a Viking prince—I do not hide, Medusa," replies Alfarin crossly. "I came here for answers. And after much research, I believe I have found them."

I can't believe it. All this time when I was worrying that Alfarin was getting into trouble or wandering Hell in despair, he was down here, thinking. Studying. He's been ten steps ahead of us this whole time.

"What have you found?" Mitchell and I ask together.

"It seems that the Dreamcatcher was not originally a child. It was something else. Something that could cope with the subconscious thoughts and images of The Devil," replies Alfarin excitedly.

"What was it?" I ask. "Can we get it back? Could we replace it?"

"Come with me; I will show you what I have discovered," replies Alfarin. "It is down here."

Alfarin strides down the path Patty told us to take. His faithful axe swings from left to right as he moves it from hand to hand, and the curved blade glows orange in the firelight that illuminates the way. I look behind us to see that Patty is following with the torch.

"How long have you been down here, Alfarin?" asks Mitchell. "You've been missing for days."

"Then I have been down here for days," replies Alfarin. "I remembered what Jeanne said by the lake—that knowledge is power. If I cannot break down the doors to The Devil's inner sanctum with my hands, I will use my head."

"What are you guys plotting?" asks Patty, but she doesn't sound scared, or even inquisitive. There's excitement in her voice.

In the shadows, Mitchell and I exchange a glance. I wouldn't trust Patty Lloyd if she were the last devil in Hell, and judging by the roll of his pink eyes, Mitchell wouldn't, either.

But she will know where we can get answers, because Jeanne was right, knowledge is power, and that power is written in these books.

Somewhere.

A huge black mass suddenly towers up in front of us. It's a statue of a monstrous beast with seven heads. The body is grotesquely obese, with rolls of fat that ooze over one another. It has short legs and long arms. I have to look twice at it before I realize what's strange about the hands. They each have seven fingers.

Each head is different, and each is looking down a different corridor. We seem to be at a central point in the labyrinthine library.

"What the Hell is that?" exclaims Mitchell. "Whoever made it must have been stoned out of his mind."

"I'd keep your voice down, if I were you," whispers Patty. "This is a life-sized sculpture of the Highers. Most devils don't come down here, so they have no idea it even exists."

"The Highers are one...one...thing?" I have no idea what to call it. It's a monster.

"No, there are seven of them," replies Patty. "Each head is responsible for one immortal domain. They're very different."

"You are wise, Patricia Lloyd. There are few in Hell who take the time to know of the Highers," says Alfarin, gazing up at the third head. It's perched on an extremely long neck that is curled in the shape of the letter C. The head is bald, with tiny ears and a flat nose. The mouth is wide and is sculpted as if the head is screaming. Two wide eyes stare down the third corridor from the left.

"Is that Fabulara?" I ask, staring at the head that has mesmerized Alfarin. I can hear a sound coming from the grotesque face. It's eerie, like wind blowing through trees.

"Indeed," replies Alfarin, and I notice a shudder convulsing his shoulders.

"Hang on, Patty. You said there were seven immortal domains. What are the others?" asks Mitchell. "I thought there were only two: Hell and Up There."

"For those like us, yes," replies Patty. "But the universe is pretty big, Mitchell."

"This is way weird," he replies, rubbing his temples. "I'm not sure knowledge is power anymore. I kind of feel like my mind's about to explode."

"We don't need to worry about anything that doesn't concern us and Hell," I say, picking up the pace. "Tunnel vision, Mitchell. The only thing that matters is Elinor."

"Who's she? Your friend with the long red hair? Where is she?"

asks Patty. She's still following us with the torch. I look back to answer her, and as I do, my eyes are drawn up to Fabulara's fierce face. I jump as the statue blinks at me.

"That thing just moved!" I cry.

"It's made of stone, Medusa," says Patty sarcastically. "Stone doesn't move."

But the hairs on the nape of my neck are prickling. I reach back to smooth them down, and I'm reminded of Elinor's habit.

"Do you think Elinor's in pain?" I whisper to Mitchell.

"I can't think about it," he replies quietly. "Because when I do, part of me is glad it isn't M.J."

"I would have done it, you know," I say softly.

"I know—me too."

"I know."

Our eyes lock again, and this time we don't look away from each other. Mitchell's pink irises look glassy in the glow from the flaming torch.

"You didn't answer my question," snaps Patty. "What's happened to your friend? And why do you really want to know about the history of The Devil?"

She pushes herself between Mitchell and me. I get her back; he gets a full-frontal assault from her chest.

"My princess has been taken by The Devil to be the vessel for his dreams," answers Alfarin.

"Alfarin!" Mitchell and I holler. We don't want Patty gossiping, and I know from bitter experience, she's Underworld class at that.

"You mean she's a Banshee?" asks Patty.

"No, a Dreamcatcher," I snap.

But Patty swings around and glares at me in the torchlight.

"Only children can be Dreamcatchers, Medusa. Your friend is too old to be a Dreamcatcher. If The Devil has taken her, he must be reverting to the original ways."

"What are you talking about?"

Patty sweeps her long, pink-tipped blond hair back and then

forward again. A smirk plays out on her lips. She's enjoying this moment of superiority over all of us—especially me.

"Medusa, you don't want information about the history of Hell, or The Devil, at all. If you're gonna save your friend, you need to start looking for The Devil's Banshee."

29. **Nine**

"A Banshee!" exclaims Mitchell in a high-pitched voice that could shatter glass. "We need to look for a Banshee? Oh, this just gets better and better."

"I can concur with Patricia Lloyd," says Alfarin excitedly, mistaking Mitchell's sarcasm for joy. "This is the information I have also found. In the beginning, when Hell was first created by the Highers, it was the Banshee who collected The Devil's dreams. According to lore, the two fell in love and were inseparable for tens of thousands of years. But as The Devil's dreams changed, and Hell became more crowded with the dead, she left him to—"

"Find herself," interrupts Patty, giving me a triumphant smile. "If you read more, Medusa, you would have known this."

"I do read, Patty," I snarl, "but there can't be a devil in Hell who has read this far back."

"I have."

"You work here."

Our bickering is brought to an end by Alfarin, who grabs hold of my hand and starts dragging me farther into the darkness.

"Come, Medusa. You have the greatest intellect of all of us. As soon as I came across a mention of The Devil's Banshee in my research, and the role she once played in filtering The Devil's dreams, I began collecting all the information I could that might help us locate her. Once we find her, we must persuade her to return to her glorious position at The Devil's side, and then my princess can come home."

I turn and look at Mitchell. He's standing there in the shadows looking shocked.

We have to find a Banshee, he mouths. *WTF.*

"If it means we get Elinor back, Mitchell..." I call as Alfarin continues to pull me away from him and Patty.

The pounding of feet is enough to tell me that Mitchell is following us. The looming orange glow that casts elongated shadows on the floor is—unfortunately—enough to tell me that Patty is coming, too.

"Alfarin, wait. You're going to dislocate my shoulder."

"My apologies, Medusa. But I am preparing for battle, and time is of the essence."

"Have you really been down here for days? We've been worried sick."

"I have forgone sleep and food. I am a warrior possessed, but one with a purpose. Come, four heads are better than one."

We turn a corner, and Alfarin's home for the last few days towers in front of us. Patty cries out as our feet trample over pages and pages of text, roughly torn from the ancient history books of Hell.

"What have you done, you Viking criminal?" she shrieks.

"There were too many words of little consequence, Patricia Lloyd," replies Alfarin angrily. "I need information on the vessels used to contain The Devil's dreams—not what his favorite flavor of ice cream is. I only took what I needed."

"I can't be seen here with you idiots!" cries Patty. "The librarians will think I was responsible. I'll be sacked and whipped, and not necessarily in that order."

"There are more important things in death than a good whipping," replies Alfarin. "Although my great-aunt Dagmar would not agree. Right now, my beloved princess is being used as The Devil's Dreamcatcher. She has...she has been taken against her will...and...and..."

I've seen male devils cry in Hell before, but never one the size of Alfarin. His face just crumples in on itself, like a piece of paper being folded into an origami shape. His wretchedness just tears at my insides. Alfarin doesn't sob, he doesn't make a sound. His grief is beyond words.

"You don't have to stay, Patty," I say decisively, stepping over several piles of dusty leatherbound books. "But please, just show us where we can find all the existing information on this Banshee creature before you go."

Another metal bracket is fixed to the rock wall nearby, and I can tell there's something dripping down the stone. It's too dark to see what it is at first. It's only when Patty places the lit flame in the bracket and accidentally smears the stuff with her hand that I see it's blood.

An image flashes before my eyes. It's of Elinor, and she's crying streams of red. It covers her clothes, like a scene from a horror movie. I shake my head to try to dislodge the image from my brain.

"Patty, please help us," I say. "We need all the help we can get to do this as fast as possible."

"Who died and made you Queen of the World?" snaps Patty.

"Septimus," reply the rest of us in unison.

The flame on the wall flickers and then extinguishes completely for a split second before relighting. The hairs on my neck stand to attention, and a shiver goes through my spine. I have the unnerving feeling we're being watched.

"How are we going to do this, then, Medusa?" asks Mitchell. His long legs ease over a stack of books, ten high and even wider. He reaches for me and half pulls, half drags me into the sea of literature.

None of it seems to be labeled or categorized. In fact, it just looks as if it's a dumping ground for the oldest, most decrepit pieces of paper in Hell. Some of the parchment is so delicate, I can practically see the edges disintegrating before my eyes.

"Patty, please." I say again. "This is more important than any of the dumbass stuff that has gone on between the two of us in Hell.

When we're done, you can go back to hating me, but I need help to help my friend."

I try to make my voice sound soft. I hear myself echoed back, and I just sound as if my brain has dissolved.

Patty crosses her arms and juts out her hip. Her skintight jeans are hung so low I don't know why she bothered putting them on.

"Please, Patty," begs Mitchell. "We really need someone who knows this place. I'll...I'll take you out for dinner, to say thank you."

Flames of jealousy shoot through my stomach and chest. If I opened my mouth now, I would roar with fire. But Patty immediately acquiesces and jumps over the wall of books into Mitchell's arms. He releases her quickly and doesn't look at me.

"It's a deal," she says sweetly. "Let's get started. Viking, your first task is to stop ripping up books and organize whatever information you've already collected on the Banshee. Mitchell, sweetie, you come with me and we'll snuggle down in row Z666 to find more. I doubt the Viking's been down that way yet." She looks at me and smiles. "Medusa, you can go get us coffee like a good little intern."

Argh! I hate her. But I'm doing this for Elinor. That's what I have to keep telling myself. I'm putting up with this for Elinor.

"Do you need some help?"

Patty screams and I jump several feet off the ground as an English voice, slow and deeper than I remember it, joins in the conversation.

"Owen!" exclaims Alfarin. "Angela! And my almost–blood brother, Johnny. What are you doing here?"

"We've come to help you—if you'll have us," replies Angela sadly. She's staring at me, and it takes me a second to realize why. She's transfixed by my pink eyes.

And even though we're all bathed in the orange glow from the flaming torch, I can see that the three angels have started to absorb the heat and fire that come with existing in Hell. Their irises, once brown, blue and green, are now milky white with swirls of pale pink. Owen's are brighter than any of Team ANGEL's.

"I'm so sorry," I blurt out. "It's so unfair, what Up There did to you."

Angela's bottom lip is trembling, but Owen merely shrugs. It's almost as if he expected to be screwed over. I feel a rush of affection for all four angels.

"Where is the warrior Jeanne?" asks Alfarin. "Eight heads are even better than four. We will have the Banshee back by suppertime, which reminds me, my need for sustenance has returned with a vengeance."

"Jeanne is still in quarantine," whispers Angela. "They won't let her out, but not because she's still toxic, but because they're scared of what she'll do. They weren't going to let us out of segregated housing either, not yet, but then Septimus arrived and one of the healers fell into something and knocked himself out. It was Septimus who told us where to find you."

"How are you doing, Owen?" I ask.

He shrugs again. His records said he was nineteen years old when he died in the Battle of the Somme, but down here, in the darkness of Hell, he looks so much younger. They all do, especially Johnny.

"Getting used to pink eyes . . . I guess," replies Owen dully.

At this, Angela bursts into tears. She buries her head in Johnny's chest, but he doesn't help her. He stands completely still, like a statue.

"Johnny?" I say quietly, reaching out to him.

"He still has my sister, doesn't he? That Devil bastard."

"We're getting her back, Johnny," I say quickly. "We've got a plan."

"We had a plan, too," says Johnny bitterly. "We were supposed to get The Devil's Dreamcatcher. We were told to rescue it from evil. We were told ye were evil. But Heaven just wanted it as a weapon, too. And now that bastard has my sister and he's going to destroy her. There'll be nothing left of her, Medusa. And it's all yer fault."

"Johnny!" says Angela.

"No!" exclaims Alfarin.

"How can you blame Medusa?" cries Mitchell.

"Owen has told me all about ye!" yells Johnny. "I knew there was something strange about ye the first time I met ye. I'd seen ye before, I was sure of it, but I didn't know where or when. And then Owen told me ye had died twice and yer records have marked ye down as a freak. And because ye are not right, my sister's been taken by The Devil. It should have been ye—not our Elinor."

"That's enough, Johnny," snaps Mitchell. He steps forward and his arm is drawn back. "She did everything she could to prevent this. You keep talking to Medusa like that and I swear I'll put you back in quarantine."

"Died twice?" says Patty. "How can someone die twice? Are you even human?"

I'm not right. I keep hearing those words in my head, and now they seem to be coming from countless voices, screaming down on me in a cacophony of doubtful noise.

I'm not right. I'm not right. I'm not right.

I push past the devils and angels and start running. My nose prickles with the sensation of oncoming tears, but I fight back against the feeling. Life made me tough; death made me tougher. That's my mantra, and I say it over and over again, trying to block out the voices that hate me and what I was and what I have become.

Left, right, right again. I just run. I have no idea where I'm going, but it doesn't matter. Nothing matters.

"Elinor Powell matters."

I skid to a stop. The voice isn't male. It isn't female. It sounds fake, almost synthetic, as if the speaker is trying to copy what it thinks a person sounds like.

Before me stands the seven-headed statue of the Highers, and it's talking to me. Or at least the head of Fabulara is. It's hideous, but I can't look away. The oversized mouth is moving, and even though the other six heads are completely still, I can see the wavelike ripples through its grotesque, overweight stomach.

It can move, walk. I'm sure we didn't come this way before, yet here it is, standing directly in front of me.

"I see through you, Medusa Pallister. Into the depths of your tortured soul and beyond," whispers the strange voice. "You have a choice before you, but neither path will be easy."

I have a choice, all right. To stay here with this monster, or to run.

Its mouth stretches even farther and a noise, like a perverse sickening laugh, barks out of the monster.

"You will not get far, devil."

The creature can read my mind.

"I am beyond the entities of this world, but I know everything in every one of you. The guilt you feel over the fate that has befallen Elinor Powell seeps through your skin like blood. I can taste your tears on my tongue. Your cries are heard above all of those that scream from the Underworld."

As it speaks to me, its long neck swings from side to side. The motion is hypnotic. I turn my head and look back up the row of ancient manuscripts and papers I've just run down, but I see and hear nothing. At this moment in time, I am the only devil in Hell, and I am face to face with the Higher that rules all of the dead here.

Elinor. I have to be brave for Elinor.

"What choice?" I dare to ask.

"You can leave Elinor Powell to her fate. The Devil's dreams will eventually overpower her, and she will become nothing but atoms in the air. He will resume his use of the Dreamcatchers."

"Not an option," I reply as confidently as I can. My stomach has tightened into such a painful ball that I want to double over.

"Then you must carry on and seek that which left The Devil. It will not be easy. The Viking is brave, yet even he will quail from the horrors you will face on the journey."

"Nothing is worse than knowing that Elinor is suffering."

The monster lurches forward with a speed that defies its size. Fabulara's gaping mouth splits apart, and teeth the size of knitting needles snap inches from my face. I fall back into a bookcase and scream from the depths of my soul. I never knew I was capable of making such a primal noise. It's beyond fear and pain and helplessness. My body is turning to fire and ice. I can see people drowning in filth; bodies being stripped of skin by wind; the condemned trapped in flaming tombs.

The monster's head pulls back and I am left a shaking mess on the floor. My stomach heaves violently, and what comes out of my mouth is vile and green and tastes like bitter fruit.

"That is but a glimpse of what you will face if you choose not to leave Elinor Powell to her fate."

"But we only want to find the Banshee," I choke. "Then we can have Elinor back."

"Three of the nine is all I have just shown you, but there are a further six."

"I don't understand."

"You will find the Banshee in the nine."

The seven-headed monster is disappearing, melting backward into the shadows. I can't walk, so I start to crawl toward it.

"In the nine of what?" I cry.

"*Medusa…Medusa…*"

It's too much. I faint dead away.

When I wake up I find I'm back in the accounting chamber. Mitchell and Alfarin are there, staring at me with concerned faces. Mitchell is stroking my hair. I can feel his fingers bouncing around my forehead.

"Hey there," he says softly. "You've been out for hours."

"That monster…"

"Gone. We heard it, and that was how we found you. Scared Patty Lloyd shitless. She didn't realize it was real. Apparently she takes dudes down there all the time. You should have seen her running, you would have laughed."

Somehow I doubt it.

"Johnny says he is sorry, Medusa," says Alfarin. He's leaning forward, arms crossed, balancing precariously on his axe. "You should forgive him. What he said was done for the love of Elinor, not his anger at you."

"Where are the angels?"

"With Jeanne, trying to calm her down. Septimus reckons she's getting close to immolation. I think he's quite impressed, actually. If she manages, she'll be the only one in Hell who's ever accomplished it."

"The monster—Fabulara—she told me how to find the Banshee."

"We heard that as well."

"Do you know what she meant? 'In the nine'?"

Mitchell swears. Not at me. Not at anything. He just swears, shakes his head and swears again.

"What did you see, Medusa?" asks Alfarin. "What did you see when the monster roared its bile at you?"

"Dead people. Their skin was being torn from their bodies by wind. And their faces, Alfarin. They were screaming, and they didn't stop, but they had no tongues and so I couldn't hear it, but I knew the noise was there, just waiting to get me. And even when the wind stopped, and their skin grew back... they knew it was coming again. The wind was like knives. It just kept tearing at their skin... again, and again. And the smell... there were others, and they were being submerged in this brown filth."

"It is as I thought," says Alfarin. "I will go alone, Mitchell. I cannot ask you to follow me."

Follow Alfarin where? What am I missing? I prop myself up on my elbows. A stabbing pain shoots through my head, from left to right, and it's quickly followed by a large black shadow that swims across my vision in the same direction.

Then I hear the howling of wolves.

Nine.

Nine wolves.

Nine Skin-Walkers.

Nine circles of Hell.

Nine.

You will find the Banshee in the nine.

Alfarin doesn't look scared, or even confused. Determination just glows from his huge body.

"Oh, no!" I cry. "This isn't happening."

"You understand already?" asks Alfarin. "Medusa, you are truly the wisest of us all. Mitchell and I have gone through the papers we collected in the library. We brought them back here with us. The written word, and those spoken by Fabulara, all match up."

Finally we're all on the same page. We know what we have to do and where we have to go.

The Devil's Banshee, the original Dreamcatcher, is with the Skin-Walkers. If we want to save Elinor, that's where we'll find her.

"We're going into the worst part of Hell," says Mitchell.

"I will do this alone, my friend," repeats Alfarin.

"There's no way you're doing this alone," I say. "We're a team."

The three of us look around the small, cluttered office. We're a team that is one woman down, but we have a plan.

We're heading into Dante's circles of Hell. Together.

30. **A Proposition**

Septimus has his fingers locked in a cradle beneath his chin. His face doesn't betray a flicker of emotion. He did hear me, right?

A single bead of sweat travels down the side of my face. I no longer feel shock over what we have to do. My spectrum of emotions has been stretched like a rubber band, nearly to its breaking point in recent days, and what I feel now is exhilaration. It's almost perverse, but I want to hold on to this gloriously terrifying feeling.

Somehow it's empowering, knowing how we can get Elinor back.

This accounting chamber really isn't big enough for Septimus, Mitchell and me, but now there's an amped Viking prince in the office, too, and Alfarin has enough nervous energy to fire up Hell's furnaces. He's like a pinball waiting to be unleashed. In a moment he'll start bouncing off more than the balls of his enormous feet.

I kept calm when I told Septimus our plan. That we knew where the original Dreamcatcher was, and we were going to get her back for The Devil. Now we just need Septimus to get us—me—into that Oval Office to explain it to the master of Hell.

Septimus is staring at something, but I'm not sure what. His red eyes are flickering with the reflection of the candle wick burning in front of him.

"Septimus, please," I say, breaking the sweaty silence. "Just get me in to see The Devil. I'm not scared. I know I can do this."

Septimus leans back in his chair. He drums his chin with his fingertips.

"Medusa," he says in his long, deep, drawling voice. "I am astounded at your bravery and loyalty. It is an ingenious plan, but one that is fraught with more danger than I could possibly explain. I will give you one chance to walk out now, and no one will think any less of you for it. Least of all me."

"No," I reply defiantly. "Elinor is the best girlfriend I've ever had. I'm getting her back, and I will do anything—*anything*—to make that happen."

"I cannot allow all of you into the Oval Office," says Septimus, taking in the remainder of Team DEVIL one at a time. "This must be Medusa's proposition. Her task will have come full circle, and she will have to go in to see the master alone. You will have but one chance, Medusa. Decide now how you wish to play this."

Play? Septimus's word flares up in my chest like a lit fuse, burning me with righteous indignation. This isn't a game. This is real and horrifying.

But then he rises from his chair and nods to me, and suddenly *play* seems like exactly the right word. I have to play to my strengths and The Devil's weaknesses. Like anyone in a position of power, he will want to be seen to be holding on to that. A puppet master holding the strings.

I need to make him think that this is all his idea. That he's still in charge.

"You need to beg The Devil to let Elinor free," suggests Mitchell. "Cry if you have to."

"Demand that he set our princess free," counters Alfarin. "Threaten him if you have to. You may have my axe."

I bite my tongue to help center my thoughts. The guys are wrong. I can't play to fear, or to anger. I need to confuse The Devil. But how? What emotion will cause the most bewilderment to a madman?

The one emotion that makes wrecks of us all, I think, suddenly recalling Septimus's words to me by the stone wall when Mitchell first immolated. *Do not underestimate the power of love, Miss Pallister. It can blind us all, for better and worse.*

"Did he love her?" I ask Septimus. "The Devil, I mean. Did he love the Banshee?"

"Yes, very much," replies Septimus. "They were married, you know, and they were actually rather well suited. He took her leaving very badly."

"You don't say," mutters Mitchell. "The sick bastard."

"What was her name?" I ask.

"Medusa, what does it matter?" asks Mitchell. "Her name is irrelevant."

"Names are important, Mitchell," I reply. "Think about it. When my name changed to Medusa, I was able to start gaining a new sense of self. You share your name with your little brother, and I know you wouldn't change that for the world. Alfarin, son of Hlif, son of Dobin, is so proud of his name it takes a week to say it, and Septimus's name strikes fear and admiration into every dead soul, whether it's Up There or here in Hell. Names aren't irrelevant. They're personal. They can mean everything."

"Beatrice Morrigan," says Septimus quietly. "Her name is Beatrice Morrigan."

Beatrice Morrigan. That's a pretty name. Its normality makes me smile. In my head I see a slender woman with long blond hair. She's floating with her arms outstretched. Her eyes are black, like The Devil's and the Skin-Walkers. It's not a vision like the one I shared with the Dreamcatcher; what I'm seeing is just my imagination. It's nice to use it and not to be scared for once.

I think back to what Patty said, deep in the labyrinthine library. That the Banshee left to "find herself." Well, I hope she's about done, because now I'm coming to find *her*.

"I'm ready," I say. "I want to see The Devil."

Suddenly I'm crushed between two chests. I don't think

Mitchell and Alfarin coordinated their hugs, but I've become the filling in a devil sandwich.

"You are the most amazing...brilliant...brave—" stammers Mitchell.

"May the goddess Hlin walk with you, Medusa," interrupts Alfarin. "She will protect you."

"Septimus," I squeak. My voice box is being crushed along with everything else, but once Mitchell and Alfarin step back, I kiss both of them on the cheek.

"Thank you," I whisper. "For believing in me."

"Always," replies Mitchell, tucking my hair behind my ears. I brush my thumb across his bottom lip.

"Crumbs," I lie.

My thumb continues to tingle as I step away and face the connecting door between the accounting chamber and the Oval Office. It's sparking with blue electric light. I remember worrying about that when I first came up here for my interview. That suddenly seems like a lifetime ago.

The door opens without Septimus's even touching the door handle. The same one that has seared me and Mitchell countless times in recent days with imprints of The Devil.

Don't let me go.

For some reason I can hear myself saying those words, but my mouth has frozen in terror.

The door closes behind us. Septimus and I are alone in the Oval Office.

"What happens now, Septimus?" My voice is a whisper, but it still echoes in the cavernous space. "Do we press a buzzer? Do we call him? Where's that little old lady who was here earlier?"

"*We* do nothing, Medusa," replies Septimus. "From here, you go on alone."

"What?" I cry.

"You asked me to get you in here, and I have done what you requested. I have more trust and belief in you, Medusa, than you could possibly know. Keep calm and as emotionless as you possibly can. There is a door behind the red drapes opposite. You will have to reach that in order to find the master."

"Septimus...will this work?"

"Death is full of compromises, Medusa. Sacrifice and betrayal. Yet in Team DEVIL I have seen more heart and soul than in one thousand living beings."

I take a step forward, my eyes drawn like magnets to the red drapes. "Was that a yes?" I wonder aloud.

The door to the accounting chamber slams shut. Septimus is gone.

I'm alone, and the room knows it.

The Oval Office is starting to stretch and distort. The curved walls, covered in the gaudiest of the room's drapery, are trying to confuse me. For every step I take toward the red curtains that Septimus pointed to, they seem to get two further steps away from me.

I suddenly feel as if I'm walking uphill, only the incline is getting steeper and steeper and I'm slipping as the room stretches and contorts itself. I focus on the huge mahogany desk in the center. There is a large gilded throne behind it. It's ostentatious and ridiculous, but it isn't moving. The walls, the ceiling and even the floor are rising and falling in rippling waves, but if the motion were real, the desk and throne would be sliding around, too. This is all fake. It's a security device to disorient intruders. The movement of the room isn't real.

"This isn't real!" I cry.

As if in response, the Oval Office pulls apart like a Slinky being stretched and then pings back to the way it was when Septimus and I entered.

Feeling nauseous, I run across the floor toward the red drapes and pull them back. There's a single door behind them. It's made of gold and has four clouded glass panels set into it, with golden stencils showing The Devil's face.

In the center is a large gilded knocker. It's in the shape of a woman. Her golden hair is floating around her body, and her hands are joined together. Her arms form a looped piece of metal.

I clasp her hands and bring down her arms. A deep ring echoes through the Oval Office.

Through the glass panels I see a figure approaching. I want to swear, but I can't form the word. My throat feels as if invisible hands are throttling it. There's a pain in the pit of my stomach, and acidic bile is lapping at my tongue.

The door opens. It's The Devil.

He's wearing black pants and a purple quilted jacket. His black goatee is curled into a perfect C. Bottomless black eyes appraise me.

"Medusa Pallister, what a delight," he says in a high-pitched voice. "Please, come in."

"I'd . . . I'd rather not," I reply, peeking over The Devil's shoulder. The room behind him is as black and impenetrable as his eyes. "Could we . . . could we speak out here, Sir? I have a proposition for you."

"A proposition, what fun," says The Devil, but his voice is cold. My skin erupts into goose bumps. "You're clearly a favorite of Septimus's, you know. I can't remember the last time he brought devils in to see me. . . ."

He trails off, as if thinking. His long index finger curls around his goatee as he looks upward with a pout.

As he does, another figure, dressed all in white, appears behind him. My knees give way when I see her.

The Devil abandons his feigned confusion and claps his hands together with theatrical glee.

"Of course, I remember now!" he exclaims. "The last time Septimus allowed devils into the Oval Office, I came away with quite the prize. Did I not, Elinor?"

"*Elinor!*"

I scream her name and try to run forward, but an invisible force field pushes me back.

"I invited you in and you declined," says The Devil, and he

makes another theatrical face. This time disapproving. His forehead is creased, his black eyes narrowed. The index finger on his other hand ticks left to right to left like an inverted pendulum. "Tsk, tsk, Medusa. You didn't think it was going to be that easy, did you?"

I'm sprawled on my ass, my hair is everywhere, and my hands are stinging from the blow. Every single ounce of anger I have in my dead body right now is making me want to grab and pull on that ridiculous goatee until tears of blood fill The Devil's eyes. But I remember what Septimus said about trying to remain emotionless.

"I know where Beatrice Morrigan is," I say in a rush.

It's amazing how those six words have a far greater effect than any physical assault I could wage on The Devil's grotesque face.

"What did you say?" The Devil's face looms up in front of me as he speaks. It's getting bigger and bigger, as if the room is distorting again. Only, the only thing distorting this time is The Devil himself. His thin face, with skin so pale and translucent it reminds me of the ancient parchment in the library, is now so large it's taking over the entire Oval Office. I scream and scramble backward. I fling an arm up to shield my eyes as a blast of intense heat is thrown at my face. I can feel his breath, and it burns.

"*What are you?*" I scream at the monster. "*Stay away from me!*"

"I am your worst nightmare," growls The Devil, and even with my eyes shut I can see his horrible leering face burning through my eyelids. "You believed that you, a minion among millions of pathetic minions, could enter here and play me for a fool? I indulge Septimus's whims, but you are not worthy to say her name, Medusa Pallister."

"I know where she is," I sob. "I can find her. I'll bring...I'll bring Beatrice Morrigan back to you."

"*Stop saying her name!*" screams The Devil. "*Stop it, stop it, stop it.*"

The room is shaking, and my hands feel wet. I squint, not daring to fully open my eyes, and I can see that the entire floor is now deep red and glistening.

Blood. The floor is bleeding. I scramble to my feet and retch as the familiar metallic smell fills the room. Thick red blood like lumpy gravy is oozing out of the center of the room like a volcanic mud pool. It's coming so fast that my sneakers are already covered.

My stomach and chest are in so much pain that I feel as if something is inside me trying to claw its way out. The Devil's face is still grotesquely stretched out across the room. I don't know if he's really expanded like that or this is just a projection of his anger, but his dense black eyes are boring into me, reading my soul like a book.

With a guttural cry I try to expel the pain. I take a step forward, and my sneakers squelch in the bath of blood that is now at calf height.

"Beatrice Morrigan!" I scream. "The original Dreamcatcher. She's in the circles of Hell. The dwelling of the Skin-Walkers…"

But now The Devil is wailing, and his cries are biting at my very existence. Stabbing, burning. My dead body, this soul I entered Hell with, is dissolving. Blood is in my mouth. My eyes, my ears, are streaming with it.

Is this what Elinor feels? Is this what The Devil dreams?

Elinor. This is all for Elinor. My best friend. My sister. And then I see and hear it all. Elinor linking arms with me as we cross my old street. Team DEVIL in my mother's kitchen. The gun spinning across the floor. Screams. A gunshot. Mitchell and Alfarin dragging me and Elinor down the alleyway.

Don't let me go. Don't let me go.

My timeline changed. I dissolved. Me, Medusa Olivia Pallister, who died on the twenty-fifth of June in 1967, was erased from the records of Hell.

"You can't cheat death, Medusa." The Devil's voice cuts through my visions. "You can buy more time, but you all come back in the end."

It's December 2, 1967. I'm climbing over the edge of the bridge. She didn't believe me. My mom didn't believe me about Rory hurting me. She's watching me. Screaming at me to get back in the car. I just want her to believe me. Scaring her like this might be the wake-up call she needs.

But the mist has fingers. It's groping at me. Pulling me.

"*Don't let go!*" screams my mother.

I didn't. But death claimed me anyway.

31. **A Second Chance**

The room is suddenly quiet, apart from my sobs. "Why are you showing me these things?" I cry.

"Your nightmares are my dreams, Medusa," sneers The Devil. "You wanted to know." I look up to find that his face is back to normal—yet somehow more hideous than before.

"I came here for Elinor," I say, trying to regain control.

"Liar. You wanted to know how you were special. And I have shown you. You are one of the rare dead. One who tried to cheat death. Septimus is one, too. A kindred spirit. But I claim you all in the end."

"I didn't try to cheat death!" I scream. Then I notice that the door behind The Devil is starting to close. Elinor. I can't lose her now. Not when I'm this close. "My timeline changed, but it was an accident. I remember now! Rory Hunter didn't die in my first time-line, but when he was killed in a paradox, it changed my death."

"*Postponed* your death," corrects The Devil. He licks his lips, and I see that his tongue isn't forked, it's black.

"Postponed my death, then. What does it matter? I'm dead. You still got me, and I'm even more messed up than before, because I'll have to exist with these flashbacks of my previous existence forever. Isn't that what you want?"

"So now you know," says The Devil, tilting his head back in triumph. "Now get out."

"No."

"Do you want me to call my guards?" he threatens. "You've seen them before. They were gentle then. You don't get a second chance, Melissa."

"Is that what she said to you?"

"What are you talking about?"

"Is that what Beatrice Morrigan said to you? That you don't get a second chance?"

"I ordered you to stop saying her name!"

Time is running out. The door is almost shut. I have to throw everything at The Devil now, including myself.

"I'm telling you, Beatrice Morrigan is somewhere in the nine circles of Hell," I insist.

"*I know where my wife is!*" screams The Devil. Spit flies from his mouth, and it sizzles where it lands. "I know everything that happens in my domain—everything."

"Then why didn't you try to get her?" I shout. "Or was it just easier to take children who couldn't fight back?"

"You think you know about love? Foolish child."

"I know it hurts," I say. "Love isn't hearts and flowers. It makes you lose control. You stop thinking. Love makes you reactive. When you love someone, you put their happiness first, even if it causes you great pain."

The Devil slumps against his desk. He steadies himself with one hand, which gently caresses the silver metal of a photo frame that is facing away from me.

"Letting her go caused me pain," he whispers.

"Yes," I reply. "She hurt you, but you loved her." I sense that his mood is shifting, and suddenly I think I might know how to play this after all. "You loved her, and so you didn't go after her. But what if she wanted you to? Your wife could be alone and scared. She might think that you—the most powerful devil here—don't want her. If I were Beatrice, I'd be destroyed. I might be too scared to come back, even if I loved you with everything I had to give."

The Devil's back straightens. He picks up the photo frame and traces a line across it with his finger.

"I cannot just leave to traipse around the nine circles, searching for my beloved," he says, his high voice cracking. "There would be a bloodbath of anarchy with me gone from the office. Septimus is my wise second-in-command, but he does not have my skills...."

He trails off, and his black eyes snap from the photo to me.

"You will go in there in my stead. You will find Beatrice. I will give you Elinor Powell back and the four of you—Team DEVIL—will find my wife and bring her back. I will have a second chance, in the same way you had a second chance at death."

"Yes, Sir," I reply quickly. "You're so clever. Death really did make me special. Don't you think it's more than a coincidence that Septimus and I are working together just feet from your office? What if this was all building to this moment? My second chance becomes *your* second chance. A second chance with Beatrice Morrigan. Your wife. Your true Dreamcatcher!"

The Devil regards me coolly, and I worry I've laid it on too thick.

"Don't overflatter me, child, or I may just decide to hang on to Miss Powell after all," he says, stepping away from me. The pool of blood parts as he walks through it. It ripples back, lapping at my legs. I try to follow him to the glass-paneled door, but my legs are stuck fast. Everything suddenly seems to be slipping out of control again.

"*Elinor!*" I scream. "Sir, please give her back to us," I beg. "She is to us what Beatrice Morrigan is to you. We love her."

The Devil stops walking and places his right hand on the doorframe. He leans forward, steadying himself. His jacket is starting to smoke.

"I told you to stop saying Beatrice's name!" he snarls.

"A second chance!" I yell, trying to redirect him. "Your plan, Sir, it really is an amazing idea. Because you have nothing to lose. At least let us try, and if we don't find your wife, then you get...you get..."

"Miss Powell back?" prompts The Devil, saying the words that even now I can't speak.

"You have nothing to lose, and we have everything to lose. Isn't that how you like it?"

The Devil starts to laugh, and as he does, the bloody pool around me starts to drain away. I look down at my legs, expecting to see thick lumps clinging to my skin, but there's nothing.

It was another hallucination.

"I do not cope well without sleep, Medusa Pallister," says The Devil. "Septimus may well rue the day he started this chain of events."

My heart soars with hope as his long, pale fingers inch across the door toward the knocker that's shaped like a woman. Trailing his fingers downward, as if he's caressing the figure's hair, he leans forward and pushes the door back.

"Elinor Powell," says The Devil. "You are wanted."

Even though it could be another hallucination, I don't care. I start running. I can't even see the room anymore or the real monster in it. All there is, is Elinor. She falls into my arms and we tumble and roll as the Oval Office spits us out with an earsplitting scream.

The four of us, Team DEVIL, are huddled together on the floor of the library. We wanted to be away from other devils, and this was the only place we could think of. It's been a couple of days since Elinor was taken. She's slept a lot and eaten nothing. Trying to give her space to get over her ordeal didn't work. We were all so worried about her, we ended up watching over her from a distance, which really just felt like spying. She finally told us to stay with her, and so we have. She may be battered and emotionally wrung out, but our Elinor is hanging on. When I asked her about her time as The Devil's Dreamcatcher, she played down the horror and wouldn't talk at all about what she saw. Apparently the nightmares weren't constant, because The Devil didn't sleep for very long most nights.

Or so she says.

*　*　*

Now Alfarin and I are on either side of Elinor, barricaded in a fortress of books we built up around ourselves, and Mitchell is leaning in so close, his legs are wrapped around hers. Without saying it, we need to touch one another, to make sure we're solid and real and here.

I'm dead, but I've never felt more alive—or more thankful.

"I will go alone," whispers Alfarin. "I will not ask either of you to come with me."

He'd better not be bringing this up again.

"Either?" whispers Elinor. Her voice is cracked and barely audible. It's not the voice of someone who is unwell; it's the voice of someone who has been shouting.

Or screaming.

"Elinor, there's no way in a million years you're coming with us," replies Mitchell gently. "And when I say *us*, I mean me and you, Alfarin. 'Cause you're not going into the circles of Hell alone."

I reach out for Elinor's hand, but I don't take it. I just let my fingers hover above hers.

She takes my hand and leans into me. Were her nails always this short and ragged?

"Team DEVIL, right?" I whisper.

"Always." Elinor squeezes my hand and I hear a tiny crack, like a wishbone being pulled apart. Elinor flinches.

"We all have to go, Alfarin. Even Elinor," I say. "When I was in with The Devil, he showed me things about my second death. It's just like Owen kept talking about. I have memories of my two timelines. They're faint, but they're getting stronger. When Rory was killed, my first death and timeline were erased from the records, because Team DEVIL altered time. But I was part of Team DEVIL when you all went to San Francisco. When everything changed, I still had to die, and so six months later, I did—again."

"I don't understand what that has to do with—" says Mitchell.

"My first death was an accident, Mitchell. It was marked down as the twenty-fifth of June, 1967. The records say I killed myself. But I didn't. I wouldn't. I slipped. I was trying to make my mom believe me about what my stepfather was doing. I've known all three of you for so much longer than we all remember, but it's starting to come back, like a whisper. It was the four of us who originally left Hell with the Viciseometer. So I was there, a devil in San Francisco, when Rory was killed."

"It wasn't just the three of us?" says Alfarin. "I knew it."

"Don't let me go," whispers Mitchell. His pink eyes are wide, not with surprise, but with remembrance.

"Yes!" I cry. "I remember those words, too."

"But why?" asks Elinor. "Why do ye think that is? Why have we all struggled with these blanks and almost-memories?"

"This is only a theory, but my guess is that even though I was erased from the paradox, there was something left behind, kind of the way a pencil still leaves a faint trace on paper when it's erased. I think it's those lines that I've been remembering.

"So with my first death and existence in Hell removed, I carried on living. But I still went back to the bridge on the second of December in 1967. It was like something was pulling me there." I take a deep breath. "See, my mom didn't believe me about the abuse, and even though Rory was dead, I still needed her to understand that what I was telling her was true. Even if no one else believed me, I needed *her* to. Does that make sense?" I'm relieved to see my friends nodding. "My head was so messed up. So I threatened to hurt myself. I went to the bridge, and when my mom found me there, I tried to convince her that I wasn't making things up.

"I never planned to die," I say forcefully. "Something dragged me off the bridge that day. For a split second, I even wondered if it was the fog. It was like death was controlling it."

"Fate," says Elinor softly, squeezing my hand again.

I nod. "Now, after everything that's happened, and knowing what we have to do next, I think this is the reason I was taken again," I say. "My second death is linked to getting Beatrice Morrigan to give The Devil a second chance."

"This is seriously hurting my head," says Mitchell. "I can't even begin to get my brain around it."

"Neither can I," I reply. "And I'm the one it all happened to."

"Remember a time when death was easy?" asks Mitchell.

"No," the rest of us reply together. The same perverse smile spreads across our faces.

"So Mitchell, Medusa and I will enter the dwelling of the Skin-Walkers," says Alfarin.

"I keep telling ye all," croaks Elinor. "Ye are not going anywhere without me."

"The Nine circles of Hell," mutters Mitchell. "I don't know anything about Dante. Does anyone else?"

"I know most of the circles," I reply.

"I don't suppose any of them involve an all-you-can-eat buffet and kittens?" asks Mitchell sardonically.

"Ye are allergic to cats, Mitchell," says Elinor, rolling her eyes. "That would be a circle of Hell for ye anyway."

Alfarin snorts. He tries to hide his laughter behind his plate-sized hand, but his convulsing shoulders knock Mitchell over. Mitchell's foot accidentally kicks Elinor, so I slap him in the stomach.

Mitchell grabs me and pulls me on top of him, roughing my hair like he's drying a dog.

"Medusa's circle of Hell would involve a comb," he calls.

"And yours would be having to bench-press something heavier than a stapler," I retort.

"Mine would be having to wear those garments called underpants," says Alfarin. "My manly parts cannot be constricted. It affects my appetite."

"Well, that is an image I did not need in my brain, Alfarin," scolds Elinor, standing up. "And I thought the dreams of The Devil were bad enough."

It's so wrong, but Mitchell and I can't stop laughing. Hell has finally made me hysterical.

"You must not joke about such matters," says Alfarin gravely. "I will never—"

But Elinor pushes Alfarin's large lips together with a pinch of her thumb and forefinger.

"We are Team DEVIL, and nothing can break us," she says softly. "Not time, not death, and not some Banshee. We have a quest. Now we need to get ready."

And she kisses Alfarin on the cheek. It's swift and yet intimate, as two pairs of gleaming red eyes meet and block out the Underworld and everything in it. Mitchell and I stop laughing and wrestling and just watch Elinor and Alfarin, who have been through the worst ordeal imaginable and still only have eyes for each other.

And to think I had to die to appreciate the purity of love and friendship.

Mitchell wants to make a quick getaway from the main entrance to the library. Not because he wants to get going into the circles of Hell, but because Patty Lloyd is walking toward us with her hips swinging from left to right like she's bouncing off the walls of an invisible rubber box.

"You guys go on," I say. "I'll meet you at Thomason's."

Elinor is sandwiched protectively between Alfarin and Mitchell. Her feet barely touch the ground as they hustle out of the library. Mitchell keeps his head low and does his best to avoid eye contact with Patty. They're almost beside an old man who is removing his clothes by the front door—the people you run into down here, I swear—when Elinor breaks free and runs back to me. She throws her arms around my neck and I hear her frail body snap and crackle, as if she's made of Bubble Wrap.

"I want ye to know I heard it all, Medusa," she whispers. "In that place, when ye came for me. I will never forget what ye did. Ye are truly a sister to me."

"And I would do it again and again until the end of time," I reply.

"Why are ye not coming to Thomason's now?" asks Elinor.

I look over at Patty, who is staring at Elinor with a strange, perhaps soft, but definitely dumb expression on her face.

"I'm right on your heels. There's just something I need to do first."

"Don't be long," she says.

I watch Mitchell, Alfarin and Elinor leave the library. The Devil's intern, a Viking prince, and a peasant from medieval England. My best friends.

"So you got her back," says Patty, interrupting the moment.

"Yeah."

"Quite the power player, aren't you? Don't think you can start lording it over the rest of us in the dorm because you're The Devil's bitch now. And if you—"

"I want to thank you, Patty," I say quietly, interrupting her breathless flow of abuse.

"What?"

"I said, thank you."

"Are you serious?"

"You were the one who confirmed Alfarin's research. And you led me and Mitchell to him, and all those other resources. If you hadn't done that, we would never have gotten Elinor back. So I'm saying thank you. Not because I have to, but because I want to."

Patty considers this.

"Don't think you being nice will make me forget that Mitchell promised to take me out for dinner," she finally replies. She looks me up and down, as if seeing me for the first time. "And don't think for one second that I don't fully intend to be his dessert."

I shake my head as a guffaw threatens to escape my chest. It's not because I think Patty's funny. It's because right now, as much as I adore Mitchell, I have bigger issues to deal with.

"You are seriously weird, Medusa Pallister," says Patty, an unsure smile on her face. "There's something not quite right with you."

Now I let out a full-on laugh.

Medusa Pallister, that's me. There may be something not quite right with me, but I'm finally okay with that.